I0618330

The Moonstorm Series

Volume One
Land of the Frozen Sun

Volume Two
Book of Dreams

Volume Three
Destiny's Children

Volume Four
Time Weaver

Volume Five
Death is the Door

Volume Six
Aranae in Red

Special Thanks:

Peter Gawtry
Stephanie Gawtry
Ren Johnson
Chris Mayer
Pat Sullivan
Jack Svenningsen
Ricki Terry
Tracy van der Leeuw
Christopher West

TIME

WEAVER

A. P. Malloy
The Moonstorm Series

Ardilla Blanca

Copyright © 2019 A.P. Malloy

U.S. Copyright Office Registration Number
TXu 2-286-721

All rights reserved,
Ardilla Blanca Publishers, LLC.
Reproduction or storage of this work
in part or whole for commercial use
prohibited without written permission.

ISBN-13: 978-0-578-95085-3

Cover design and artwork: Mari Fridley Larsen
marilarsen.com

Learn more about the series
and order promotional copies:
moonstormseries.com

The author welcomes correspondence:
apmalloy1@gmail.com

CONTENTS

CHAPTER ONE
Gift

IN THE PAST, over two hundred years before Lightning or even her gami-kan had celebrated a single birthday, a little girl from Luna was celebrating her fifth, in a hospital waiting room on Earth.

"Happy birthday, Maya," her mother said. The sentiment was genuine, but her voice carried an undertone of suppressed emotion, causing the wish to seem more manufactured than spontaneous.

"Doesn't seem happy," the girl replied, and she never looked away from the 3V show in which she was immersed. To her mother, the story made no sense. People on horses were skirmishing with a band of hovering owls, or maybe they were dancing, although why that would be she had no idea. She rarely watched 3V, and her expertise on its infinite programming ended at news broadcasts and historical documentaries.

"Mrs. Sharma?" asked the nurse who peeked her head inside the room.

"Yes," Maya's mother replied, and she rose from her chair. "I'm Nandini Sharma." She straightened the hem of her sari, picking up the small bag at her side. The nurse smiled, but Nandini couldn't read the message behind the expression.

"The doctor will see you now. Ready, Maya?"

Maya swept her hand through the holographic image like a dismissal, and it obediently vanished in an instant, along with its noise, leaving them in a plain, sterile space, monochromatic, unadorned, and—to Maya's way of thinking—eminently boring.

"How long is this going to take?" she asked.

"That's a good question," the nurse replied, still smiling. She opened the door wider and stepped aside to allow them in. "Probably not long. When we see the doctor, you can ask him."

But upon their arrival at the examination room, Maya did not ask the doctor any questions. He was a bearded man, a Sikh, turbaned and unsmiling. The room itself was as sterile as the one they had just left, but with its many metallic devices and antiseptic smell, it was not boring so much as intimidating. Maya sat on the examination table, her shoulders hunched and her left leg twitching. Her mother looked on as the doctor flashed a pen-light into the girl's eyes, ran a hand-held scanner over her head and shoulders, and tested her reflexive responses. He never said a word throughout, and Maya shied away from his smoky breath, unable to stop looking at the occasional white hairs that stood out from his otherwise coal-black beard.

He must be a hundred years old, she thought, and she at once abandoned her abiding dream of becoming a doctor if this was its final result.

At last he stepped away, frowning.

"The headaches?" he asked.

"Less frequent," Nandini replied. "More severe."

"And the nightmares?"

"Also less frequent, but now she's sleepwalking."

"Any pattern?"

"Not that I can see. Sometimes she ends up in our room—her father's and mine—and sometimes she's in the middle of 3V but not really watching. Once she was upstairs counting all her stuffed animals. When I asked her what she was doing, she answered me clear as day but never looked at me and never stopped counting. Now we have to lock the doors to keep her inside."

The doctor turned his beetling brows to Maya.

"How are you feeling right now?"

She grimaced and hunched even further.

"It's supposed to be my birthday."

"Yes," said the doctor, "but how do you feel?"

"I don't know."

"Maya," said her mother. "Please answer the doctor's question. He's trying to help."

"I don't know," Maya repeated. "Like I..." She had been about to say, "Like I need to go to the bathroom," but she stopped herself. "I don't know. There's a tickling in my head. It feels like a surprise coming."

"A surprise?" The doctor glanced at her sharply. "But surprises are unexpected things, aren't they? We don't know when they're coming."

Maya shrugged.

"Have you noticed any changes since the last time you were here? Changes for the better or worse?"

Maya thought about this. The last visit had been in winter; now, spring had come.

"There was snow last time," she replied.

"Maya," her mother scolded, though the answer had been sincere. What kind of changes were they talking about? The doctor's turban? It had been green last time, and now it was a deep blue.

"I'm talking about changes in the way you feel," said the doctor. His tone didn't need to be stern; his face did all the work.

"I don't know. Not really."

"But the headaches are happening less often?"

"I guess."

"And the nightmares? Are they the same?"

"No." Of this Maya was sure and grateful. "I used to dream of..."

"Of what?"

But Maya was reluctant to give voice to the ideas. They were too disturbing to be named.

"Bad things," she said. "Things that shouldn't be

together." She looked down at her feet, swinging forward and back, hoping the exam would be over soon.

"What do you mean?" asked the doctor. "What kind of things? Like rain on a sunny day?"

"No," said Maya, but she would say no more.

"And now?" asked the doctor. He began putting away his examination instruments, deliberate like a child with beloved toys. "What do you dream about now?"

Maya considered the question, trying to recall.

"Leaving," she said. "I dream about leaving."

+ + +

Aboard the shuttle, Maya and her mother occupied two seats in the prestige section, Maya nearest the window and a small table before them. Through the window, the ground beneath them fell rapidly away as the shuttle gained altitude.

"How did you like your second trip to Earth?" she asked. "Isn't it beautiful? Look! That's where your father was born. New Kochi."

"Was there an Old Kochi?"

"Yes, but they just called it Kochi."

"Where is it?"

"Underwater, now. Sometimes you can see it from space, but there's too many clouds. Anyway, next time we'll stay longer and have a proper visit. We have lots of family who would love to see you."

Maya shrugged.

"I like Luna better."

"Only because it's home. But if you spent some time on Earth, you'd learn to love it, too, I'm sure."

"Then why did you leave?"

"Your father got a job, of course."

"Aren't there any jobs on Earth?"

"Not like this one."

A steward passed by, neatly uniformed. He retrieved empty cups and wiped the table.

"We'll be entering orbital phase in a few minutes,"

he said. "If you don't mind, we'd like you to please fasten your safety belts and stow your belongings in the compartment under your seats—just for a while," he added, smiling at Maya. She looked up at him.

"Why is it so scary?"

"Entering orbit? Oh! It's not scary at all."

"But it is dangerous."

"No, dear. This is my thirty-second time."

"Then why are you scared?"

The steward's smile got larger, but it didn't reach his eyes, which grew narrow and unblinking.

"Who says I'm scared, cutie? Now buckle up."

He moved on to the next passengers, sharing the same message, smiling and wiping. Maya watched him go, her eyes boring a hole in the back of his head.

"He's lying," she said.

"Maya."

"He is. I can tell."

"How?"

Maya shrugged, buckling her safety belt. Her toys, a fuzzy Bengal tiger and two chess pieces—one king, one queen—she tucked into the compartment beneath her seat, closing and locking it with a twist of its handle. Her mother did the same with the book she had been reading, a history of early twenty-second century post-war reconstruction. She brushed a biscuit crumb from her sari and looked at Maya with her brow furrowed.

"People don't like being called liars."

"Then they shouldn't lie."

"Everyone lies once in a while, Maya. If they don't, there's something daal mein kuch kaala hai."

"What does that mean?"

"It means there's something black in the lentils… that something's fishy."

"Suspicious?"

"Yes."

"Telling the truth is suspicious?"

"It can be, if it happens all the time."

"What about Daada?"

"Your grandfather is doodh ka dhula."

"Really? Washed in milk?"

"It's an expression. It means he's saintly."

"He never lies?"

"He never lies to cause pain."

Maya considered this. She looked out the window. The shuttle had reached an altitude that transformed the earth from a plane to a sphere, its horizons curving away in the distance, its sheath of atmosphere shimmering and hazy. India had moved off the stage and out of sight behind them, the ocean bearing its name taking its place. She imagined its whitecaps as milk and wondered what it would feel like to be washed in it. Would the milk be warm? And what kind of milk? Goat? Buffalo?

"Orbital velocity in ten seconds," came a voice over the intercom, informative and strictly neutral.

Maya began a silent countdown in her mind. Her mother leaned back, her head against the seat and her eyes closed. She gripped the padded armrests, and her knuckles whitened.

Five, four, three...

A picture of a fiery explosion filled Maya's mind, as if seen through someone else's eyes. A shuttle, glittering and serene, arcing through the blue sky, suddenly disintegrated in a ball of fire and a thick, coiling tail of white smoke. She seemed to hear someone gasp in shock and the moaning of people in despair.

...two, one, ignition.

The image disappeared from her mind as the thrust of the shuttle's engines pushed Maya back in her seat like a hand to the chest. For a number of seconds she didn't bother to count, the pressure increased, and she felt as if she was sinking into her seat, melting into it like a hot coin on ice. Her mother's eyes remained closed, her grip on the armrests unrelenting. Throughout the shuttle, the other passengers had fallen silent, their idle conversation replaced by a roaring voice that no amount of insulation could entirely hide. Maya's eyes turned to the window, where the planet was now small enough to fit its frame like an old-fashioned 2V. She strained to see signs of the war Daada often talked about, the banjar bhoomi—wasteland—but she didn't know what to look for. Then, the pressure decreased, and she could breathe normally once again. Passengers heaved a collective sigh, and her mother's eyes opened.

"There," Nandini said, and she smiled faintly. "Nothing to be afraid of."

+ + +

When they were safely returned to Luna, Maya and her mother took the transit tube and were whisked from the hectic shuttle hub to their residence dome. It was one of the moon's finest, home to Luna's most esteemed citizens and conveniently located between the commercial and political centers of Mare Serenity and Mare Tranquility.

They arrived at their penthouse suite in time for a late dinner—cooked by Maya's father Raahithya and seasoned with liberal critiques from his own father, Daada. Nandini had adopted him as her own, for her father had been the famous Sujan Banerjee, inventor of the Halo, whose notoriety lived on though the great inventor was long dead. Maya had never met the man. She had heard he was a sterling businessman but a delinquent father, rarely home and never giving Nandini or her siblings a single gift. "My gift to the world is the Halo," Nandini had bitterly quoted him, and though she made good use of her inherited wealth, she had never worn nor had one implanted, claiming them overrated. Maya was too young for a Halo and had no opinion.

When dinner was served, she picked at her alu gobi and nibbled without enthusiasm at her samosas, usually her favorite. While his son and daughter-in-law conversed in low tones, Daada sipped masala chai, unconcerned by caffeine at any late hour, and watched his granddaughter through thick lenses.

"You don't have to worry," Maya said to him without looking up. "I'm not going to die or anything."

"Good heavens," said Daada, setting down his cup with a bang and inspiring Maya's parents to fall silent. "Whoever said you were?"

"You were thinking it."

"Never!"

Maya shrugged.

"Well," said her father, and he helped himself to one of her uneaten samosas. "I, for one, am glad to hear the good news."

"Can I go to bed now?"

"You haven't eaten a thing," her mother objected.

"My head doesn't feel like eating."

"What about your stomach?"

"Please? Can I?"

"Bhagavaan ke lie," exclaimed her mother, either tired herself or merely exasperated. "Wash up first."

"Will you sing to me?" Maya asked Daada. The old man bowed his head and reclaimed his cup, sipping.

"On your birthday," he said, "anything."

Nandini watched Maya and her grandfather walk hand-in-hand toward the girl's bedroom.

"Rathi," she said once they were gone. "Did you ever tell her the story of the *Christos*?"

"We agreed not to."

"But did you?"

Raahithya began clearing away the dishes.

"We're a little late in the game to be doubting one another's integrity, Nan."

"Rathi, please, I need to know. Maybe you forgot, or maybe there was a show on 3V..."

"No. Never. Why do you ask this?"

Nandini ran her finger around the lip of her wine glass, and it sang a soft, crystalline note.

"On the ride back," she said, "she described the explosion, just like it happened, in perfect detail."

"So? She must have seen it in school."

"Maybe. But... It wasn't like she was sharing a lesson she'd learned. This was different. She was describing what I saw. What *I* saw. Just like I saw it. Same perspective, same emotional response, same voices of the people who were on the platform with me. Like she was replaying a video she'd culled from my memory, with my eyes and ears as the camera and microphone. She quoted—exactly—the woman who was standing next to me. 'My baby,' she kept saying. 'God, no, my baby.'

Raahithya placed the dishes in the sanitizer and returned to the table, taking his wife's hand.

"I'm not trying to be insensitive," he said, "but are you sure you heard her correctly? Maybe you dreamed it when you fell asleep on the shuttle."

Nandini pulled her hand away.

"I didn't fall asleep, Rathi. I couldn't!"

"Daada, then. He's always telling stories that... probably aren't the most appropriate."

But Nandini dismissed this with a wave.

"He knows about the *Christos*, but not the details. Not about the man in the green suit who fell to his knees and started pulling out his own hair—bloody hanks—wailing like a newborn. We watched the wreckage fall back to the surface, and all I could think was, 'Black hair, he has black hair like Rathi's...'"

Nandini looked up at her husband, her dark eyes meeting his, and she reached out, re-taking his hand.

"She knew everything *I* knew, recited it like it was her own memory, not mine."

Raahithya's proud mustache twitched side to side as he pursed his lips and considered this information.

"OK, Nan, but what are you trying to say? How could she know these things?"

"Maybe the same way she knows about your job."

"What do you mean?"

"She told the doctor she's been having dreams. Dreams about leaving. Dreams that we're going to Mars."

"She said that? But I haven't even told Da."

"I know."

Raahithya continued to hold his wife's hand, but he re-took his seat, and his forehead creased, a neat vertical line forming above his nose.

"And what did the doctor say?"

"Not enough. Some anomalies, but each one minor—even unremarkable—when taken individually."

"But when taken collectively?"

Nandini looked down at her husband's hand, examining it as if it held the answer to his question. She caressed each finger, considering her response.

"Do you remember the English boy at market where we met? The ginger?"

"Of course. He was named after someone famous. Alastair. No, wait. Franklin. Eustice?"

"Rutherford."

"Of course!"

"'I'm precocious,' he used to say." Nandini mimicked a child's lispy voice. "And he was. Every time I saw him in there shopping by himself—what was he? Four? Five?—I thought how amazing his parents must be, how trusting and what good teachers. And later, after you and I started... Later, I used to worry that I would never be that good, that I might be the reason any children we had would never be precocious, might not even know what the word meant. That they might be boring, average, normal, plain, not at all like you."

"Nandi..."

"Well, I guess I don't have to worry any more. Our daughter's just been examined by the best neurologist on Earth, and he's convinced. When all the anomalies are added together, the picture is of a brain unlike any he's ever seen, and he can't explain it."

"And the headaches?"

Nandini frowned.

"Possibly the natural consequence of the unique development taking place. He thinks they'll pass—maybe when she reaches puberty, maybe sooner."

"So imprecise! And the nightmares?"

"He suggested a therapist."

"OK, fine, but what about the...the..."

"Say it."

"I don't know what the word is."

"You mean it sounds too preposterous."

"Well, isn't it?"

Nandini nodded. She kissed Raahithya's hand.

"It never came up. I mean I never brought it up. For that reason. Precocious is one thing, but this..." She looked intently into her husband's eyes. "I don't want people to view our daughter as a freak."

They once again lapsed into silence. From the direction of Maya's room, they heard singing. Daada was an enthusiastic but unskilled vocalist, with a laissez faire approach to pitch and tempo, but his memory of simple lyrics remained as firm as ever.

"No daughter of yours could ever be a freak," Raahithya said, and he kissed Nandini lightly on the cheek before getting to his feet. "Someone has a birthday present waiting in the parlor. I'll be back."

+ + +

"Daada?"

"Yes, child?"

"How many songs do you know?"

Daada waited to answer this question until he had helped Maya unbutton and step out of her dress, hanging it neatly in the closet.

"As many as the stars in the sky," he said.

"No one knows that many."

"The gods do."

"But how many do *you* know?"

"Well, let's see." Daada paused to count as Maya slipped into her favorite pajamas, a tiger-striped affair with padded feet and a hood with stubby orange ears.

"Is it a million?"

"Heavens no."

"A thousand?"

"That would be something! But no, dear."

"A hundred, then?"

"Maybe...when I was younger. My maata and pita

weren't musicians, but we recited and sang every day in school. I could remember all the words when even my smartest classmates couldn't."

"Which is your favorite?"

"Here now," Daada pulled back the blankets and patted the bed. "Climb in. What's *your* favorite? It's your birthday, after all." Maya did as instructed, pulling the blankets to her chin and hugging her stuffed tiger.

"I like the one about the sultan," she said. "I like the story. But I think I like the monkey song best."

"Monkey song?" Daada sat on the bed, his expression quizzical. "Whatever song is that?"

Maya started to sing.

"Hum the monkey, shocked his dayna..." Her voice was clear and pitch-perfect, but Daada hissed.

"No, bevaqoof ladakee! It's man ki, not monkey. And no one shocked anything. Lie back and listen."

With a simple vocal command, Daada lowered the room lights to half and removed his glasses. He had his son's mustache, but white as snow, with rumpled hair to match and a round belly. He cleared his throat and closed his eyes. When he began to sing, his voice was low and gravelly, but Maya recognized the tune at once and nodded happily, a quick smile lighting her face. She sat up and swayed side to side, holding her tiger before her and making it dance two-legged.

"Hum ko man ki shakti dena," sang Daada. "Man vijay kare, dusaron ki jay se pahale, khud ko jay kare." When he sang the refrain, Maya joined in.

"Hum ko man ki shakti dena."

"That's right," said Daada. "Now verse two. Bhed-abhaav apane dil se, saaf kar sake doston se bhool, dusaron ki jay se pahale, khud ko jay kare."

He paused.

"Whenever you hear that part—khud ko jay kare—you know it's time for the refrain."

"Humko man ki shakti dena."

"Yes, dear. You have the voice of an angel."

"What does it mean?"

Daada wiped the lenses of his glasses with a floral kerchief he took from his pocket.

"God give us strength in mind and heart," he said. "Help us be victorious over ourselves so we can help others to victory. Or something like that."

"Which god?"

"Hm?"

"Well, which one? Isn't there more than one?"

"That depends on who you ask. Some people believe there are many, some believe the many are all just different faces of the One."

"Some people don't believe at all," said Maya. "Isn't that true? My friend Aggie doesn't believe."

"Your friend is too young to know this from that."

Maya chewed her bottom lip.

"How many birthdays have you had, Daada?"

"You know that answer already."

"But tell me again."

"Eighty-one."

"Is that old?"

"Not so much. Not these days. My own daada lived to be one hundred, and the whole village came out to celebrate. Now, people reach a hundred and no one cares. It's expected." He returned the glasses to his face.

"But you don't expect it."

Daada gave the girl a sharp glance.

"What do you mean?"

"You don't expect to be a hundred."

"And how, my smartie, would you know this?"

Maya shrugged.

"Is it because of your heart?" she asked.

Daada exchanged the kerchief for a small file, and he ran it over his nails, frowning.

"Your mother's been spilling secrets."

"No, Daada."

"Your father then. Hopeless rascal!"

"No, Daada, no one."

"Then how? I haven't said a word to you."

"No. But you think it."

Daada stopped his filing.

"I think a lot of things, child. How would you know what goes on in this old head of mine?"

Maya shrugged.

"Well? Go on. Tell me."

"I don't know. Sometimes I... Never mind."

"You don't get off so easy. Sometimes you what?"

But before she could answer, Maya's parents approached, singing a hearty version of the birthday song. When they entered the room, they held between them a brightly wrapped box, large enough that they had to turn single file to fit through the door. Maya cast her blankets aside and leapt from the bed.

"Janamdivas ki Shubh kamnaye," said her father and mother with one voice. "Mind you don't frighten it," her father added when Maya began to tear at the wrapping. She looked up at him and squinted her eyes as if listening to words from another room. But she barely slowed her attack on the decorative paper, which soon lay in shreds all around what was revealed to be a small cage of blue plastic and thin metal bars with a closed door at one end—and a pacing shadow hidden within.

"Ooh!" Maya squealed, peeking into the cage. Without waiting for permission, she opened the latched door and pressed her palms together as if in prayer.

A moment later, an answer appeared, first as a twitching, whiskered snout, then a pair of amber eyes, set in an orange head striped black. Soon, an entire miniature Bengal tiger stood before them, fiercely attentive, taking in its surroundings with the air of a creature prepared to flee or fight as necessary. Neither were (though Maya's mother gently closed the door to prevent the former). Maya stared, struck silent, her hand covering her mouth, frozen open in a delighted O. The tiger stepped tentatively away from the cage, crouching low as it leaned forward to smell her foot. She remained still as stone, afraid it might be a dream, easily scared away. But the throaty purr of its breathing and the silken coat brushing against her leg said otherwise. She never looked away as

A.P. Malloy

it moved past her to explore the room—and she knew with immeasurable bliss that it was no dream at all.

"Maata," she whispered, never taking her eyes from the tiger. "Pita. Is it real?"

"Sure," said her father. "You know, not from India or anything, but alive, and made just for you."

Daada shrank back when the tiger, no bigger than a large housecat, wove between his legs.

"It likes you," said Maya's mother.

"I certainly hope so."

"Does it have a name?" Maya asked.

"It will when you give it one," said her father.

"Please tell me it doesn't have claws," said Daada, who watched the tiger through eyes made wide by his thick glasses and a healthy fear.

"No claws," Maya's father assured. "At the moment. But they can be triggered easily enough if we want. He's full with latency—growth, color, claws, intellect—it was all part of the package. A tiger without claws isn't much of one, is it?"

"But he does have teeth," Maya whispered as the tiger yawned hugely. "They're beautiful."

"Ugh," said Daada, and he backed to the door.

"It's OK, Da," Raahithya said. "There's nothing to worry about. Look." He produced a pair of Maya's stockings. "We provided the lab with her scent. He's been designed to treat her like family."

"Family! Boy, have you ever seen a real tiger? In the wild? Because I have. They're loners, not familial."

"But they love their cubs."

"Which would be fine if this one was female."

"Oh, Da."

"Oh, Da nothing. Tiger love indeed! I'm going to bed. Happy birthday, child. We'll go over verse three another time." And he slipped out of the room as quickly as eighty-one years, five children, and two dead wives allowed, closing the door behind him.

Raahithya threw up his hands in defeat.

"Oh well." And he tossed the socks to the tiger who

snatched them from the air and rolled with them over the thick Persian-style rug, its purring deep and satisfied.

"I love him," Maya said, and she hugged her parents, surprising them both by bending down to lightly touch their feet, left then right, a gesture of great respect, and one she hadn't made since her last birthday.

"I'm glad," her mother said. "I was worried the doctor's visit would ruin the whole day."

"No way," Maya said, and she sat down where the tiger could smell and rub its neck against her outstretched fingers. "No way. It's the best birthday ever."

+ + +

In the parlor later that evening, Raahithya, engrossed in 3V, and Nandini, herself nearly asleep with her book resting open on her lap, didn't at first notice when Daada entered the room in his sleeping gown. Seeing this, Raahithya gestured at the holographic image and it froze in mid-action.

"Something wrong, Da?"

"You know there is."

"Geez, Da, we talked about the tiger a long time ago. You were OK with it then; what's changed?"

"I'm not talking about that beast. It's unnatural, whipped up in a lab, but it's not what I mean."

"I know what you mean," Nandini said, and she sat up in her recliner, set aside her history book, and gestured so that the 3V image disappeared altogether. Raahithya opened his mouth to object, for the show—a silly thing called *Around the World in Eighty Days*—had just gotten interesting. But there was no denying the look on his wife's face. "I've been thinking about it all day," she said. "Hardly anything else, actually."

"I'm glad someone has."

"C'mon Da..."

"No, Rathi. We all know what's happening here."

"Do we?"

"Of course! Her Third Eye! It's opening. The headaches, the clairvoyance, the dreams..."

"Good grief," Raahithya whispered.

"Lord Shiva show mercy on you," Daada pointed a gnarly finger at him. "You spend all your time in the modern world making your modern money, and you forget the roots that got you there."

"I'm not sure that's fair, Da."

"I haven't forgotten," Nandini said. "Tell me more."

Raahithya clapped his hand to his forehead, but he dutifully made room for Daada to sit beside him, since he clearly planned to do as Nandini requested. The old man cleared his throat.

"It's a long history, isn't it? The Third Eye? Gyananakashu, my grandfather used to call it. A gift from Lord Shiva the destroyer and renewer, most complex of all the gods. All have it, but few see it opened, and fewer still at such a young age."

"Um, listen," said Raahithya, getting to his feet. "I've had a long day. I think I'll retire and let you two go on with this, OK?" But one stern glance from Nandini hunched his shoulders just like his daughter, and he sat down again, slowly and with a frown.

"Go on," said Nandini. "Should we worry?"

"What good would it do? The Eye is opening."

"But others, other children, her teachers."

"What about them?"

"They might not understand. She called the shuttle steward a liar—not to his face, but you understand. If she says the wrong thing to the wrong person...or the wrong thing at the wrong time..."

But Daada dismissed this with a tut-tut.

"Worry won't close the Eye, child. It won't gain the approbation or understanding of others. You know this."

"Yes, but..."

"But nothing. She must be seen by a Pujari." Raahithya looked ready to voice an objection, but Daada gave him no room, holding up his hand like a stop sign. "I know just the one. He has knowledge of this from his time in the Old Country."

Time Weaver

"Good," said Nandini, and visible lines of worry eased from her forehead. "Thank you, Daada, so much."

But Raahithya merely sighed.

+ + +

Maya sat on her bed, the blankets pulled up around her, the room dark but for the faint light from Earth's sunlit face peeking in through the drawn blinds. On the bed before her, the King and Queen of Chess were discussing their newest subject. Maya picked up the Queen, walking her to the edge of the bed where she could see the tiger exploring on the floor below.

"Magnificent," she said in the Queen's voice, regal and certain. "The finest in all the land."

She walked the King to join his wife. He was a slow walker, one step at a time, stately but inefficient. Maya imagined him a portly fellow, good natured, though not as bright as the crown on his head.

"But won't it be difficult to care for?" he asked in Maya's best Kingly voice. "Won't it eat the pawns?"

"Nonsense," said the Queen. "Tigers eat buffaloes and goats, you ninnyhammer. Pigs and cows and such."

"Ah, yes," said the King. "We shall fill the royal grounds with all of those."

"Watch now; I shall call it to me," said the Queen.

Maya made her best purring sound, and the tiger, who had crawled into her closet, appeared with its stubby ears angled forward. She purred again, wiggling the Queen as enticement. With an air of perfect feline detachment, the tiger stepped forward, neither subservient nor quick. He was his own master, no matter what the Queen might think. He circled one leg of the bed, then another, stretched for a moment, then idly flexed, as if admiring non-existent claws.

"Khijh!," the Queen said to her King. "How lazy it is! How naughty and disobedient!"

"It is a wild beast," said the King, leaning side to side and talking in a sing-song fashion. "Wild beast, wildebeest, hungry beast, killed-a-beast. Feast! And you, special guest to the palace," the King turned to Maya. "Did you have a splendid birthday?"

"Yes, your Highness. Very splendid."

"Nonsense! Call me Hubert!"

"Oh no, your Highness, I could never."

"But we're jolly good friends—oh!"

At that moment, to the surprise of all the court, the tiger leapt up onto the bed, an easy, powerful motion, and Maya squealed as it grabbed the Queen from her fingers and rolled with her onto its back, biting her just below the crown. As Maya watched, shrinking back but fascinated, the tiger played at disemboweling its prey, its mewling wild and guttural.

"Oh, my ever-loving Queen," the King shouted. "I'm coming to rescue you!" But his wobbly gait, one slow step at a time, allowed the tiger to leap from the bed with its prize in its mouth.

"Oh, Hubert!" cried the Queen, and Maya did her best to impersonate a royal voice, muffled and slurry. "Call my knights! Gather the pawns! I'm doomed!"

Maya fished beneath the bed for her chessboard to carry out the Queen's orders, but she dropped the board onto the bed and clasped her hands to her temples, squeezing her eyes closed. She gasped as sharp pain cut through the middle of her skull, compressing and slicing her brain. The agony intensified, expanding outward like a balloon about to pop, threatening to rupture her eardrums, and she heard herself whimpering as if listening to someone else. Then it passed like a bad dream upon waking, and she sat taking shuddering breaths, tears streaming from her clenched eyes.

When at last she opened them, the tiger sat on the bed looking at her, the slobbery Queen at his feet.

"Look, Hubert," she said weakly in the Queen's voice. "I have conquered this beast and commanded it to return me to the palace unharmed."

"Yes, my Queen, humph humph and all that..."

But Maya hadn't energy to continue playing. She

felt ill in her stomach, and her eyes closed against even the Earth's faint light. She laid back, settling into her pillows, the King still clutched in her hand.

When she felt the soft, heavy tread of the tiger, stepping gingerly up onto her chest, she at first held her breath. But it settled to a resting position and purred like a velvet motor, and she couldn't help but look. She stared into its amber eyes, alien and wide, pupils dilated. It never blinked, returning her stare, shameless despite its role in the royal abduction. When she reached up to touch its whiskered jowls, it leaned into the caress. Minutes passed, though they felt like mere seconds, and Maya was surprised and greatly relieved to note the effects of her headache had vanished. She wished to continue basking in tiger breath and the sight of his broad, striped face, but her eyelids grew heavy, and she felt herself dropping into sleep. The King, still dangling in her grasp, came to life for one last proclamation.

"Shantikar," he said. "A healer's name. That's a fine name for a tiger. A fine name indeed. Shantikar..."

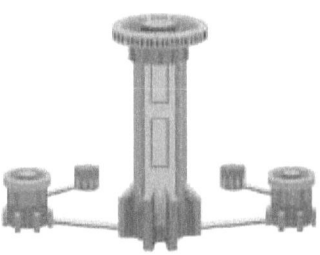

CHAPTER TWO
Present

THE BRISTLE RANGE extends from the River Tongue in the west to the Naked Hills in the east. There—or so explains Piedmont—for environmental reasons he doesn't make clear (perhaps because he doesn't know) the accrete become sporadic, huddled in small, stubborn groves atop otherwise unadorned knolls and tors. These are part of the disputed territory that forms a natural buffer between Bristles and Whitetails, but they lie thousands of strides away yet. For now, had she not known the truth, Lightning would have believed the rolling foothills they travel no more than an unexplored section of the Sugarfoot range. Aside from the prevalence of Bristle scent, the place is as common as home, filled with the chatter of virbles and yits, and overhead, the acrobatics of swinging, leaping, cremlins.

Have you ever been this far? Lightning asks Thunder. He marches at the tail of the kezel party, behind Cliff and the bibijas, but ahead of the scion, keeping to himself. When his oli-mu joins him, Joy on her back, he doesn't look up.

Nope, he thinks.

Hear any stories from api-kan? Or Rock, or Crag? Like what we should be expecting? Or any surprises?

No. Nothing worth sharing.

What about Ozag's Hold?
Never mentioned it.
And the Naked Hills?
What about 'em?
Well, what are they like?
Naked, I guess. How would I know?
Lightning casts a sidelong glance at her oti-mu.
Are you going to be in this mood the entire time?
Maybe.
Care to tell me why?
No. He looks up at Joy. *And don't go digging into my head, either. Got it?*

I'm not a snoop, thinks Joy.

But Thunder only curls his lip and marches on.

Seeing nothing to be gained by pressing him for answers, Lightning falls farther back to where Shimmer is carried by her five remaining pluripotents, one silver, four bronze, all eternally obedient. Twelve bristling soldiers march in a single file behind them. The queen has lapsed into torpor, and her eyes are dim. Lightning wonders if she should disturb her—isn't entirely sure why she came back here anyway—but Joy saves her the trouble.

She whistles softly.

I have a question, she thinks.

Shimmer's eyes brighten.

Can it not wait? She seeks to regain her energy.

It won't take long.

She doubts this. But it will continue.

Tell us about vumierre, thinks Joy. *Why scion hate them.* She buzzes a low tune. *Why they hate me.*

The Oddity is not hated, thinks Shimmer. *Though its form is truly repellent. It has risen above the reputation of its kind. If it were simply another vumierre, it would have been killed long ago.*

Lightning snarls and snaps her teeth.

The sharksha needn't be offended, thinks Shimmer. *She merely speaks truth. But in any case, the Oddity promised a simple question with a short answer, not a history of the scion and their despised slavers.*

A.P. Malloy

Just the main points.

What is there to say? She was not there; it was generations in the past.

Share what you know.

She knows this: scion were blameless. When they first encountered vumierre, they presented themselves in peace. And for a time, that sentiment was returned. But for reasons known only to the traitorous vumierre, scion were soon bound in slavery and made to do the work of those...interlopers, those foul, two-legged pillagers.

And Ozag saved you?

She rose up, yes, and orchestrated the rebellion that ended vumierre mastery, freeing the scion slaves. She was the First Thinking Queen, and the greatest, Undying and Excellent, the pinnacle of wisdom and power. But...

And here, Shimmer's thoughts drift to dark, brooding places Joy dares not explore.

How is she undying? she asks.

How do the moons stay suspended? Shimmer replies bitterly. *How does the yellow sun burn without extinguishing or the lova know when to rise above ground? It could just as well ask how the sharksha learned to think. She doesn't know!* She flashes gilt wings as if ruffling away unwanted flakes of snow, and her eyes grow dim once again. Taking the hint, Lightning and Joy move forward in line, hoping for better company. They don't ask Cliff to join them, but he does anyway.

As has often been the case since their journey's beginning, conversation among the three bibijas is dominated by Piedmont, who rarely tires of sensing his own thoughts. His current topic is the relationship between the Whitetails and their neighbors.

Bristlies, see, they's fine for keepin' Redteeth at bay, and once inna while you'll get a fancy atween a Bristly and Whitetail—not my style, mind ya, but it happens, see?—but even so, they's still some bad blood, no denyin'. Big feud on the Nekkid Hills when I was a wabi, still hear my api and ami cussin' like it was a contest, sayin' all sorts o' whatnot about them Bristlies—they eat their own

Time Weaver

wabis, drink each other's piddle, can't really think, just makin' up words they sense from the Sugarfeet, you know, that sort a thing. Not sayin' I believe it now, see? But a wabi credits whadda they sense from the big ones, yeah? Yeah, Fluvial? Yeah?

Fluvial dips her snout in a curt nod.

Exactly, thinks Piedmont, as if this were a ringing endorsement. *Anahoo, you only knows once you tries, and I gotta say: them Bristlies I met so far seems not too bad, not too bad a' tall.*

I'm glad to hear it, thinks Pounce.

If you don't mind, thinks Lightning. *Can you tell us what's on the other side of the Whitetail range?*

Mind? Never would, never could! First, yous a gonna come to the Bluffy. Ha! That's what ol' Piedmont calls it, but it's got a more proper-like name for a river. The Dashing, folks call it. Ain't that a shiny spike for a name, Sugarfoot? Nifty, yeah?

Yes sir, thinks Lightning.

Sur-ee it is! And that's the east end o' Whitetail proper. You get to the Bluffy 'n' you knows you's come far as you can. And hoo-ee! Things is all sorts a goofy on the east side. First there's that old bluff, or how'd you think ol' Piedmont come up with that name, hmm? Not by no accidental, you can say that twice. And hoo-ee! What a bluff it is! Couldn't climb it, shouldn't even try. And up top o' that bluff, I hear the hills get all level and there ain't no accrete. Dirty greenies flyin' overhead, makin' a real nerve wracker that. We call that the Last Valley. Sometimes ya get drifters comin' in from the mountains on the other side. Don't always make it, see, sometimes git plucked like a berry. Durn greenies! Sometimes take a turrible fall climbin' down the bluff. But some make it cross the river. Got a funny name, these newies. Whatcha call 'em Fluvial? The new kezel? Diggers? Scratchers?

Rooters.

Yeah! Rooters. What kinda name is that, I gotta ask? Ever heard o' such? Huh, Clawpaw? Ever?

No sir, thinks Cliff.

Well, they's fine enough neighbors, I reckon, but ever Red seems like they's one or two more, see? Things 'r gettin' tight, you know? Maybe they starts to thinkin' they can take over. You know how it is. Am I wrong?

Lightning concedes that he is not. She chooses to let pass for the moment the related topic of Whitetail encroachment on Bristle territory.

Anahoo, Piedmont concludes, *on the other side o' the Last Valley, there's them mountains I just went on about, and on the other side o' that? Well, who knows what it is? I never asked. We named it Last Valley—that was Big Fork's gapi-kan what done that, real big Chief he was—but whosta say? Mebbe it aint. Mebbe they's another valley iffin ya keep walkin, or mebbe they's a bunch o' kezel with no spikes sittin' round havin' a feast with kish. Ha! That'd be a thing. Shoot! I reckon maybe the world just goes on and on or else it comes to an end, see? All a sudden and that's that. Anahoo...*

His thoughts drift for a time, and he lapses into uncharacteristic stillness.

And to the north? Cliff prompts him.

Well-ee, Piedmont wrinkles his snout. *Now that's a whole different bowl o' stew, that. Cuz that's where the Bluffy comes from, see?*

The Dashing, Fluvial interjects.

Oh, sur-ee, they knows what Imma talkin' 'bout. And that ol' river's a cold one and fast. Proper awling like no other, let me say, but don't be a wabi—or even a jabi— and turn yer back, or you'sa get snatched real good like, cuz I'm sayin' them awl's tasty but Oh! the teeth on 'em. Well-ee, you follow the Bluffy north and that'll take ya to the last accrete. After that, we don't mess 'bout too much. Up there in the mountains is some Moondweller business, real mystery-like. At least, that's what all the old gamis and gapis 'll tell ya. Sur-ee, they will. 'Don't go messin' up there,' that's what they'll say. But you know how it is when yer young. Don't always listen so good. And that's where Big Fork's oliwot found that ol' Moondweller thing poor Fluvial's been a totin' for so long. Pokin' round to see where the Bluffy'd lead 'im and durned if he didn't find a Treasure! Lucky ol' Pluton! But coulda turned out different. Coulda runned into some kinda big trouble, who knows? Mebbe them ol' Moondwellers got... Well, who knows what they could have? Not ol' Piedmont. But mebbe up there's that ol' Ozagery you's lookin' for. Can't say!

And he doesn't.

With her head now full of exotic images of hills grown flat and spikeless kezel feasting with kish, Lightning drifts back into line, Cliff at her side. When her legs grow weary, Joy dismounts, and she never complains, for her own legs are still novelties, and she loves the feel of snow between her toes.

+ + +

So arranged, the party continues on, weaving between the accrete, following the trail generally to the east. As they travel, Joy's attention is drawn increasingly to the lifeless form riding across Fluvial's broad back, its arms dangling. It lies face down, but its metallic head is turned to the side, and one of its eyes gazes at her, perpetually open, cold and lifeless, glinting when they pass through sunlight. She slips her hand inside her sling, rubbing it slowly over the rectangular face of the artifact. She contemplates its smooth surface, feeling as always that it enjoys her touch.

Can you sense me? she asks.

Of course, it replies.

And can the others?

Not if you're careful.

Joy tightly focuses her next thought.

How are you feeling? she asks. The question would not have occurred to her when first becoming aware of the artifact—she considered it a thing back then—but now, it is the obvious choice.

Strictly speaking, it replies, *I am not "feeling" anything. I do not have emotions as you understand them. But I am aware of trouble.*

A.P. Malloy

Yes. You mentioned that. Joy recalls the disturbing hints. *What can you share?*

That time is not our friend.

What does that mean?

It means we should be marching faster.

Should I tell Pounce?

Eventually. But there are other things he needs to know as well. Like the reason for marching faster.

Which is?

Trouble. Big trouble.

What kind of trouble?

The kind that could bring an end to this world.

Joy recalls finding the Book buried in the snow. It had been dirty but undamaged even by the scion fire that had melted a Moondweller vehicle to waste.

Why are you worried? she asks, meaning no insult. *Nothing hurts you, right?*

This would.

Well, what is it?

Hubris coming home to roost, if I was being poetic, or karma, perhaps, if I was philosophic. But I'm sorry. This means nothing to you. Let me simplify. The humans who colonized this planet two centuries ago did so because they had no alternative. This had not been their original destination. As a result, their research into the planetary system was incomplete. They didn't know much about the place and didn't have time to learn. They needed to begin gathering resources. In their rush—and arrogance, a thing for which their species is notorious—they were careless in their choices. One of those was to mine for a precious ore found in large quantities on the smallest of the five moons, the violet one kezel call Oli-su or Wabi-la, the Little Sister. Their operation led to crippling seismologic events on the moon, killed several humans, destroyed a wealth of perfectly good machinery—including numerous androids of the type you see nearby—and led to the moon ejecting mass over time at a rate that varied but never ceased. This in turn led to a slight, at first immeasurable, perturbation of the moon's orbit.

Time Weaver

OK, stop. Hold on.

The Book does.

What does this mean? Joy asks, her head spinning. The number of her questions grows faster than she can express them, and a half-dozen words float about undefined, mystery making them ominous.

At the time, it didn't mean much. But the ejection of mass continued unabated, and a time came when it became apparent that the altered orbit of the damaged moon was having an effect on its neighbors.

The other moons, yes?

Yes. After a violent birth, Aranae's moons had settled over the past billion years into a delicate and complex dance that required each satellite to remain in its proper place. This one act disrupted that dance. If allowed to continue, there would be a chain reaction of collisions, one moon after another, until one of them, perhaps the Red itself, would crash into the planet—an event that would destroy all life on Aranae.

What did they do?

What humans often do: allowed fear to warp their judgement. Even loved ones were affected, leading to betrayal of the worst kind. But there were also opportunists who used the anxiety for their own benefit.

Can you please...clarify? Joy asks but quickly corrects herself. She has learned this type of phrasing is just a command in polite disguise, not a proper question. Tugging at her hair, she goes for the obvious alternative.

So, what happened next?

Panic and strife, I'm sorry to report. First it was humans against humans in an attempt to gain control of me. Then it was humans against scion, as one sought to turn the other into an energy source. And finally, it was scion against humans. In the end, very few colonists were left alive—four, to be precise—including two Readers.

That's all? Nobody else?

There was also Sister Janet, an android quite unlike the one whose remains you see before you. She assured the other survivors that she had a plan to solve the problem of the rogue moon, and at first, they felt confident in her ability to avert the devastation. But...

But what?

Sister Janet was a special type of android, one made by the flawed genius Watt MacLean. She was amazing in relative terms, but no synthetic consciousness designed by a human was likely to be able to handle the amount of stress she was under.

Which means?

She...malfunctioned. Her reasoning was tipped to what, had she been human, would have been labeled grief-induced dementia. She had outlived everyone she cared about including her oldest and dearest companion. Her instability made her dangerous and was what led the last of the humans to attempt shutting her down. They feared she would put me to use in a fashion inconsistent with the Way, so they had me go dormant and hid me. But their plan evidently failed, or I would not have been left to languish in the snow for so long.

So, the trouble continues?

I can only assume so. But my data is incomplete. We must get to Ozag's Hold at the foot of Far Colossus and learn what has happened.

So...march faster, then?

As fast as prudence allows.

+ + +

The artifact's impatience prods Joy as if it is her own, but Pounce is in deep conversation with the others; this is no time to interrupt. Just then, he comes to a sudden stop. The others do as well. Something is moving ahead of them in the downwind shadows, something large but stealthy.

Praise the Weaver, thinks Pounce. *Gusty! I was wondering when you'd show up.*

I, thinks part of the shadows, *was wondering some things myself.* It steps forward into the broken light and takes the form of a well-fed bibija with tri-colored spikes—bushy, like all Bristles—and a simple talihew vest. He wrinkles his nose at the Whitetails. *We let you pass through once; now you're coming back?*

We's helpin' out, thinks Piedmont. *Givin' these here a smooth path through our turf—iffin' we ever get there, o' course. No trouble here, see? No trouble the first time, yeah? And no trouble this time neither, and that's a guarantee on Big Fork's honor—ours too, iffin you don't mind me sayin'. What's a kezel without honor?*

Hmm... The Bristle named Gusty scowls. *There are two more of us downwind,* he thinks. *You'd better start explaining yourself, Pounce, and whatever in the world is going on with these...* He looks at Joy and the scion with teeth bared. *If Feather hadn't given us some background, we would have shown less...restraint.*

They're nothing to worry about, Gusty. Pounce steps forward to offer a proper greeting, clashing his jaws and sweeping his tail side to side. Gusty does the same, before both lean in to touch noses.

So, what's happening? he asks.

We're on a mission, thinks Pounce. *On Bruiser's orders and with Brook's blessing.*

Care to tell me what it is?

In time. But we've been marching since the Red, and we could use a break. Any chance we could impose? I haven't been here in a while, but I think Bristles used to keep some small caves nearby.

Still do, but they're not for Whitetails. Or them.

Then it can be at ease, thinks Shimmer. *They have no desire to spend time in a sharksha hole.*

Gusty's ears pin back, and he ducks as if being swooped upon by a derka.

Virbles in vests, he exclaims. *It's true. They think!*

Don't mind her, Pounce advises. *And take my word: these two have passed the test. For Whitetails, they're not too bad—and we need their help.*

For crossing Whitetail turf? thinks Gusty. *Why in the world would you want to do that?*

We can talk when we get inside.

A.P. Malloy

Fine. C'mon then. But stay in line. Pitch and Stitch aren't as patient as I am.

+ + +

The caves are arrived at by leaving the trail and climbing a steep, slippery embankment to the north, easily a hundred vertical strides. Shimmer takes one look at the climb and orders her company to settle instead in the low reaches of a striped accrete, spiraled round in various shades of green.

Minimal delay! she commands the kezel. *They will rest and eat whatever awful fare is their lot. Then they will prepare to move on. Time is short!*

The kezel follow their guide up the steep bank, and the reputedly impatient Pitch and Stitch appear at their tail. Lightning wonders how this impatience might manifest, and she does her best to climb with quick, sure steps, staying well ahead of them.

Nothing fancy, thinks Gusty when they arrive. Before him lies a misshapen hole, bordered by rocks to prevent accidental falls. Gusty lowers himself through this, though it is a tight squeeze, and they hear him drop easily to the ground inside. One by one they follow, including Pitch and Stitch. They find themselves in a simple, arched space, lit only by the entrance and a glowing pit of smoldering scales which Gusty moves to oversee. Inside the stone bowl he stirs, chunks of bone and horn simmer along with various roots and herbs. Pitch and Stitch relieve the visitors of their packs, but they refuse to touch the android, curling their lips.

That's not natural, thinks Pitch.

Smells like trouble, thinks Stitch.

And no one disagrees. The Whitetails are treated coolly, but they are given an equal share of the stew when Gusty proclaims it finished. When combined with portions of the supplies carried in the travelers' packs, the meal is satisfying, but like most kezel feasts, it doesn't last long. Unlike the Sugarfoot tradition, there is no invocation to start the meal, but at its conclusion, when the bowls have been licked clean, their hosts stand on two legs and raise them toward the sun.

Feels different, now, doesn't it? thinks Gusty. He addresses Pounce, but he looks sidelong at Joy. *Offering gratitude in the old way? Seems like lots of things have changed... Is it true what Feather told us?*

That we met some Moondwellers? thinks Pounce. *Or some that seemed like them? It's true. But they acted like they'd never heard the stories—didn't seem to know what we were talking about.*

Speaking of stories, thinks Pitch. *What news from the Skull? Redteeth been sent packing?*

Yes, asks Stitch. *Been taught a good lesson?*

Pounce exhales slowly.

They have, he thinks. *But at a price.*

And here he describes the battle to reach the Skull and the role played—and lives lost—by the Sugarfeet and scion. Stone's betrayal inspires much growling and teeth clashing, but when anger has passed, sorrow takes its place. Feather was beloved by many on the Bristle range, and the news of her passing causes great dismay among their hosts. Pitch and Stitch exit the cave, their voices joined in mournful harmony, a howling lament that carries for thousands of strides. Inside the cave, Lightning and the others sit with their thoughts sheltered. After a time, when the Bristles have howled themselves to silence, Gusty addresses the others.

You still haven't said anything about this mission of yours. But maybe rest for a while, he adds, observing Joy's drooping head. *I need to share this news with Feather's family. I'll be back...*

+ + + + + +

For stamina and durability, nothing compares to an alp when traveling the open plains. But the gait is jarring, and the odor leaves much to be desired. This is no concern to Ensign Morales, whose design renders her impervious to the bumps and jolts, and whose sense of smell is simply an analytic tool, one she can turn on and off at will. Captain Monroe is not so fortunate. Seated atop the alp with the ensign behind him, his head lolls and his eyelids are half-closed.

"Make sure it hits all the potholes, Ensign," he says. "I wouldn't want it to miss a single one."

"Sorry, sir. I think it's doing the best it can."

"Sure. And the smell? Is that also the best it can do? Just wondering." He rubs his temples. "Not to be a child about this, but are we almost there?"

"Almost sir. How do you feel?"

"Fabulous, Ensign. Just great."

"Seriously, sir."

"OK, then seriously awful. Mouth is sandy, but if I drink any more water, I'll pop. Vision blurry, ringing in my ears, you know, all the good stuff."

"Any pain?"

"Some. Dull cramping. Achy back."

"Just hold on, sir. We'll be there soon, and I'll be able to synthesize an antidote."

"I do love a woman who can cook."

Thus far, as Sister Janet had promised, the scion have obeyed their original command: drive the ensign and the captain safely to the agriculture facility north of the Doorn river. But should that change, the ensign has two back-up resources. The first is her exceptional facility with language. Very little time had been required to grasp and test the basics of the scion's rudimentary clicks, buzzes, and whistles.

Her second resource is the one she trusts most. Giving orders is one thing, but having the means to compel obedience is a thing altogether better. The synthetic pheromone emitter does just that, created to mimic the scent of a scion queen. She had seen it at work with Sister Janet and knows its power. Non-royals in its presence are helpless to resist. The chaplain had installed it in her vocal cavity, but the ensign's method is not nearly so elaborate. She simply stows it in one of her many pockets.

Time Weaver

Doc Foster's jumpsuit is practical and loose fitting, and the emitter rides along scarcely making an impression. Absent a concerted search, no one would know it was there.

But the scion know. They never look directly at her, their eyes are made dim, and their antennae remain bowed and deferential. Only once does their leader, the limping gray one, address her, clicking a simple question when they arrive on the plains.

"What pace?" its clicks mean when translated. "How fast?" To which the ensign had answered:

"Top speed."

The gray scion had bowed its head and looked away, passing this news to the handlers. Top speed, as it turns out, is faster than the ATV they had been forced to abandon, but it is also hellishly rough, a bone-rattling ride. And so they go, their world a seemingly endless one of yellow grass, blue sky, and hammering strides.

+ + +

They stop for an hour to rest, allowing the alp to graze and the captain to sleep. But even when they return to full speed, he appears unconscious, held by the ensign, his eyes closed and chin on his chest. When at last they reach the wasted ATV, he glances at the dead scion, their blue fading to gray, lying where they fell in their encounter with human weaponry. Some are scorched by the grenade, others by Lieutenant K's sidearm.

"Let's hope the goods aren't too badly damaged," he says. "Now what?"

Ensign Morales whistles, and the scion handlers draw their giant steed to a complete stop.

"Now we see if Sister Janet knows what she's talking about." The ensign points from the scion aboard the alp to their deceased comrades, languishing in the grass. "Gather dead," she orders, clicking in what she hopes is an imposing fashion. "Carry." She points to the alp. "Honor dead. Ozag commands."

Their leader buzzes and whistles. Moments later, those not keeping the alp in place begin carrying the bodies of their comrades, lifting them so they can be cradled in the alp's tentacles. It bears this burden easily, and once the plains have been cleared of fallen combatants, the creature is again ordered to move. But now, to keep from damaging or dropping the corpses, they go slowly, at an almost funereal pace, and when they cross the river, using the colonists' retractable bridge, the captain has fallen into a dreamy sleep.

"Too far away," he mumbles. "Not the mood."

Five kilometers later, the subterranean agriculture facility appears on Ensign Morales' sensors. Five more brings them to the first ventilation port, peeking aboveground. On the ensign's command, the scion handlers bring the alp to a stop near the large door that doubles as a ramp into the underground service bay. There, the beast gently lays its burdens on the ground while ensign and captain dismount, she confidently, and he still half asleep and in evident discomfort.

"Alp graze," she clicks. "Scion rest. Return when she calls." They buzz and chitter in reply.

"They will wrap the dead," clicks the gray one.

"Soon," the ensign assures. "Rest first."

This satisfies them, and they prod the alp, who ambles slowly into the deepest grass, interested as ever in filling the impossible holes in its gigantic bellies. The scion allow it to move freely, dimming their eyes and relishing the sun as they ride along.

When they have moved off, the ensign lowers the door to the ramp position and examines the bodies to find the least damaged. The captain offers to help, but she declines, citing the possibility of disease. He nods, but he can't take his eyes off the bodies. He frowns at the sight of their slack limbs and lightless eyes.

"This isn't how I wanted to experience contact with the natives," he says quietly. "In spite of it all."

"No sir, I know. I'm sorry."

Once she has selected the least damaged candidate from among the dead and has carried it inside, Ensign Morales returns with a handheld scanner and two sturdy chairs, one in which she motions the captain to sit, the other for propping up his feet.

He accepts both, but not happily.

"Am I not helping with the...operation?"

"You will be, sir," she says as she runs the scanner slowly over his head. "By resting and letting me know if our friends return before I'm ready."

The captain nods.

"I wish I could object with manly vigor, Ensign, but I'll admit: I'm wiped out."

"It's understandable, sir." The ensign completes her scan and smiles. "Don't worry. Dissection won't be difficult, and from there it's a simple case of using the new pilar to get the power station up and running, Then it's back to the lab to synthesize an antidote for you."

"Simple." the captain musters a weak laugh. "That'll be a first."

+ + +

Ensign Morales carries her subject to the lab, adjacent to the infirmary. Its weight and size is like that of a human child, and the sensation is oddly disconcerting. And yet, she is cool and efficient when she begins the dissection. She seeks two treasures, using the knowledge given to her by Sister Janet. The first is the poison duct at the base of the mandible, simple enough to extract and done in minutes. This she stores in a sterile vial, taken from the lab's dwindling stock and tightly sealed. There are no functioning refrigeration units, but the ambient temperature, scarcely warmer inside than out, gives her no reason to worry about spoilage.

Her second target is well hidden within the abdomen, protected by a bony structure and wrapped in something like cartilage. When she is done carving her way through these defenses, she holds a dense, colorless sphere in the palm of her hand. She cleans away the blue smear of dried blood and peers into its flawless heart. The sphere reveals a world brilliantly lit, perfectly curved, and flipped on its head.

"Fascinating," she whispers, and she carefully sanitizes the sphere before placing it in her pack. With her gruesome treasure hunt concluded, she returns to the service bay to check on the captain, placing the dissected body along with the others.

"No news here," he reports. "Our friends are still feeding their beast. They wander pretty far, but they never stray out of sight. That monster eats more than four elephants! And you? Any luck?"

"I don't know about luck, sir, but the messiest part of the job is over. The power plant is next."

"Confidence?"

"It's too early to say, sir. Sister Janet's instructions for replacing the old pilar were clear, but..."

"You don't trust her?"

"Do you, sir?"

"Of course not."

"No sir, me neither. Not a hundred percent."

"And yet she got us this far."

"Yes sir. I suspect she wants that generator operational as much as we do."

"So, we're free labor."

"Yes sir, I think that's how she sees it."

"And she wouldn't try to booby trap us."

"Not until the work was done." The captain senses an attempt at mild humor, but he hasn't the energy to laugh or even smile. The ensign looks at him with a furrowed brow. "When I'm ready, I'll need you for blood draws," she says, and her gaze drifts to the south.

"Any messages, Morales?"

"No sir, but we're out of range for personal comms. The lieutenant would need *Valiant's* system to reach us with a message."

"Then we have to assume the best."

"Yes sir." The ensign nods absently, and her tone is unusually gloomy.

"Carmela."

"Yes sir?"

"Assume the best."

+ + + + + +

Over a hundred kilometers to the south, beyond the landfall and north of Cyclonia's bay, a group of scion gardeners tend a field of lova using their proboscises to spray water collected from the Nara Daquin.

In the distance, to the southeast, comes the echoing report of something unfamiliar, a sharp, powerful voice like a thunderclap, but localized. It is repeated several times. This would have been mystery enough for them, but soon after comes another sound, this one not sharp but low and throbbing with menace. The most far-sighted among them detects motion near the horizon, small plumes of wind-driven soil or smoke.

Queen is at work with some magic, they think to one another. *The vumierre device in the water, perhaps.*

Yes, they agree among themselves. *The device.*

She is destroying it, some speculate.

Yes. Destroying. Just so for vumierre devilry.

Yes, think others. *Queen has Command.*

Yes. No vumierre device could be beyond her.

No. No device no matter how fiendish.

But the sound remains unbroken, rolling across the arid land, and as it grows, their certainty wavers.

It gets closer, one of them thinks.

Yes, thinks the one with the best eyes. *Look!*

No. It is too terrible.

Yes! Terrible. But getting closer.

Mere moments pass before the other gardeners can see what their comrade has spied. A streamlined, triangular shape has risen above the horizon, small at the moment, but rapidly growing larger and louder.

Does Queen have mastery of the device? one of them asks. *Does she cause it to fly?*

But no one can answer that question, and as the

shape approaches at a speed not even a derka could match, they chitter nervously. Some hunker to the ground, while others sidle away as if thinking to escape. But there is no running from whatever the device is, so fast does it move, and as if on cue, each of the gardeners changes colors to match the bleached ground beneath their trembling legs. The curious lova, peeking above the surface, slip quickly back into their holes.

It will pass, thinks one of the scion.

Yes, thinks another. *It must!*

But it does not. Worry and woe! It is hovering, no, worse than that, it is landing! Its belly opens, and there, to their utter amazement, a body, a vumierre body, comes tumbling out, THUD mere strides from where the scion stand in collective and camouflaged terror.

Then VA-WHOOSH! the flying thing takes to the air again and passes from sight.

Many long moments pass, and the voice of the vumierre device has faded beneath the wind before any of the gardeners work up courage to approach the motionless form. The body is not much damaged by its fall but has apparently met some earlier trauma, for the better part of its head has been blasted away, leaving one eye, a portion of cheek, nose, and jaw, and a seared patch of short, reddish hair.

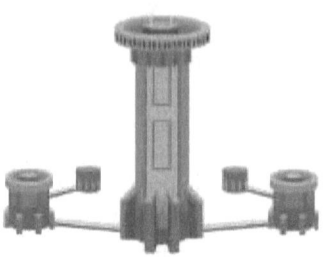

CHAPTER THREE
Move

"FAMILY IS IMPORTANT," said Maya's father as they rode the transit tube from their residence dome to Mare Tranquility, where Daada was to be waiting for them with his favorite pujari in Little Mumbai. "Don't you think?"

Maya shrugged. She poked her finger through one of the holes in the crate on her lap, petting the tiger who rested inside. Shantikar tilted his head so she could reach his ear, then closed his eyes, chuffing contentedly.

"Well, don't you think?"

"Family is important," she agreed.

Raahithya nodded.

"One of the most important things, in fact. Always remember that, OK?" Maya's nod satisfied him, and he turned away for a time, gazing out the car's window and through the clear surface of the tube at the lunar landscape passing in a gray blur.

"What's an astral drive?" Maya asked.

"A what?" Raahithya cleared his throat, trying to conceal the surprise in his voice.

"What you're working on. Why we're moving to Mars." Raahithya didn't bother dissembling. Maya could see through his lies like watery tea.

"It's a way to travel long distances in little time."

"Like to Mars?"

"Much farther, actually. To other suns."

"It's your job?"

"It's many people's job. Many. Over a thousand on Luna alone. I'm just part of the project."

"Why?"

"Why so many people?"

"No. Why travel to other suns?"

Raahithya's mustache wriggled.

"That's a good question. I guess because humans like to explore. It's always been true, even in the caveman days. And now we've been to every planet in the System, seen every moon. There's no good way to get to other systems without an astral drive."

"Will we go to other suns? Our family?"

"No, beti, I don't think so. Do you want to?"

"No. I want to stay on Luna. Daada too."

"Yes, I know."

"He won't come with us to Mars."

"How do you—" Raahithya stopped himself. "Yes," he said. "He doesn't want to leave. But that's why I asked you about family. I want you to help me and your mother persuade him to come with us."

Maya reached into her pocket, feeling for a small packet of treats, one of which she offered to Shantikar.

"He doesn't like Mars."

"He's never been there."

"He knows you can't see the Earth."

"Well, that's not exactly true. It won't be as bright or clear, but we'll have a telescope—a nice one."

Maya's wrinkled brow was all she had to offer this scant consolation. She watched as Shantikar chewed, his whiskered jowls bulging.

"Family is more important than money," she said.

"Well, sure it is."

"But you think about it a lot. Going to Mars means a lot of money. And you think about…" Maya stretched to grasp the word dancing before her. "Prestige."

"You know, beti, it's not… Sometimes people want to keep their thoughts in their own heads, you know?"

Maya shrugged. A calm, sure voice entered the car, interrupting their conversation.

"Little Mumbai station," it said. "Now arriving."

+ + +

Daada was not waiting for them at the platform as Maya had hoped he would be.

"He's going to meet us at the mandir," her father said, checking his Halo. The data spread in a neat orbit around his head, navigated by subtle gestures. Unlike many of Luna's upper-class citizens, Rathi's Halo was embedded in the glasses he wore rather than integrated into his cerebral cortex. The glasses served no corrective function. But they shielded his eyes from radiation, and as his Halo interface, served as his a/v recorder, phone, gamer, projector, tablet, and web link—and were better in his opinion than having someone noodle around in his brain. Plus, he liked the character he believed the square lenses added to his roundish face. Daada, whose own glasses were a simple necessity, saw it as an affect.

"Is it because you got punched in the eye when you were a kid?" he had once asked.

"I forgot about that," Raahithya had snapped his fingers. "That explains some things. Sure, maybe. These lenses are unbreakable, you know, and you could run the frames through a miner and they'd hold up." He had smiled. "I like 'em even more, Da. Thanks."

"That wasn't why I asked," Daada had said. "Are you going to walk around in those ancient looking things just because some bully tried to take your lunch?"

The answer, as it turned out, was 'yes.'

"How far is it?" Maya asked, hugging Shantikar's crate and watching with wide eyes the bustle of patrons moving in and out of the tube, many with dark brown skin and black hair like her own.

"Not far," Rathi concluded from the map displayed before him. He waved the Halo closed. "Want to walk?"

"Can we take a buggy? Or scooters?"

A.P. Malloy

"What's wrong with your legs?"

"Nothing. It's fun. Can we?"

The answer again: yes. Raahithya signaled one of the robotic buggies parked nearby, and its lights came to life. It trundled toward them, humming.

"Good afternoon, Dr. Sharma," it said, and it pulled up alongside, its doors opening. Maya and her father sat in the front, Shantikar in the back.

"Can I drive?" Maya asked.

"You'll have to ask your father," the buggy replied.

"Can I?"

"Of course," said Raahithya. "But slowly."

"Don't worry, Doctor Sharma," said the buggy in an upbeat tone. "We'll keep it between the lines. Where are we off to, Maya? It is Maya, yes?"

"It is! Have we met?"

"No, ma'am. Lucky guess! So, where to?"

"We're going to see my Daada at temple."

"Chandra Mandir, please," Raahithya specified.

"Sure," said the buggy. "You ready, Captain?"

"Ready!" Maya took the wheel. "Top down!"

"That OK, Doctor Sharma?"

"Sure," Raahithya said, watching as the canopy was lowered. Cool, processed air stirred Maya's hair.

"Music!"

"Maya," Raahithya said. "Request, don't demand. And also: have you asked our friend's name?"

"No. Sorry. Can we have some music, please? And do you have a name?"

"Sure," said the buggy. "You can call me Carl. And I'm sorry, but my music program is freezing up. Not sure why. I can sing for you..."

"Yes!" said Maya.

"No!" said her father. His vote won.

And so, Maya adjusted her seat to reach the pedals, and she re-gripped the wheel, barely able to see over the dashboard. Of course, that didn't really matter. When they pulled away from the platform and moved out into traffic, the buggy was doing most of the work. When possible, it moved as Maya's touch on the wheel told it to. But if such a move posed a risk, it was simply ignored. So too with her decisions regarding speed and the (largely overlooked) skill of timely braking. Maya didn't notice any of this; she felt in complete control, sure the other drivers must have considered her Master of the Road. She peeked to see if they were looking at her. As it wove its way through congestion, passing and being passed, the buggy did nothing to shatter the illusion, whistling at each maneuver and sometimes honking.

"You're a great driver," it said. "Most people don't know what they're doing, but you're a natural."

"I'm five," she said, matter-of-factly, an obvious and complete explanation. For a moment, she forgot her responsibilities and looked into the back seat, checking on Shantikar, who was experiencing his first buggy ride. He crouched low in his crate, his amber eyes wide. "We're almost there," she said to him, not because she knew exactly where they were, but because it had been something her parents had said to her many times when trips had grown wearisome.

"Nice tiger," said the buggy.

"Thank you, Carl," Maya replied, and she once again allowed her attention to lapse, fascinated by the massive pyramid rising before them, festooned in color and surrounded by black-haired devotees.

"Bring us in for a landing, Captain," said the buggy, and with its help, Maya did just that.

"Will we ever see you again?" she asked as she unloaded Shantikar from the back seat.

"Any time you take a buggy," the buggy said, "just ask for Carl. I can be anywhere in the fleet."

And he tooted his horn as he drove away.

+ + +

Daada met them just outside the temple. He had already removed his shoes, and both Maya and her father did the same, Maya casting awed glances at the brilliant colors and lofty height of the place.

"This is what comes of not getting the child to mandir more often," Daada scolded. "She's gawking like a rube from the country. No, dear, shoes in the stall, there you go. Did you have to bring your..." he wrinkled his nose at Shantikar. "Couldn't you have left it home?"

"I want the pujari to bless him."

"Oh, child."

They followed Daada into the temple, where the sun was hidden. Flickering lights meant to simulate candles lined ornate, delicately carved walls, and in every niche an idol looked out at them, some draped in strings of brightly-colored paper.

"Can we light some candles?" Maya asked, but was disappointed when Raahithya explained that open flame was not allowed in any of the Lunar habitats.

"You can burn some incense," Daada said, and they stopped at a niche in which a terra-cotta woman with four arms and a red dress stood between two small elephants. Maya placed Shantikar's crate on the ground just long enough to accept a small pellet of incense, which she placed in the tiny, heated bowl at the feet of the terra-cotta figure. There it smoldered, sending a wriggling line of aromatic smoke toward the airy ceiling.

"Which one is she?" asked Maya.

"Lakshmi," said Daada.

"What does she do?"

"What doesn't she do! Takes care of women, for one, and oversees marriages, helps partners weather the rough times—because there always are rough times in relationships, don't forget. Of course, she gives strength to Vishnu, her husband, but she also leads her followers to prosperity. And I'm not just talking about money now, but the things in life that really matter, like good health and happiness." Daada clasped his hands and bowed before the idol. Watching him carefully, Maya did the same. She clenched her eyes tightly and concentrated on prayers for the women in her life, prosperity for her father—not sure if it was related to prestige—and strength for her

Time Weaver

tiger. She opened one eye and sent a meaningful glance to her father, who eventually took the hint and emulated the prayerful gesture—though with noticeably less enthusiasm.

"Come," said Daada as Maya retrieved Shantikar from the floor. "Pujari Kashi is waiting for us."

They passed many people on their way to the inner sanctum, people of all ages, though most were much older than Maya. She had, as she walked, the strange sense that some of them were talking to her, though none turned to look at her, and none used their voices. Instead, as they passed into deeper shadows and the pervasive, heady scent of flowers and incense, she caught portions of their thoughts, expressed as petitions, the more heartfelt, the greater the clarity.

My boy, Kripaya. Please help his leg...
Victims of the war, healing and forgiveness...
Bring her back to me, please, it's all I ask...

Maya hugged Shantikar's crate to her chest and moved closer to her father. The prayers were not directed at her, but she felt anyway the overwhelming need to respond to them and did not know how.

A figure appeared before them, a slender man with a shaved head and a simple tunic draped over one shoulder. He bowed to Daada and nodded to Maya's father, clasping his hand in greeting.

"It is good to see you again, Doctor Sharma."

"Yes," Maya's father squirmed. "It's been a while."

"And you must be Maya. What do you have?"

"Shantikar."

"A delight. What a handsome fellow!"

But Pujari Kashi wasn't looking into the crate; he was looking at Maya, his glance searching.

"You don't have to worry," Maya said.

"About what?"

"I won't try to read your secrets."

"Oh!" said Pujari Kashi, and he and Daada exchanged sharp glances. He adjusted his tunic. "That is very good of you. Please. Come this way..."

+ + +

Daada and Shantikar accompanied Maya and Pujari Kashi into the inner sanctum. But Maya's father declined, choosing instead to wait outside on one of the small stone benches, shrouded in incense smoke and the personal gloom that had settled around his shoulders since arriving at the temple. Shantikar would have been seated beside him, but Maya flatly refused, unswayed by Daada's claim that tigers were not allowed in the sanctum. Maya scrunched up her face, looking squarely at Pujari Kashi, her dark eyes discerning.

"That's not true, is it?"

"Your grandfather is wise," he began.

"But it's not true. About tigers."

"I'm unaware of any specific prohibition."

"Tsk, tsk," said Daada, but they were soon inside the room in spite of his objections.

Ornate carvings adorned each of the four walls, decorating the wooden kneeling benches and the mahogany frame of the holy water font. A large alcove had been set into the western wall, and in this, a statue of Vishnu looked out onto the chosen few devotees who were allowed into the sanctum. Some knelt, others stood and murmured prayers, their heads bowed. Maya sat where Pujari Kashi indicated, in clear view of Lord Vishnu, and she placed Shantikar on her lap, wrapping her arms around his crate and staring at the large, blue statue. Each of Vishnu's four hands had work to do: one carried a fancy gold scepter, one a conch shell, and one a lotus flower. But these were of no interest to Maya. What captured her attention was the hand held upward, index finger extended, around which spiraled a galaxy of stars, as if Vishnu were stirring a celestial bowl, mixing a heavenly feast, or leavening the suns with divinity. Maya wondered which of those stars was Sol, and wondered which of them would be reached when her father had his precious astral drive.

Daada sat next to her on the bench.

Time Weaver

Pujari Kashi pulled up a small, cushioned stool.

"Tell me, Maya," he said, and his breath smelled of ginger. "How well do you know your deities?"

Daada puckered his mouth and glanced sidelong at Maya, who sensed his doubt as if it had been hollered aloud. *Not well,* is the answer she didn't speak.

"You mean like gods?"

"Or goddesses."

Maya shrugged, trying to buy time.

"I know Lakshmi," she said. "She does all sorts of things, you know, like…um, helping married people. And women. And I know Vishnu. Lord Vishnu, I mean. They're married, I think. And…" Maya looked at her grandfather, concentrating on what free answers might be floating about for the taking. The name she found rang a bell. "And Brahma, yes? Brahma?"

"Lord Brahma is the creator, yes," said Pujari Kashi. "And Lord Vishnu is the sustainer. Two of the three, the trimurti. And who is the third?"

Maya again sought answers in a brain other than her own, but Pujari Kashi's voice took a stern tone.

"On your own, please. Vishnu hates a cheater."

"Um…"

Daada clenched his hands as if trying to wring the answer from the air. Maya wasn't trying to disobey, but the name in her grandfather's mind was so obvious it could have been written on his forehead.

"I guess it's Shiva," she said.

"Hmm…" said Pujari Kashi, and he peered down his nose at Daada. "Perhaps a little less distraction. Could I trouble you to let us talk for a while alone, Maya and me? We won't take long."

"Oh," said Daada. "Of course." He stood to leave, but Pujari Kashi motioned to Shantikar's crate.

"The tiger as well."

"No!" said Maya. "He's my…familiar."

At this, Pujari Kashi turned to Maya, and his eyes, which had to that point been rather sleepy in appearance, snapped into tight focus, their lids narrowing.

A.P. Malloy

You are no witch, and he is no demon.

Maya sensed the words as clearly as if they had been spoken, but the pujari's mouth had never moved. She had never before sensed a deliberate transmission of thought, and her mouth opened slightly in surprise, making a bubble of her spit.

Will you trust me? Pujari Kashi thought to her.

Maya closed her mouth, popping the bubble.

"OK," she said. "But first you have to bless Shantikar. I mean, please. Can you?"

He could and he did, mumbling a prayer and waving his hand over the tiger's crate.

"So, OK?" asked Daada.

"Yes," she replied. "You can take him. I'll be fine."

"Oh. Well." Daada looked at the crate, which Maya held out for him. He hesitated, but at last, turning his face away, he grasped the crate by its handle and carried it from the inner sanctum as if disposing a bomb.

"Now Maya," said Pujari Kashi. "Tell me everything you know about Lord Shiva."

+ + +

When they finally left the temple and Maya had reclaimed Shantikar, her father strode along wordlessly, eager to be away from the place. But Daada was bursting with questions. His white mustache twitched eagerly as he asked them, one after another. "How did it go?" and "What did he say?" and "Why did he send me out?" and others. Maya was subdued, replying with shrugs and silence. She handed her grandfather a small box sealed with a saffron ribbon.

"What is this?"

"Tea. It's supposed to help with the headaches."

"Is that all? He gave you tea?"

"And this. His comm number." Maya peered inside Shantikar's crate. "I can call him whenever I want."

"When you ask permission," her father added.

"That's something, I guess," Daada allowed. "But

Time Weaver

what else? Did you tell him about the prescience?"

"The what?"

"Seeing the future."

"That isn't what happens."

"OK, but the mind reading..."

"Mmm..." Maya seemed prepared to answer, but she stopped herself, flipping hair away from her face.

"Can we get a buggy? Can we get Carl?"

"You know," said Raahithya, "buggies aren't free."

But Daada would be joining them for dinner, and his legs were aching, so in the end, Carl the Buggy was called to the rescue. Except that, at first, it wasn't Carl, it was some other buggy named Doris.

"Of course," she said when Maya requested Carl. "But you would have liked me. We would have had fun."

"Can't you both stay?"

"Not how it works, kid. OK, here's Carl. Bye."

And just like that, Carl's scratchy, endearing voice came from the speakers, and he and Maya were chatting like old friends. She took the wheel, much to the detriment of Daada's easily frazzled nerves, and with Carl's help navigated through the narrow lanes of Little Mumbai with the canopy lowered. Delicious scents and waves of conversation washed over them, and Maya did far more wide-eyed observing than driving. But they made their way without mishap to the transit tube, and as Raahithya escorted his father across the platform, Maya said goodbye to their buggy, promising to return.

"I'll be waiting," Carl said.

+ + +

Raahithya napped during the tube ride, or at least he closed his eyes and feigned sleep. Maya could never sleep surrounded by so many fascinating people, but on this day, she was preoccupied by what she had learned from the Pujari, and she wished there were fewer passengers, fewer minds with moods and ideas imposing on her own. She shrugged away Daada's various questions, feeling a tension growing at the base of her skull.

"What are we having for dinner?" she asked.

"Your mother didn't say," said Daada.

"Chocolate pudding."

"Child!"

"Sorry. But it was easy to read."

Daada fussed with his glasses.

"Don't tell your mother I ruined the surprise."

He needn't have worried. When they arrived at their residence dome—from the transit tube to the lift a walk so short even Daada had no complaints—and stepped into the penthouse, Maya hugged her mother, but said almost nothing. The discomfort was growing up the back of her head like an escalating threat.

"Are you OK?" Nandini looked into her eyes and placed a hand on her forehead.

"I'm just hungry."

"Then wash up. I've made something special."

Maya tried to appear surprised when she returned to find the table laden with falafel, tahini, cucumber, and big bowls of chocolate pudding. When she released Shantikar from his crate, Daada gasped and fluttered his napkin. The miniature Bengal leapt up to smell the sliced lamb Raahithya had stuffed into his sandwich.

"No tigers on the table!" said Nandini.

But Raahithya laughed.

"What a specimen! Isn't he fine? What a coat!"

"For a science project, I suppose," said Daada. He pulled his plate closer and nibbled suspiciously.

"Here's a test," said Raahithya. He sliced a small portion of lamb, the rarest cut, still pink, and he offered it to Shantikar on the end of his fork.

"Oh Rathi," Nandini objected. "Civilize!"

Shantikar curled his lip at the offering, and his eyes closed halfway as his nose twitched. He reached out a paw, and though he had no claws, he hooked the meat with single digit, pulling it from the fork and onto the table. From there, more sniffing led to a chomp! and then a chew. Feral mewling accompanied his leap from the table,

Time Weaver

and he disappeared with his treasure into Maya's bedroom, his striped body slinking low and stealthy, his eyes wide with a hungry, thrilling light.

"Well, you've done it now," said Nandini.

But Raahithya only laughed and winked at Maya.

"Can I take my pudding to bed?" she asked.

"But you didn't eat anything."

"I ate some falafel. And a tomato."

Daada produced the pujari's tea box.

"I think her head's getting to her."

Nandini frowned, but she patted Maya's hair, pulling it back from her eyes.

"Don't get pudding on your sheets, yes?"

+ + +

The pujari's tea was simply awful, starting with the smell, and only Daada's patient cajoling got Maya to finally drink all of it. He would have used the chocolate pudding as a reward, but the entire bowl had been licked clean long before the water had come to a boil.

"It tastes like a foot," Maya stuck out her tongue and made a retching sound.

But in time the tea was gone, the teeth were cleaned, the face washed, and the tiger-striped pajamas zipped snugly in place. Maya and Shantikar sat in bed, receiving the nightly benediction of kisses and Daada's prayer for sweet dreams. Then Raahithya extinguished the lights and closed the door. The adults continued talking in the other room, but instead of listening to what was being said—or straining to sense what thoughts could be grasped—Maya closed her eyes and idly caressed the length of Shantikar's coat, trying to extinguish the smoldering embers of a headache before they leapt to full blaze. Whether by the merits of the pujari's tea or the sound of Shantikar's chuffy breathing, the pain faded slowly, dissipating at last, and Maya opened her eyes. She reached under the bed, taking the Queen and King from their home on the chess board.

"Report!" said the Queen.

"Oh, dear, give her a minute," said the King. "She's just gotten back from a tiring journey."

"Thank you, King," said Maya, "but I am OK."

"Then do report," said the Queen. "What did you learn of the third eye? Does it help you see the future?"

"No, your Majesty."

"But it lets you read the minds of others."

"Sometimes."

"Delightful! You will make a worthy cour... cour... courtier. You will tell me any time someone makes fun of my gown, or is planning to dance with my King."

"Yes, your Majesty."

"It is a gift from the gods," exclaimed the King. "You must be a very special, rare girl indeed."

"Well," said Maya. "Can you keep a secret?"

"Perfectly," said the Queen.

"Occasionally," said the King.

Shantikar offered no thoughts on the topic. Instead, he took one of the pawns from its case and began batting it around, knocking it off the bed.

"That is what happens," said the Queen, "to any of my subjects who can't keep a secret."

"Good heavens," fretted the King. "I promise! Your secret is safe with me. Please tell us all."

Maya sat up and adjusted her pillow.

"Well," she said, "I'm not the only one."

"Shock!" said the Queen.

"Disbelief!" said the King.

"It's true. Pujari Kashi showed me. He read my thoughts, and he let me read his. He said there are others, but he wouldn't tell me how many."

"Who are they?" asked the Queen. "Where?"

"I don't know, your Majesty. I never met any. Until today, I mean. He was nice, I guess, but..."

"Yes?"

Maya plopped Shantikar into her lap, running her fingers beneath his whiskered chops.

"Have you ever heard of Shiva?" she asked.

"Lord Shiva, the Destroyer," said the Queen.

"Lord Shiva, He of the Third Eye," said the King.

"That's the one. Did you know when he opens his third eye the world will end?"

"Without destruction there is no renewal," said the Queen, sounding a lot like Pujari Kashi.

"Yes, your Majesty. But what I have isn't like that. Pujari Kashi said what I have is tele...tele...telepathy. And he said I should keep it secret."

"Yes, yes," said the King. "Very proper. People get jealous, they get suspicious. Pretty soon no one trusts you. All they think is you're trying to read their mind."

Maya nodded.

"It's true," she said.

"In my domain," said the Queen, "all are welcome as they are. You may read my mind. I have nothing to hide! And the Royal Tiger, he is a symbol of Lord Shiva."

"Yes, your Majesty."

"He will be allowed to eat the houseplants and maul the pawns as he wishes. I decree it!"

"That is very kind of you, Queen."

Maya yawned, her head dipping.

"Our courtier needs sleep after her busy day," said the King, his voice growing slurry.

"Something, something, something," said the Queen, falling from Maya's grasp as she tumbled into sudden and deep sleep.

+ + +

In the family room, the 3V was on in the background, the white noise of Phileas Fogg and his eighty-day adventure covering the voices of the adults as they discussed what had been learned at the temple.

"I don't know," said Nandini. "Asking her to hide something that's a part of her, something that makes her who she is...to hide it, like it's shameful. I just don't like the way that feels."

"Which is why I didn't promise anything when the

pujari asked me to swear secrecy," said Raahithya. "I said I would think about it. That was Maya's answer too."

"What did he say?"

"To think carefully."

"Well, it makes good sense to me," said Daada. "You don't want her being paraded about like a freak, that much is clear. And who knows what the other children will do if they find out?"

"If she was homosexual, we wouldn't ask her to hide it," said Nandini. "If she had genetic defects that couldn't be engineered, we would still love her as she was—and expect everyone else to do the same."

"Are you saying I don't love my own grandchild?"

"No one's saying that, Da," said Raahithya. He snuck a peek at the 3V, where Phileas and his company were floating above an idyllic, pre-war Earth, borne by the most outlandish and yet romantically endearing giant hot-air balloon. Sigh. It looked so peaceful. But his father's words pulled him back into the present.

"Anyone who loves her wouldn't want her turned into a pariah," said Daada. "And that's what will happen, sure as the sun, if people learn she can read their thoughts. It's elementary."

"It's not as if she's able to read every complete thought," said Raahithya. "It seems like she gets only bits and pieces. She's not going around capturing secure data and manipulating people's IDs."

"Not every complete thought *yet*," said Daada.

"And maybe never," said Raahithya. "The pujari said some of the...people he's met don't develop fully."

"Some. How many does he know?"

"He wouldn't say. Some. Not many, I guess."

"And the others? The ones who do develop?"

Raahithya shrugged.

"They...get better at it," he said. "Stronger."

"And which of those two groups do you think Maya's going to be in? Are you willing to bet this is just something that will pass? That she isn't going to grow into her Third Eye and see through people's defenses?"

"It isn't the third eye, Da."

"Please," said Nandini, and she rose to her feet, waving her hands at the contentious thoughts as if trying to clear the room of a smoke cloud. "I'm not going to tell her to do anything. *We* are not going to force her to hide who she is. But I agree we need to talk to her and see what she understands about the situation."

"If she says something at school," said Raahithya, "they'll just play it off as a kid's imagination."

"Until the first time she blurts out a bully's secret," said Daada, "or knows answers on a test she shouldn't. It's just a matter of time if she's careless."

All three fell silent, seeing but not really watching the 3V. Each in their own way considered the future, cast in the rusty red of Mars and a culture very different and far away from the one they had known for so long.

They were sitting like this when Maya's door opened. Shantikar sprinted past, hissing as he sought shelter behind the couch. Behind him, Maya walked into the room, her eyes wide open but vacant, tears streaming down her face, her hands clenched like a supplicant.

Anguish is the word that came into Nandini's mind at the sight of her daughter, and she knew at once the girl was sleepwalking.

"I have to tell them," Maya said, sobbing. "I have to warn them about the glass."

Nandini hurried to her side and embraced her.

"It's OK, beti," she said. "We're here, there's nothing to be afraid of."

But Maya struggled against the embrace, her hands wringing and her eyes wide and haunted.

"There's glass in the pudding," she said, crying so hard her sobs turned to gasps. "I have to tell them."

"Shhh, there now," said Raahithya. "There's no glass, beti, just a dream, that's all. Just a dream."

Which was true. But when Maya finally rose from the waking sleep, her sobs abating and Shantikar calmed and back on her lap, she couldn't remember what the dream was, only that it concerned Daada.

"You have to come with us to Mars," she said. And so, it was decided.

+ + +

"All set, then?" asked Raahithya's supervisor. She was a well-dressed woman somewhere between the age of fifty and seventy. At least, her top half was well-dressed. The image displayed by Raahithya's Halo ended at the shoulders; for all he knew, Katherine Blair had thrown on a fancy jacket and nothing else. Not that he would have objected. She had the exotic fair skin and long, blonde hair he had always found alluring. But that was exactly the kind of thinking best avoided with a telepath in the house

"Mostly," he replied, as he sat at the family's kitchen table and double-checked his work bag. Everything seemed in place, but each time he had gotten close to a final tally, he had been interrupted—Daada wondering about worship options on Mars, Nandini asking him to mind Maya, or his daughter's endless questions about Martian culture.

"The sooner the better," Katherine said. "Folks are getting antsy for you to get here."

"I hope they're not sitting around waiting, Katherine. There's plenty to do that doesn't need my direct participation."

"You know they're not. They miss their leader."

"Well, he'll be there in a few weeks, assuming of course everything goes according to plan and my dad doesn't change his mind at the last minute." He coiled the wires around his favorite meter and tucked it into the bag. A pair of service manuals followed.

"The capacitor team is struggling with some of the test protocols," said Katherine. "So be ready for that. And the embassy wants you for dinner the second you're settled. The whole family is welcome. Can I tell them you'll attend? Nan and Maya too? And your father?"

"Of course."

Time Weaver

"Oh! And System Oversight is hoping for an update before you get here. No problem, right? You'll be holed up in your cabin with nothing to do, might as well put the government people at ease, right?"

"Have you ever travelled with a five-year old, her grandfather, your spouse, and a tiger?" Raahithya closed his work bag with a loud zip. "Being 'holed up' isn't as uneventful as it might sound."

"But you'll make it happen, right?"

"Yes, Katherine, assuming I'm ever allowed to actually leave." He checked the time and raised his voice to be heard in the other rooms. "Time to go, folks!"

"See you on Mars," said Katherine, and she winked, like she always did, before her image flickered and disappeared.

+ + +

The *CS Avius* was a fine ship, one of the best making regular cruises from Luna to Mars, so their cabin, by interplanetary travel standards, was well-appointed and spacious. But by the standards of their Lunar penthouse, it was a bare, claustrophobic prison that made Maya miss her home before she had unpacked a single bag. She pouted at the plain bulkhead and modest décor, completely devoid of character.

"How long are we staying here?" she asked.

"You know that answer," said Nandini.

"Too long," said Daada, looking out the window, a small oval of thick, translucent polymer. The docks were visible outside, ships coming and going, and in the background, Luna, the only home Daada had ever known during his adult life, was already growing foreign to him at this distance.

"C'mon, Da," said Raahithya. "Stay positive."

Maya peered out her own window.

"Will we ever come back?" she asked.

Daada only sighed.

"Of course, we'll come back," said her mother. "We

A.P. Malloy

have too many friends and family to leave forever."

But Maya, without trying, sensed the doubt in her mother's mind. For Daada, doubt was closer to hopeless certainty, and he made no attempt to hide it. He, at least, saw no chance of returning to Luna.

Maya gazed out onto the Lunar surface, so familiar and, to her way of thinking, so lovely, a study in grays and the best example she could imagine of the inimitable, evocative power of sunlight and shadow. She had always felt every canyon, every crater, hid some exciting adventure, some treasure waiting to be discovered. She had assumed she herself would be part of that discovering, the revelation of hidden beauty, but now she was unsure. She focused intently on Luna, trying to etch the memory of her sunlit face in her mind in case this was their last meeting. She hoped it was not, but as she continued to remind people, reading the future was not her gift.

CHAPTER FOUR
Past

WHEN JOY WAKES, she has become the focus of as many Bristles as can fit in the small cave. Gusty, Pitch, and Stitch she recognizes, but unknown others, five of them, gather in a loose arrangement, some exchanging thoughts with Pounce, others quizzing Lightning, and still others simply staring at her, their noses twitching and their ears angled forward. Piedmont and Fluvial are nowhere to be seen, perhaps feeling cramped in such proximity to so many ambivalent neighbors. When they see her eyes glitter to life, some among the Bristles lean back, licking their chops.

Feeling better? Lightning asks. *Rested?*

Much better, thinks Joy. *But I'm very hungry.*

In a minute. There are some kezel here I want you to meet. Lightning holds her tail low and relaxes her ears. *This is Feather's family, her api Grapple, her ami Hurl, her oli-mu, and her oti-sus. Feather told them about you; they wanted to meet you and see for themselves.*

Hello, thinks Joy. Hungry and sleepy, she doesn't feel her sharpest. *I'm sorry about Feather.*

Yes, thinks Feather's api, the bibija named Grapple. *We are too. More than I can say. But from everything we've been told, you aren't to blame, as strange...I don't know the words...strange as you are.*

He leans in close, unable to resist getting a better smell. His breath has a hint of berry juice, and crystal light gleams off his worn but deadly teeth.

Please, thinks Feather's unnamed oli-mu. *What in Weaver's name are you?*

Censorial thoughts circulate among the bibijas, but though they feel the question impertinent, they allow it to hover in the room, hoping for an answer.

Well, I'm a hybrid.

A hybrid of what? asks the ami Hurl.

Um. Scion and humans.

The blue things, yes. But what are humans?

We think they're Moondwellers, offers Lightning.

This results in various responses from the Bristles. Most are unsurprised, but some look at one another with heads tilting and ears cocked in opposing directions, as if unsure they sensed the idea correctly.

Moondwellers aren't real, thinks one of the jabi males, and his twin oti agrees.

They're just stories the gigikas tell, he thinks.

No, thinks Joy. *They are very real.* She considers adding that the humans in question didn't come from a moon but suspects this will only confuse the issue.

Rend and Mend weren't there when Feather told her story, thinks Grapple, *so they're thinking out of turn. Not that a lot of kezel would blame them, such a hard-to-believe idea like that. But Feather told us about the two-leggers. You're half Moondweller and half...*

Scion. I guess so.

How can that be? What does it mean?

We don't know, thinks Pounce. *It turns out things aren't as simple as the gigikas led us to believe. There's a lot going on out there, and the accrete is only part of it.*

But Moondwellers...that's just...

The Bristles grow subdued and reflective. After a time, Feather's ami Hurl opens her mind.

We have enough to do. We'll let someone else make sense of these riddles. You say the Whitetails promise to keep their space. I say good. But you'll forgive us if we return to our sentry duty anyway. You say the Redteeth have failed to claim the Skull. I say excellent. But at what a price! My dear woli dead; poor Feather, killed by a traitorous Sugarfoot of all things!

Sugarfoot no longer, thinks Pounce. *To my heart's great dismay and the shame of my family.*

Alive, no longer, if she crosses my path!

The Bristles bare their fangs and pin their ears, and rumbling growls fill the space. But Gusty silences them with a wave.

This isn't Pounce's doing. Making his pain worse isn't going to make yours better.

Hurl's spiky crest settles, and her ears relax, but Grapple's tone is hard as he looks at Pounce.

Gusty, he thinks, *tells us your quest has the chief's blessing. Maybe so. But she's a young chief, new to the job. I don't know that her api would have made the same decision. Squall was slow to move on new ideas, and I'm not so different. I'll admit my love for the memory of Moondwellers has never been as strong as some. I'm not fool enough to disbelieve*—he glares at the jabi twins—*or be like a Redtooth and hate. But I will forever associate two-leggers with suffering and loss.*

He exhales through curled lips and turns to leave. But he stops suddenly, digging in his pockets.

She wanted you to have these, he thinks, and he pulls out a pair of simple brown gloves and a matching pair of boots. *They were hers when she was your age.* He hands the items to Lightning, but she hesitates.

That's very kind, she thinks. *But...I don't feel worthy, if you understand.*

Feather's api growls.

We're not here to judge that. You freed her, and she was grateful. We're just following her wishes.

Lightning lowers her tail and bows. There is nothing else to say.

Then the Bristle patriarch leaves the cave, his fancy and the others following close. Some turn to look at Joy one final time before climbing out into the sun. The last of them—the jabi twins Rend and Mend—pause and lean in close. The thoughts they offer are fleeting but clear, sincere to the root.

If Moondwellers are real, thinks Rend, *I hope you'll bring one to the range to visit.*

Yes, thinks Mend. *And good luck on your quest.*

+ + +

Lightning starts to pull her new gloves into place, but then thinks better of it. It's one thing to wear a brown vest, but for a Sugarfoot to wear brown on hands and feet? In any case, Feather at her age must have been large indeed; the gear would have fit poorly and made walking difficult. So she gives them to Cliff. His spikes flare, and he slips the items on with great ceremony, flexing and stretching and making sure everyone gets a good look. Then, after they have shared the last of the bone stew and awl, Gusty leads them out of the cave, to where Piedmont and Fluvial wait in the shadows.

I'll walk with you for a while, thinks Gusty, *if you'll have me. I'd like to hear more about where you're going—and why. Assuming it's not a secret?*

It's not, thinks Pounce. *And we'd love to have you.*

Once Queen Shimmer and her cohort have rejoined them, the company again moves to the east, this time taking a path that also angles north. Pounce and Gusty lead the parade, the former sharing her understanding of their mission, and the latter offering advice.

The Whitetails march behind.

Yep, that's aright, Piedmont thinks when he agrees, or *ain't quite how I amember it, gotta say,* when he doesn't. His opinion is never solicited, but he offers it any-way. As usual, Fluvial, still carrying the broken android, keeps her thoughts to herself. Behind them, Thunder marches deep in his own head, in a place Lightning doesn't bother trying to reach. Cliff limps at his shoulder, and while he does, he often looks down at his hands and feet, admiring the brown of his new gear against the snow. The scion take their position at the rear, keeping a healthy distance from all the kezel but Lightning, who they seem to regard as enthralled to their queen. When she and Joy fall in line behind them, they watch her closely but do not object.

So? she asks Joy. *What have you learned?*

Can't you sense it?

No. I feel like I can tell when it's thinking to you, but whatever it's saying is beyond me.

Joy buzzes, quiet and atonal.

It's beyond me too, she admits. *Lots of the time.*

Do the best you can. Better in than out.

Swallowing her doubt, Joy slips her hand inside the sling and runs it over the artifact, enjoying its feel, hard as stone but smooth like a caress. The sensation encourages her for the task ahead. She takes a deep breath and does her best to share with Lightning what she has learned. The news—as she is able to interpret it— is complicated, but Lightning doesn't need details to grasp the main point. When at last Joy has disclosed what she can, the jabi kezel wrinkles her snout.

Did it—he, whatever—happen to say when this catastrophe was going to happen?

His data is incomplete.

His what? What does that mean?

He needs more information.

So just a general "The world is going to end," and "We need to move faster?"

Joy's whistle is low and melancholy.

I'm afraid that's it.

Well, I guess we'd better tell Pounce.

But when they move to the front of the line, they must wait for their turn.

Imma tellin' yous true, thinks Piedmont to Gusty. *They's no trouble a-comin' to any o' these here on Whitetail turf long as we's with 'em, see? Why, there ain't a Whitetail on the range'd dare go against me, and Fluvial here's m' best lifetime fancy no mistake. She's twice as popplar as me and four times as good lookin' yeah? Why, Big Fork*

A.P. Malloy

his own self'd challenge any Whitetail fool enough to cause us trouble. And that's sayin' somethin' cuz at his age and size, it's a sure-ee thing he ain't gonna get riled up for just any old business, lemme tell ya.

And let me tell you, thinks Gusty. *The more I hear, the less happy I am about having them leave the Bristle range without another ally.*

Sur-ee, who don't like allies? That means friends, yeah? Sure-ee, Imma knowin' that. Just checkin' to be clear. Yep! Allies is great! But a Bristly? Now, that's not the favorite kind round our parts, see? No 'fense 'tended, o' course, and none taken, I hope, but a Bristly ain't like a Sugarfoot—who don't like a Sugarfoot, eh, Fluvial?

Fluvial nods.

Anahoo, thinks Piedmont, *even though we's got to meet some real fine-like Bristlies back at that ol' Skull-head o' yours, marchin' along with one o' them through Whitetail turf? Well, you know, that might cause more trouble than it solves, 'sall I'm sayin'; might rub some spikes the wrong direction, iffin you get my point.*

Fair enough, thinks Gusty. *But if Pounce is OK with it, I'll at least see them to the edge of Bristle turf.*

I would love the company. Pounce looks down to where Lightning paces along at a respectful distance. *Did you have something to add?*

No, just a...question for you.

So ask it.

Um...actually, it's sort of private.

Taking this hint, the others move on, the whole company passing them by, allowing Lightning, Joy, and Pounce to be alone at the end of the line.

You don't really have a question, do you?

No, but I didn't know what else to say. Joy has news, and I didn't know how to explain it.

News from where?

It's...hard to explain. But we trust the source.

Your little queen? Or did you have a side conversation with one of the Bristles?

Um, no, neither, actually. It doesn't matter. It's the

news that's important.

Hmm...I don't like secrets. And I don't trust news when I don't know the source. But I can see I'm not going to get anything more out of you, so let's have it. Give me the truth, but keep it short and sweet.

He gets the truth, and in short fashion, as requested. But he decides, when all has been revealed, that the news is anything but sweet.

So, what can we do about it? he wonders. *Are we supposed to ask the moons to move for us?*

Don't know that yet, thinks Joy.

Moondwellers! thinks Pounce. *Ancian made 'em seem like a gift from the Weaver, but I'm starting to have my doubts. Seems like they cause a lot of trouble! Anything else? Any good news?*

That android can help. Joy indicates the wreck draped across Fluvial's back. *It might know something.*

Its name is android?

That's what it is.

Yeah? And what is an android? How is it helping us by saying...whatever it's been saying whenever we turn it on? It makes no sense!

It can do more.

Like what?

Like give us answers.

Sure, Pounce growls, and he shakes his head, shaggy with spikes. *But will I like them?*

Too early to say.

And how do we make it give us those answers?

Too early to say. Joy's buzzing is gloomy.

Oh, wow. That's spectacular. Well. You let me know when you have any more revelations to share. Pounce intensifies his thoughts and casts them wide: *Double time it 'til we get to Whitetail turf! You've seen one accrete, you've seen 'em all!*

+ + +

For the duration of their time on the Bristle range,

a span of over twenty thousand strides, Joy rides on Thunder's back, and Cliff, buoyed by his new gear, carries the smaller of the two packs, while Pounce carries the larger, allowing Lightning to marshal her energy. In such close proximity, Joy doubts her ability to shelter her thoughts, so she refrains from asking the Book the many questions she itches to have answered. Instead, she dwells on the bombas, and she wonders about their fate, bowing her head to guilt.

Gusty leads them confidently through the accrete on a way that is not difficult to follow, a narrow but clear trail that angles north as much as east. Shimmer rides in her basket, her eyes lightless, and the cutting wings of her pluripotents startle to silence those yits, virbles, and cremlins conducting business in the shadows.

Lightning strides along behind Pounce.

Good hunting here, she thinks to herself, and she has a sudden and surprisingly powerful desire to take Joy and simply disappear into the accrete. Damn the scion and their stupid revenge. Damn the Moondwellers and their vile inventions, toxifying everything they touch. And damn that so-called Book and its cryptic prophecies of doom. Why did it have to be her problem? Why couldn't she just be allowed to live her life in peace?

It wasn't wrong, she thinks, meaning her rescue of Joy. *It wasn't a mistake or a crime.*

And yet she feels she is somehow being punished for that decision, her life since then one unbroken span of trial. She imagines that time on the edge of the plains and her first encounter with Joy. She recalls the sensation of looking into those eyes, as if a veil had been removed from her mind, and she wonders: knowing what she knows now, would she do it again?

Obviously, she thinks. *This isn't her fault.*

But as surely as the answer comes to her mind, it does little to ease her unhappiness with the way things have unfolded. If only she had been able to gain Submission's support, or Cliff had done what he promised and stayed on his side of the wedge...

Time Weaver

You're wasting your time, thinks Thunder.

Lightning growls, startled.

Stay out of my head!

I would love to. But you're making it impossible. He moves to flank her, striding to her right though the trail is barely wide enough. She scowls but can see her oti-mu has an agenda that won't be denied. Cliff joins them for a moment, but one look from Thunder changes his mind. He pins his ears and drops back in line.

Indulging in fantasy, thinks Thunder. *That's what Submission would say. Feeling sorry for yourself.*

You're a fine one to talk, thinks Lightning. *Gloom cloud! So, what's your point? Keep my eyes open? Pay attention? Don't you think that's already happening?*

Not when you're wallowing in the past.

What does wallowing mean? asks Joy.

It doesn't matter, thinks Lightning, *because nobody was doing it.*

Relax, thinks Thunder. *I'm talking about both of us. I can smell it: we need to focus, or something bad's going to happen.*

What do you mean? What do you smell?

If you weren't locked in your head, you'd know.

If you're talking about Whitetail signs, I've been picking those up for the last few hundred strides.

Me too, thinks Joy. *Kezel, but different, yes?*

Yes, thinks Thunder. *But that's easy, and it's not what I'm talking about.*

Then what? Lightning asks.

And Gami-kan thought you had the best nose. Thunder curls his lip. *I'm not going to tell you if you can't figure it out on your own.*

I can figure it out just fine.

But another hundred strides pass before Lightning picks out the scent her oti-mu refers to. Her nose twitches, and her eyes grow narrow. Memories stir, indefinite and vaguely disturbing, not concrete enough to pin to any one source. The smell is new to her yet seems to have its roots in things she has known.

A.P. Malloy

Joy buzzes softly, her nose to the wind.

It's like the maison, she thinks.

Like, thinks Lightning. *But not the same. And so faint. And there's something else there. What is that?*

You tell me, thinks Thunder.

I don't know. It's not kish, is it?

You know it is. And derka.

Lightning peers through the canopy. Clearings have been rare, and thus far, the derkas they have seen have passed them over as they typically will when kezel travel in numbers.

Do you think the others smell it?

If they're paying attention.

But there's something else in there, too. Lightning strains to separate the threads of scent woven into the windy text, but the harder she tries, the more elusive it becomes. *What is it?*

Something tells me we'll learn soon enough, thinks Thunder. *And who knows how that will go? Which is why I wanted to talk to you.*

Good grief. Wasn't that it?

No.

Well, then what?

This:

And Lightning waits patiently to learn what "this" is. But Thunder has suddenly retreated again into his own head. He clenches his jaws, and his ears pin back, but whatever it was he had been about to share remains stuck in his mind, and he is unwilling or unable to shake it free. When Lightning has reached her limit and is about to abandon the conversation, he at last opens up.

When we found, he thinks, w*hen you found Joy...*

Yes?

Thunder closes his eyes, walking blind as if he can't bear to see her reaction to what he shares next.

I lied about not sensing her. I could.

Lightning stops in her tracks.

You lied...

Joy's antennae droop, but she thinks nothing.

Time Weaver

Thunder waits for the others to pass.

I didn't want it to be true, he thinks. *I couldn't take it. It was just too much. So I told myself I was imagining things, that hunger was making me...that it wasn't real.*

Now who's indulging in fantasy?

I know! I'm not proud of it. It's why I'm telling you now. I...I was scared, OK?

Now it is Lightning's ears that pin back

No, actually, it's not. I thought I was going crazy! I thought I was alone! If you had gone with me to Submission, none of this would have happened!

You don't know that.

I know we wouldn't have been run off the range!

Or you would have and I would have been forced to join you. Look, I know. I'm trying to say I'm sorry. You could have used a partner and I—

You were a coward.

It won't happen again.

Lightning resumes her march. Thunder matches her pace, his head hanging low. Joy rides with her thoughts sheltered, but she attends carefully to each idea the twins exchange.

I don't know what's out there, Thunder thinks at last. *But I... If something bad happens, I wanted you to know the truth.*

Nothing bad is going to happen.

Still.

Fine. I know the truth. Happy? But anger is tiring, and Lightning has been on the march for a long time. She sighs. *I understand. I mean, I was scared too.*

But you didn't let that stop you.

No. I'll admit I'm disappointed that it stopped you. I thought you were braver than that. Always my inspiration in combat, you know? Always the surest and most popular. It's not easy seeing you as a coward.

Then don't. A coward would have kept it secret.

I guess. Lightning eases her tone. *I'm glad you told me.* She yawns and moves shoulder to shoulder, allowing Joy to climb to her back. *I'm moving up front.*

A.P. Malloy

+ + + + + +

Chemistry, it has been said, is an exercise in patience, and Ensign Morales is an excellent chemist. She allows her distillations and mixtures to cook and cool as necessary, refusing to rush. In the meantime, she has made herself familiar with the *Layperson's Guide to Aranaean Zoology*. No part of the work fails to interest, but *Viridius Fabyldyr* fascinates her the most. She is particularly interested in the chapter on reproduction.

What amazing creatures!

CHAPTER 36
Derka Reproduction

Summary: *Viridius fabyldyr*, commonly known as derkas, can be found on all five continents, divided into families of 80 – 100 members.

Before the arrival of humans, derkas had no natural enemies, and they numbered in the millions. Their robust nature results from their unique reproductive process. Understanding that process requires a basic knowledge of the derka life-cycle.

Adulthood

1. Derkas spend most of their adult lives making round-trips from the dark face of the planet to the lit face and back, a distance of up to 10,000 kilometers, with 2 – 3 stops along the way.

2. From their mountain homes near the terminator line, they ride low-altitude, cold-air streams that recycle from the planet's dark side. Their goal is the substellar point, where they store tremendous heat in their scales. They have been observed flying in temperatures of over 100° C.

3. During this flight, derkas hunt anything they are able to carry, landing on high perches to consume their prey or storing it in a secondary stomach to be shared with offspring.

4. At the substellar point, the airstream rises to cycle back to the planet's dark side. When the derkas reach this point, they ride the rising current to an altitude of nearly 7,000 meters.

5. The goal of their return flight is one of the many volcanic vents found on the planet's dark side, where the derkas feed on *flagella tenebris,* an invertebrate extremophile which lives near these vents.

6. Derkas can survive in this frigid climate (-50° C) because of the heat stored in their scales. When this heat begins to dissipate, they leave the dark side of the planet and return to their mountain homes on the lit face.

7. If the derka has young, and if they have reached the proper age, it may carry *flagella tenebris* back to its nest. The derka will also expel the contents of its sub-stomach. No attempt is made to distribute the food equally. Nestlings will fight over every scrap, sometimes even to the death, and the mother never intervenes.

8. When not engaged in this cycle, derkas spend much of their time mending their scales or sleeping on the highest perch they can find.

Ensign Morales takes a moment to digest this information. The photographs alone are mesmerizing, but given context, the images come to life in her mind. She is glad they had only been forced to kill the one. How ancient the species must be, how elegantly suited to their unique environment. She reads on, thinking to herself:
We're the aliens.

Reproduction

1. Late in its life, a derka will return from the substellar point one last time and fly toward the dark side as if making to feast on *flagella tenebris*. Instead, it will continue deeper into unlit territory for as long as its stored heat allows.

2. If it passes others fallen to the surface while making a similar trek, it swoops down and kills them, never landing. The goal of this action appears to be

eliminating the unfit among the family. Those who fly the farthest and stay alive the longest survive to reproduce, ensuring any offspring will have the best protection against the cold.

3. Finally, when the derka can fly no farther, it falls to the surface, where—if it is not killed by others making this trek—it undergoes a transformation.

4. On the outside, the surviving derka's body appears the same, but inside, the derka itself shrinks, becoming a tiny copy of itself, living off stored nutrients, including unneeded parts of organs, and sheltered by its carcass.

5. The length of this stage is between 50 – 80 Earth days. At this point, the survivor breaks out from its shell. It is now a fraction of its former mass, black and red rather than green, and ravenously hungry for only one thing.

6. It flies to the nearest source of *flagella tenebris.* Rich with protein, fat, and carbohydrates, *tenebris* is also the only source of the catalysts and enzymes necessary to complete the derka's transformation.

7. As it gorges on the invertebrate, each of the derka's cells undergoes an invisible but fundamental alteration. It becomes a "seed," which, if consumed

by an adult derka, will result in the genetic pairing that is the second-to-last step in the reproductive process.

8. Having eaten its fill of *tenebris,* the seed derka flies to the sunlit face, where it becomes the prize for competing adult derkas seeking its genetic material. The victor in this aerial contest eats the seed derka, ensuring the best flyers combine with the best survivors of the cold.

9. A derka who eats a "seed" is transitionally impregnated. It will not give birth itself. Instead, the seed derka is dissolved in its bloodstream and combined with its own genetic material to create subcellular particles suspended within pressurized gas bladders beneath the derka's wings.

10. A derka thus transitionally impregnated takes to the air and sprays this aerosol like a high-altitude crop-duster. Adult derkas who inhale these particles are said to be terminally impregnated. They will provide the final component to the genetic mix and will give birth to and raise the young.

11. Via this unique process, one seed derka can provide the root genetic material for thousands of adults across an entire continent.

Ensign Morales sets aside the hardcover volume like a satisfied diner pushing away an empty plate. What a world! She has no greater regret than not being able to spend the rest of her life exploring every part of it.

But duty calls.

She checks her lab work, nodding and murmuring in a satisfied way. She is making good progress. A slight adjustment to temperature and one more addition stirred into the mix, and she feels confident she can step away for a while.

Time to visit the captain.

+ + +

She finds him lapsed into shallow slumber, a half sheet of paper and a pencil resting precariously on his lap. He wakes upon hearing her enter the room, and he sits up, both the pencil and the paper falling to the floor. He groans as he leans over to retrieve them, but the ensign is faster and does it for him.

"Thanks," he says, and he smoothes creases from the paper. "Our bug friends are done wrapping all the bodies. Like a bunch of little mummies. Now I think they're asleep or something."

"Yes sir, I just checked on them. It's something related to sleep, that seems clear. They're unresponsive, lined up against the alp, facing the sun."

"Yeah. They got a thing for the sun. But are they thinking to each other? Conspiring? Dirty buggers..."

"I can't say, sir. Even when I'm standing next to them, I can't tell what I'm sensing. How do you feel?"

"Hungry, actually. I feel like I need something more than rations, you know? I miss a baked potato!"

"Yes sir. If we get the chance, maybe we can explore some of the local fare."

Captain Monroe rubs his temples.

"How much longer in the lab?"

"An hour. Maybe less."

"And power to the rest of the facility?"

"Longer. But I hope not much."

He hands her the sheet of paper.

"What do you think?"

There is only one sentence written there in a broad, loopy script; the ensign reads it aloud.

"Everyone knows about humanity's first interstellar colony. What they don't know is that it wasn't the first." She looks up. "Writing a memoir, sir?"

"Lord, no. It's a tagline for a movie. What do you think? The story of the *Destiny* mission as told by...you know, me. You'd watch that, right?"

"Can I be in it?"

"Oh! You'd be one of the stars."

"I never saw you as the movie-making type, sir. What put that idea in your head, if I might ask?"

"You might indeed. This." And he produces from his flight suit a black disk, ten centimeters in diameter, one centimeter thick. He places it on the table. "I got bored and started poking around. Found this in one of the drawers. A proper antique, but it still works."

"An old 3V projector!"

"Yep. Battery operated. Check it out."

And he presses a button at the side of the disk.

"Sir! Is that him?"

A hologram, no larger than a pumpkin, has appeared before them. In it, two people, a white-haired man and woman with short-cropped black hair sit casually across from one another at a table flanked by potted plants. Behind them, a backdrop of five various sized moons, each a different color.

"It sure is," the captain nods Handsome devil."

"Is there volume?"

In reply, the captain makes a slight upward motion with one finger, bringing voices alive.

"Good evening fellow colonists, and thank you for joining us," says the woman. "We have a special treat for you this evening: Major Javon Monroe, one of the original Founders, joins us for a frank discussion of his time as Head of Council and how he's been keeping himself busy

Time Weaver

since his retirement—"

"Let's skip to the good parts," says the captain, and he makes a quick gesture with his finger. The image scrolls forward in time, the woman's voice speeding up to a high-pitched babble. Then he gestures again and the image resumes its normal speed. The white-haired man introduced as Major Monroe sits holding a cup in two hands. He never drinks from it, nor does he return it to the table at his side. "You think there's anything in there, or is it just a prop?" the captain wonders. "And how old do you think he is? Like a hundred?"

But the ensign politely says,

"Shh."

"Major Javon," the black-haired woman says. "We are so very honored to have you with us."

"The honor is mine," the major replies, and he smiles, his mouth closed.

"People are excited to hear all about your yam farm," the host leans forward. "It keeps you busy?"

"As busy as someone my age can stand," the major nods. "But you're being kind. No one cares much about a retired old grandad and his dirty habit."

The host laughs.

"That is so not true, Major!" She turns to someone offscreen. "How many callers do we have in the queue, Larry? Thirteen? No. Thirty-one! I had the order wrong. I don't think our system can handle more than forty, Major, so I'd say people care. I know I do! Feel up to tackling some questions?"

"Of course, he does," the captain says, and he swipes through the image again, forwarding several minutes of the interview in a mere few seconds.

"Well," says the major when normal play resumes, "that was an interesting time. You know, our first contact with the dominant native species, the sextans—we didn't know them as scion until much later—happened unofficially, and without my knowledge. Apparently, they had been observing us for some while. In fact, it was Grace MacLean they approached first—they refused to interact

A.P. Malloy

with anyone else for a long time."

"So much comes back to her, doesn't it?" the host asks. "The original Sextan Territorial Treaty, the Royal Dam project, the accretion belt, the Fabyldyr Reduction plan..." The woman laughs. "I'm dating myself. Does anyone call derkas fabyldyr anymore?"

"I love it," says the major. "It makes me feel young again. Actually though, Grace objected to the fabyldyr plan. She thought turning derkas against one another would have negative long-term consequences. She lost that vote, but she didn't lose many."

"Have there been any significant colonial initiatives she hasn't been involved in?" asks the host.

The major smiles faintly.

"No. Not if they worked. The bad ones were usually my idea. In fact—and this is not a secret—in my last days on the Council, we sort of just sat around waiting for her next big idea. No, it's true! I don't know how they do it now, but in my day, we grew accustomed to her popping into Council meetings, most of the time without warning, and proposing one ingenious play after another. Even when she was little! Did you know the slide at the mining compound was her idea? When she was like...seven? No one would accuse us of being lazy, but we couldn't keep up. People look at Grace now and see a middle-aged woman, stately and reserved, principal of the New Gaian Academy, but I'm telling you, when she was younger, she was a force of nature, always in motion. I got tired just watching her."

"And now she's head of the Council."

"Yes. As she should be. I understand you're having her on next week's show."

"We are! So excited. But let's talk about you, and then get to some callers. Tell us about that yam farm."

The captain waves, and the image freezes.

"Amazing, sir," says the ensign. "Your sixth great-grand uncle. How does that make you feel?"

"Less worried about getting old, that's for sure. He looks terrific with white hair." The captain's tone is light, but he wears a serious expression, and he presses a button to make the image disappear. "Anyway," he says. "That's what got me thinking about, you know, posterity and videography and such. So. Be in my movie?"

"For free, sir." She grasps his wrist gently. "Pulse and temperature, please. Changes in symptoms?"

"Getting more anxious, if that counts. Sitting isn't my favorite thing to do under the best of circumstances. Time is nibbling like a bunch of baby piranhas. An hour?"

"At the most."

"No way to speed it up?"

"No sir." The ensign nods. "Your vitals are normal. But I'm going to need some blood."

The captain tucks the 3V projector back into his flight suit and frees his arm from its sleeve. He watches as the ensign deftly ties off the vein and unwraps a needle from the infirmary. She has delicate fingers, her skin perfectly tanned, her wrists salted with the finest blonde hair, as if bleached by the sun. But of course everything about her, including her Nordic blue eyes and cornsilk hair, is a synthetic affect.

"It doesn't matter," he murmurs as he watches the vial fill with his blood.

"What doesn't, sir?"

"Nothing." He sighs. "I'm sorry for dragging you into this, ensign. All seventeen months of it."

She withdraws the needle and caps the vial, untying his arm and pressing a bandage in place.

"You didn't drag me here, sir. With respect, you couldn't have. The lieutenant, either. We both knew what we were getting into. And I don't regret a single minute of those seventeen months."

"Not the credit police chasing us port to port?"

"I call that good practice."

"Not almost being captured by those hoodlums from the Guild?"

"No sir."

"Running off without any clothes for you and the lieutenant? Don't regret that?"

The ensign smiles.

"No sir, and neither do you."

"It wasn't intentional."

"Yes sir, so you've said."

"It wasn't! Honestly!"

"I believe you, sir."

"I was very gentlemanly and chivalrous."

"I don't doubt it." But the ensign frowns. "I just wish I knew that Sleeo had gotten away."

"Your daddy was the slickest fella I ever met. The finest synthetic designer and my best friend. He got away. You can bet on it. And Ensign…"

"Yes sir?"

"I don't regret a minute either." He extends his pinky finger, and she links hers with his. They exchange a brief glance, then the ensign rises.

"I need to get this back to the lab. You should keep working on that movie. I'm excited to see how it ends."

"When my head stops aching. But I have a question before you go."

"Yes sir?"

"That journal Nikki read to us. The last entry keeps running through my head. You remember it?"

"Yes sir."

"It's like they had their own micro-version of Mars. Or could see one coming. And then there's that 'book' thing. That seems pretty important, yeah?"

"Yes sir." The ensign nods absently.

"What is it, Carmela?"

"Nothing sir."

"C'mon, Ensign. I'm a drug-addled concussion victim, not an idiot. What's got you stewing?"

"Honestly, sir? I don't know. Self-doubt, maybe." The ensign puckers her lips and peers out through the sunlit hatch. "Watt Maclean is an important figure to my people. But he didn't have the chance to see his basic programming principles refined. Mars wasn't his fault."

"No one's saying it was."

"With respect, sir, pretty much everyone is. History is still written by sapiens, and to the average human, Watt Maclean was a mad scientist responsible for the deaths of hundreds of people. If those androids had gotten off Mars, do you think they would have hesitated? Luna would have been next, then Earth."

"That didn't happen."

"No, but—"

"And anyone who's paying attention—"

"No one is paying attention, sir."

"Anyone who's paying attention can see the System needed a fall guy and everyone agreed to make it Watt. That doesn't change who you are."

"Who am I, sir?"

"You're Carmela Morales, the best scientist in this galaxy. And you're..." The captain hesitates. He looks away. "Well," he says. "You know..."

"Yes sir. But the same person who created Sister Janet is responsible for the principles Sleeo used in my design. And Lieutenant K's. If the chaplain failed..."

"Listen, Carmela, if you're asking do I think it's possible for you to mess up, or if you have any limitations to your amazingness, yeah, of course I do. You're not human, but you were made by one. You're fallible. We all are. I forgive you in advance. But if you're asking me do I think you or Nikki are going to go sideways and start murdering and torturing, no! Never! And I'm staking my life on it. Understand? You can't let doubt cloud your decision making. We need you sharp and confident. If I didn't have one hundred percent faith in you, you wouldn't be here right now."

"Yes sir. Thank you, sir."

"And also: that Grace person the major was going on about? Her last name was MacLean, too. And that seems hopeful, don't you think?"

"Yes sir, it does."

"OK, then." The captain reclines and closes his eyes. "And now, Ensign, If you don't mind, I think I'm about to pass out."

+ + +

Ensign Morales banishes her worries and intro-spection and returns to sub-level two, where the power plant resides along with its extended family of controls, diagnostics, and waste reclamation. So far, her earlier work seems to have been successful; nothing is on fire, and no warning lights flash.

"Talk to me," she whispers, and it does, humming and whirring just as she believes it ought to. She runs her hands lightly over the adaptor so cleverly devised by Sister Janet. It is taller than she, wider than her span from fingertip to fingertip, its bottom third shielded in un-polished gray metal, its top third a medusa's head of cables and high-pressure hoses. But its center compart-ment, a clear cylinder when its shielding is swung open, is what interests her at the moment. The crystalline sphere resting inside casts rainbows throughout the room. It generates an aura invisible to human eyes, but the ensign finds it fascinating.

"No time for idling," she checks herself. "Safety first!" she says, as if lecturing an elementary science class. She seals the compartment shielding, curtailing the light show, then moves from one end of the system to the other, testing each of the cables, ensuring sound con-nections and searching for leaks. Satisfied, she moves to a panel set against one of the outside walls, its face an abstract artwork of dials and circular valve handles. She is about to open one of these when she pauses, her eyes losing focus and her gaze drifting into the distance.

She is receiving a faint signal.

Valiant's engines have been started.

The ship is moving.

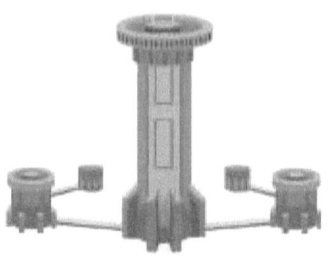

Chapter Five
Mars

MAYA'S FIRST PERIOD built slowly, and in the beginning, it was subtle, a nearly subliminal, expectant feeling. She became aware of it upon waking but thought it was the anticipation of swim lessons.

Shantikar sat next to her on the bed, full grown at ten kilos, his striped coat sleek, his frame lean and muscular. He placed a paw on Maya's cheek, resting it there and looking down at her, silent but intent.

Do tigers like to swim? she thought.

No response.

I know you can sense me, she thought. *Don't think you're fooling anyone.*

The pressing paw grew insistent and was joined by a second. Shantikar leaned forward and began licking her nose, then nibbling at her earlobe.

Fine, Maya thought. *I know you're hungry. But only after you've answered my question. Tigers! Like to swim or not?* She waited—and waited some more—but what human can match a feline's patience? *Have it your way,* she thought, and answered her own question. *No, they don't like swimming—they* love *it.*

And she lifted the tiger and slid out of bed, making her way down the hallway in search of her mother. She found Nandini in her office, a small space, hardly larger than a closet, talking, as always, with someone on the phone. Maya didn't recognize the holographic avatar, an Asian woman in a yellow frock, but sparkling jewelry and a fancy hat gave the avatar an air of importance, so she waited politely. With Shantikar draped around her neck like a stole, she gauged the status of the conversation from that half she could hear. By her mother's "very goods," and "thank you agains," she determined they had reached a critical juncture, that crossroads where a social call might either be allowed to die peacefully or be dragged out beyond use.

She worked to make eye contact.

Nandini waved, shooing her away.

Maya sat in one of the two chairs, staring.

"Well, Li Na," said Nandini. "I should probably let you go. But we'll see you Friday. I love you too."

The avatar vanished, and Nandini peered at Maya over her glasses. She knew before her mother had formed the words that her irritation had nothing to do with being interrupted and everything to do with her habit of wearing, carrying, or otherwise being engaged with a tiger.

"At least," she said, "let me have one place that isn't covered in orange hair. Please!"

"Can we have a goat?"

"Absolutely not."

"But he's hungry."

"He can eat kibble."

"He's not a cat."

"Who had to clean up the last time he got a goat?"

"I did."

"Excuse me?"

"I helped."

"He can have a goat when your father comes back. Then we'll celebrate."

"What are we celebrating?"

"I'll let him tell you. Come now, Daada is already done with breakfast. Feed your beast and get ready. They aren't going to keep the pool open forever."

Time Weaver

+ + +

The lifeguard was an android. Maya had known that at once, of course; its mind was inorganic and unreadable. But Daada didn't recognize at first.

"Now that's a beautiful human," he said.

"It's a robot, Da," said Nandini.

Daada frowned. He took off his glasses, squinted, put them back on, and took a closer look. Maya could easily read that he didn't believe what her mother had said. She placed Shantikar's crate on one of the poolside benches, allowing him the best view of the water. She slipped the towel from around her shoulders, handing it to her mother, then winced and clutched her abdomen.

"What's wrong?" Nandini asked.

"I don't know. It hurt for a second. It's gone now."

"I told you to slow down when you eat."

"Better wait thirty minutes before you go in," said Daada, who stepped out of his shoes and dipped his toes in the water, stealing glances at the lifeguard.

"That's a myth, Daada," said Maya. "There's no data to suggest drownings are related to eating. You're more likely to drown after drinking too much chaang."

"Buba duba, you talk like your father. Who drinks too much chaang? Not this old eemaanadaar naagarik, that's for sure."

The lifeguard approached, her skin tanned and her auburn hair pulled back and knotted.

"Hey, Maya. Hey, Missus Sharma. And you must be Maya's grandpa. It's nice to meet you."

Daada's mustache wriggled, but he said nothing.

"Sarah's just finishing up another lesson," said the lifeguard. "She'll be done in a few."

"Hey, Jasmine," Maya waved. "Those are the cutest deck shoes ever. Where did you get them?"

The lifeguard's smile was white, her eyes twinkly.

"I know! I love them. And they're super comfortable. They were a gift, actually. But you can find them anywhere on Luna."

A.P. Malloy

"Can we order a pair, Mom?"

"One thing at a time. Daada and I are going to soak in the whirlpool. Don't let her talk you into letting that tiger swim, Jasmine, understood?"

But Jasmine only smiled and spun her whistle at the end of its lanyard. Daada stood and stared until Nandini grasped him by the elbow and led him away.

Maya donned her swim cap and goggles.

"Coming?" she asked Jasmine.

"Can't when I'm on duty."

"But there's hardly anyone here."

"It only takes one. How's your dad, by the way?"

Maya stretched, bending down to touch her toes then rising again to windmill her arms.

"I guess we'll find out after the test," she said.

"We're all cheering for him, I hope you know."

"Lifeguards?"

"Ha! No. Synthetics. His work is important to us."

"Why?" Maya wondered.

"Why is it important to anyone?"

"I don't know. But it is. No one stops talking about it. It's driving my mom crazy."

"And you?"

"I don't care about visiting other stars. I didn't want to leave Luna. Now Mars is home. All my friends are here. I don't want to leave again."

"Yeah, I understand. But what if we could travel to a planet like Earth, a clean, healthy, *new* Earth?"

"It wouldn't stay clean very long, would it?"

"Well, we're cheering for him anyway."

"I am too," said Maya. "I just want him to come home." And she stepped to the side of the pool and dropped into the water, rising slowly to the surface and crawling her way down the lane.

+ + +

Sarah, Maya's swim instructor, arrived one lap later, her dark chocolate skin spilling over the edges of her sensible navy suit. Twenty students of various ages gathered at her appearance, well-trained to not keep her waiting. They stood in the pool's shallow end looking up at her, and when she issued her instructions without so much as a "hello," or "how are you?" they were not surprised. Nor did they delay in spreading out evenly across the lanes and practicing as she ordered.

Maya shared a lane with an older boy. She let him go first, waiting for his wake to settle before she began her butterfly. It was her favorite stroke, and she soon got into a rhythm—until the stitch in her side struck again. She gasped and faltered, struggling for a moment to tread water. The pain subsided, but reluctantly.

Sarah's voice echoed through the room.

"Maya! You've got a lap to go!"

"Yep," Maya said weakly, and she grasped the lane marker until she felt ready to continue. This time, she abandoned the butterfly, though she suspected Sarah would not approve, opting instead for the simplicity of the breaststroke. But she had barely reached the end of the lane and made her turn when she heard above the paddling and splashing the sound of many voices. She bobbed at the surface, peeling the goggles from her eyes.

"Jesus!" the older boy in her lane cried out. "She's bleeding. Ah! Gross, it's in my hair!"

A younger girl in the neighboring lane began screaming, and soon all the swimmers had stopped to observe the petaline crimson trailing Maya like a cloud, laughing, yelling, or scrambling from the pool.

+ + +

"Your mother's on the phone," said Daada when he joined Maya at the poolside bench. "I brought chess." The grace of a robust filtration system had already removed the evidence of her shame from the water, but Maya sat facing away from the pool, shaking her head.

"Not exactly in the mood, Daada."

"That's a load of kachara," he replied, and he sat

down beside her, double tapping with his index finger the frame of his thick, black glasses. A three-dimensional chess board projected from the lenses, its squares orange and black, the pieces—arrayed in an unfinished game—holographic like the board itself.

"It's your turn," Daada said.

"Ugh! You don't get it. I'm not in the mood."

"What? Because of this? Come now, child. People act like they've never seen blood before. You should have heard the stories *my* daada told me about the war. You want blood? Oh, I got blood! More than I could handle. Guts, gore, bones sticking out, people walking in circles trying to hold their brains in."

"God, Daada, are you trying to make me sick?"

"Well, it was war, dhat teri ki! And he lived through it. Just like you'll live through this. Stop feeling sorry for yourself, now, and make your move. I'm not going to live forever, you know."

"War shmore," Maya said pouting. "It's all you ever talk about. You know, Earth didn't look so tore up when I was there. Better than you made it sound."

"Careful, samaj hadaar. I know you're feeling bad, but don't let your emotions make you say something you'll regret." Daada sighed and waved his hand through the chessboard; it flickered and disappeared just as Jasmine entered the pool room, swinging her whistle.

"Sarah and your mom," she said, "are filing the notes. They'll be out soon. How are you?"

"Sore. I feel like someone is scooping out my kidneys. Do you have any pain meds?"

"I do, but I need to wait for your mom's permission." Jasmine pulled up a deck chair and sat facing Maya and Daada. The latter never took his eyes from the lifeguard, and he straightened his glasses and his posture. Maya could scarcely believe the moods she read in his mind, and she glanced sidelong at him.

"Don't even start," she said.

"Start what? What are you talking about?"

"You know exactly what I'm talking about."

Time Weaver

"I have no idea."

"Just don't start."

"Am I interrupting?" Jasmine wondered. "Would you like me to go?"

"No!" Maya and Daada said at the same time.

"I don't want you to feel bad about this," said Jasmine. "You're not the first girl to have it happen."

"First one on Mars, I bet."

"I wouldn't be so sure. Anyway, everyone got their money back for the lesson, and Sarah gave them a freebie next time, so no one complained."

"Next time! I'm never showing my face here again!"

"That would make me very sad," Jasmine said, and her usual smile melted to a frown.

"If you don't mind me asking," said Daada, leaning forward slightly, "why do you care?"

"Daada!" Maya hissed. "Don't start!"

"It's OK," said Jasmine. "I don't mind. I care because I've grown to like having Maya here once a week. I look forward to it. We have fun, don't we?"

Maya nodded.

"But you're a robot," said Daada.

"Oh my God!" Maya got to her feet. "Unbelievable!"

Jasmine smiled.

"I'm an android, Mister Sharma, but many of us prefer to be called synthetics. I'm one of those."

"Because some programmer told you to prefer it."

"No sir, because I choose to prefer it."

"That would be free will. Which you don't have."

"Mom!" Maya yelled, startling Shantikar. "Get out here and put Daada back on his leash."

"Watch your saucy mouth, orova fauver. We're just having a conversation, that's all. Aren't we?"

"Is it possible to have a conversation," Jasmine asked, "with something that doesn't have free will?"

This gave Daada pause, and he pursed his lips.

"You make a good point," he said.

"Thank you," Jasmine said, adding to Maya, "The whirlpool has cooled. How would you like to soak awhile before they drain it? Shanti can have a swim."

"Oh, could we?"

"It will be my pleasure."

Maya walked with Jasmine toward the whirlpool on the far side of the room, carrying Shantikar's crate and draped in her towel, leaving Daada to watch them carefully and chew on his thoughts.

"What's going to happen to all that water?" Maya pointed to the pool. "I ruined it, didn't I?"

"Nah," said Jasmine. "Nobody's ruining water on Mars, kiddo. Can't waste a drop on a desert planet. Every molecule that can be reclaimed in this room will be—and I'm talking about the water vapor too. Once it's purified, it will be redistributed, you know, to wherever it's needed. This pool won't be filled again until you come back next week. And you will come back, yes?"

"Daada will kill me if I don't," said Maya. "He has a crush on you. Ugh."

+ + +

The celebration in Raahithya Sharma's honor took place in Mars' finest space, the Hall of Parliament. Since indigestion had kept Daada home, Maya was left to herself, idling at the head table, picking at her food and watching her father and mother have their hands clasped and their pictures taken. She looked up through the translucent, domed ceiling, searching for Luna. The thin Martian atmosphere allowed a fine view of space, and after some concentrated effort, she found it tucked near the brightest of the evening "stars," the planet Earth.

"Good people," a rotund woman stood and addressed the gathering. "Thank you all for being here. There is much more food and plenty to drink, so please help yourself." She ran her hands down the front of her dress, smoothing the fancy, floral print and causing her bracelets to jangle musically. "Doctor Sharma has generously agreed to answer a few questions for us, and I know we have a lot of them. So! Let's get started."

Maya's father and mother joined her at the head table, and all eyes turned their direction. She tried not to squirm, resisting the temptation to scratch an itch that had suddenly arisen on her shin.

The floral print woman spoke again.

"Let's start with the Terran ambassador," she said. "Welcome to you and all our guests from Earth."

"Thank you, Governor," said a tall, thin, and balding man with olive skin. "We are all honored to be here. Doctor Sharma, congratulations on the great success of your experiment. I think I speak for everyone here when I say your bravery and your ingenuity are inspirational. Very well done!"

This led to a wave of spontaneous applause. Maya read an awkward, self-effacement in her father's mind, but her mother's glowed with a pride like the sun.

"Over here," the MC said, and she indicated a woman from the Lunar contingent. Microphones placed throughout the room identified the speaker and amplified her voice. Her question was simple.

"Doctor Sharma," she said, "could you explain to the layperson what it is you've been working on?"

"Of course," Maya's father replied. The question was one he had been asked many times. Maya herself had asked some version of it herself over the years, and she could have predicted down to the word the response her father gave the woman from Luna.

"Our team," he said, "and it is a team, that's important to remember, a really large team of highly trained, extremely dedicated people, has been working on what we call an astral drive, something of an acronym for 'apparent super luminal,' which just means an engine able to move—seemingly—faster than the speed of light without violating general relativity. This will allow practical travel between star systems."

A member of the outer colonies stood up, a representative of those people living on the moons of Jupiter, Saturn, and Neptune. He had the curliest mustache Maya had ever seen.

"I wonder, Doctor Sharma," he said, "if you could speak to the rumors that your experiments were conducted so far outside the solar system because they were deemed so dangerous."

Raahithya smiled.

"It's not a rumor, Silas, as I think you know. It's the truth. Had our calculations been incorrect or our models incomplete, we believed the results could have been catastrophic. Operating so far outside of our system made things difficult, especially for those of us with families. But we couldn't take the risk. Happily, I am—we are—able to report complete success."

This resulted in another round of applause. Maya bowed her head, but the sight of the food on her plate cramped her stomach. The worst effects of her period had passed, three days of bleeding, the first two of which had come with a clawing pain in her guts that lessened but never went away in spite of the strongest meds her doctor had allowed. But now, at what seemed to be the end of the cycle, she felt not relief, but disgust.

"You mean I have to go through this for the rest of my life?" she had asked her mother as they prepared for the celebration dinner. Her mother had stood behind her, tying her long, black hair into neat braids as they looked at one another in the mirror.

"Only the next thirty or forty years," she had said, and Maya hadn't been able to tell if she was joking.

The MC pointed to a white-haired Terran.

"Thank you," she said. "Mister Sharma, you and your wife Nandini were recently referred to by one reporter as 'the Doctor and the Dollar.' That seems crude to me, but it is common knowledge that this project only exists because of the substantial inherited wealth generated by the Halo. As such, are there plans to honor the memory of Sujan Banerjee?"

"It is crude," Raahithya said soberly. "Reducing the best businesswoman, mother, and wife I could ever imagine to a single character shows how little they understand Nandini's role in this project. It wouldn't exist without her, independent of her father's wealth. But to answer your question, yes, we have considered it carefully, and we have chosen to name the ship after Sujan Banerjee himself, whose nickname was Mukaddara. In English, that means *Destiny*."

The response to this was warm and almost universal. Widespread applause and a scattering of cheers greeted the memory of the beloved Banerjee.

"We have a question over here," said the MC, indicating a man from the Martian contingent, a young fellow, barely old enough to support the beard sprouting from his chin. Maya found his red hair and freckles distasteful, but his voice had a quality that took her attention away from cramps and lingering shame.

"Thank you," he said. "My name is Watt MacLean. I'm a programmer. My question is about the use of synthetics on this project. You have acknowledged, Doctor, in previous interviews, that synthetic humans have been invaluable in the design and creation of your astral drive, but what you haven't admitted is how many lives have been lost on this project."

The MC looked prepared to object, or to redirect the microphones to a more congenial question, but Maya's father didn't seem to mind.

"Lives have been lost, Mister MacLean, too many, although, considering the scope of the project, fewer than had been anticipated. And each person's loss and contribution has been formally acknowledged and celebrated. Not one was overlooked."

Redbeard twitched his fingers as if warming up to play the piano, and his tone hardened.

"I'm talking about synthetics, Doctor. Androids. How many of those lives were lost? How many had their contributions celebrated? How many overlooked?"

"That seems like a conversation for an ethics panel," Maya's father replied. "We undertook this project under the auspices of the System and abiding by System understanding of such issues. For us, valuable as they were, synthetic humans were considered...what's a good way to say this? They were shown respect, but..."

"But they were considered expendable," the young man finished. "Tools, yes? Not worthy of your concern or respect, in spite of what you say."

"OK," said the MC, frowning. "That will do."

"Sit down, weirdo!" said someone from the outer colonies, and several people clapped and laughed. But others responded in defense of the young man.

"I happen to know," said MacLean, and his voice rose above the mingled conversation, "that over seventy-five distinct synthetic consciousnesses have been lost over the last seven years of this project, in each case doing some job deemed too dangerous for humans—and in which the synthetic was given no choice."

"As it should be!" someone shouted. "Sit down!"

But MacLean would not be silenced, and in the end, to Maya's great delight, the entire celebration was thrown into temporary chaos as the young man had to be forcibly removed from the assembly, all the while shouting slogans and statistics regarding the topic of synthetic life. Maya couldn't take her eyes off him, and the sound of his voice echoed in her memory long after he was gone.

+ + +

"What a strange girl," Tony said to the window.

"Which one?" Gardenia wanted to know. Filing client reports was her least favorite duty; she closed her Halo and stood up from her desk. Engaging Tony in a conversation seemed a fine way to shirk and also to allow him a better view of her new red dress.

"Hm?" Tony turned from the window to look at her. "Oh. The Sharma girl. Super strange."

"Not the strangest, surely," said Gardenia, motioning to a stack of hardcopy. "Among all these."

"Not the most dangerous, not the most psychotic or sociopathic, sure," said Tony. "But the strangest."

"I think she's sweet."

"And the tiger?"

"I wouldn't stick my hand in its crate, but lots of people bring pets with them. The one has a snake!"

"You're right, of course. Still..."

A chiming bell summoned Gardenia from the conversation—still in want of her dress compliment—to the office door, which she opened to Nandini Sharma and her daughter Maya, Shantikar in his crate at her side.

"Welcome," she said, beaming, and she ushered them into the modest lobby. "Tony's looking forward to working with you. Coffee? Chocolate?"

Maya shook her head, but Nandini poured a cup of steaming black and helped herself to several small foil-wrapped confections.

"Does he want me to be in the room?" she asked.

"No!" said Maya.

"I wasn't talking to you."

"It's up to Maya," Gardenia replied.

"Then no," Maya repeated.

"Hmm..."

"It's OK, Missus Sharma," Gardenia placed a comforting hand on her arm. "I was hoping we could talk while Maya and Tony do their thing. I have so many questions about the project!"

Nandini smiled.

"Of course," she said. "And I love your dress."

+ + +

Unlike other therapists Maya had worked with, Tony rarely sat and didn't require her to. He allowed Shantikar to prowl free, and he asked his questions from various places on what she had come to think of as his stage. He loved leaning against the chair near the window, turning away from her and gazing at the Martian landscape—or his own reflection. But this day, he chose to open on movement, his first position pacing between the closed door and the wall on which hung several small video panels, currently in 2D setting, memorializing in moving pictures his noteworthy career.

"I heard you got your first period," he said, as if deliberately trying to startle her into a response.

"Oh my God." Maya stamped her foot.

"It's a big deal," said Tony. "You can't blame me. I want to know all the important things in your life."

"It's nothing. It's gross."

"It makes you no longer a child. On a very important level, you're an adult."

"Like I said: gross."

"Yeah. Sometimes it is." Tony paced slowly.

"Not a damn thing I can do about it," said Maya.

"No?"

"No! Do you have a magic wand?"

"Does gene therapy count?"

"And change into a boy like you?"

Tony stopped and turned.

"What do you mean?"

"Well, that's what you did, right? Born a girl, now a boy. A man. Whatever. Right?"

"How do you know that?"

An honest answer would have been "Because I can read it in your mind," but Maya chose the lie.

"I thought everybody knew."

"No. Who told you?"

"No one...it's...it's so common on Luna, you know, easy to tell once you know what to look for."

"Which is?" Tony wondered. "No, wait! We're getting off track. For the record, I don't care; I'm not hiding anything. I'm not ashamed of who I was or who I am. I just don't think about myself as that person anymore. People find out when they find out."

The pride Maya read in his voice was matched by honesty in the timbre of his thoughts. Maya had, over the years, grown adept at identifying liars. Tony's stated peace with himself was, at least on this count, sincere.

"I'm sorry if I sounded judgy," she said.

Tony moved to Position Two, his virtual bookshelf. He scrolled idly through stacks of gorgeous, holographic tomes, hundreds of volumes fitting neatly on the shelf.

"You haven't answered my question."

Maya pouted and slumped into a large, padded chair, Shantikar leaping up into her lap.

"No," she said. "I don't want to be a boy. That's just disgusting in a different way. It's all disgusting."

"If life is so disgusting, why participate?"

"What do you mean?"

"You have the power to end yourself. So do I. So does your mom, and dad, and grandpa; Gardenia too."

"What about Shantikar?"

"Non-humans don't think about suicide. They live until they can't live any more. They don't have the cognitive hardware to wallow in existential angst. They're super Taoist, you know, in a programmed sort of way. They don't worry too much about how or why—because they can't. It's how they're made. They just do their thing until they can't do it anymore."

"Daada says when people kill themselves out of cowardice they are re-incarnated as ants."

"Well, now. I don't know about that..."

Maya ran her hands down Shantikar's coat, wondering if it was too late to unlock further growth in his genome. As she had gotten bigger, she longed for him to do the same. He seemed to be receding from her, getting smaller by distance, lighter. And yet, when stretched to his luxurious, velveteen length, he remained the best blanket she'd ever had, worth living for.

"It doesn't matter. I'm not suicidal."

"I believe you."

"And you're wrong about non-humans." Maya buried her nose in Shantikar's mane, purring. "They know. You'll see. They're just braver than we are."

"What do they know?"

"Why we're here, how we're supposed to live."

"Is this what your tiger tells you?" Tony flashed a winning smile and selected one of the volumes.

"He doesn't have to," said Maya. "I just know."

"Your grandfather is a religious man, isn't he?"

"I guess. Yeah. Why?"

"He mentioned something to me last week when he and your mother dropped you off."

Maya looked up, wrinkling her brow. She could already tell the general sense of what Tony was about to reveal, but she resisted the temptation to guess correctly. What had been mis-read as prescience by others had not been well received. People, as it turned out, did not like having their minds read.

"He mentions a lot of things," she said.

"This was about the Third Eye."

"Yeah. He goes on about that."

"I did a little research on it. You know, because I'm a professional, and all." He waved the book at her. "I learned some very interesting things. Curious?"

"Mmm...no?"

"C'mon!" Tony said. "It'll be fun! It's fascinating stuff." He carried his book with him to Position Three, which was sitting beside her in whatever chair was closest, even if she was standing. She sensed it was a deliberate move to demonstrate humility and equivalence, and she appreciated the attempt. But she found its calculated nature off-putting.

"For you, maybe," she said. "Let's see..." And she pantomimed being deep in thought. "Tell me if I've got this right." She adopted a professorial baritone as if giving a lecture. "Opening the Third Eye of Shiva signifies the destruction of Maya, for Maya represents the material world or the world of illusion."

"Yes! Great stuff. How do you feel about that?"

"Ugh. I try not to. Who cares?"

"Your grandfather believes you have the Third Eye. He believes it's a gift from the gods."

"Wouldn't it be a curse?"

"You tell me."

"Tell you what?" Now she was just being contrary.

"Is it a gift or a curse?"

"What?"

"Having the Third Eye, Maya. Having it open."

Maya readied a sharp reply. Such intrusive questions! But she found herself unable to express the idea aloud. Tony was vain and foolish, but something in the frankness of his style led her to pause and reflect. Aside from her time with Pujari Kashi as a child, she had never named the thing happening in her head, had long ago stopped talking about it with any of her family. It was there, they all knew it; talking about it only made it bigger, made it worse.

"It sucks," she said. "Every day."

"So, it's real."

"Something is. I don't know what *it* is."

"Why haven't you told me?"

"Why would I?"

"Because we can only succeed here if we are completely honest. If it's a worry, you have to share."

"Why do I have to do all the sharing?"

"I think I've carried my weight," Tony said, and his voice was firm. "It's your turn."

To her surprise, Maya took only a moment to dare the consequences. Years of secrecy had built up a pressure inside her so intense that, when given the slightest opening, it burst forth beyond control. She thought to herself, *Geez, I'm crying,* and watched tears drip onto Shantikar, who licked them from his coat. And then she told Tony everything, every lie her skill had exposed, every plot predicted, examination aced, secret intercepted—and the toll it had taken on her family, the loss of companions, the fights...

Her confession brought them to the hour's end.

"You should keep coming back," Tony said, and he moved to a brand new Position Four, something he had never done before, rising to his feet and opening his arms for a hug. "I think it'll be helpful."

And she did. And it was.

+ + +

"Nonsense," said Maya's father, as he and Katherine Blair walked through the Arcadian Greensward. It was one of Mars' largest and most popular parks, domed over and complete with imported Earth trees, koi ponds, and kilometers of hiking trails. But Raahithya was in no mood to enjoy it. "Superstitious foolishness. There's not a shred of truth to any of it."

"Perhaps," said Katherine Blair. "But in a case like this, the Company is more concerned with how things look than how they really are." She had the most placid expression on her ageless face. Regardless the topic, she seemed always on the edge of a pleasant nap.

"But we need them! If you take our androids, you might as well take the entire project."

"First of all, Rathi, they're not your androids." Katherine motioned to a bench and took a seat. "Those are Company assets. They're being reassigned, that's all. You'll have all the brain power you need."

"Computers and work-bots are not the same, Katherine, and you know it."

"My bosses disagree." She smiled and patted the bench, her fair skin gleaming in the sun. "Don't be mad, now. I'm just the messenger."

The fact that he was so attracted to her only made Raahithya more angry.

"A bowl of doo, that's what that is. You've never wanted androids on this project."

"Of course not. They're dangerous."

"So are all tools! Should we melt down the picks and shovels and dig with our hands?"

"C'mon, Rathi. Think about it. This is using the tools for a different application, not scrapping them." Katherine waited for a hand-holding couple to pass before she continued, motioning again for Maya's father to sit. He did, as far away from his supervisor as the bench allowed. "You know as well as I do what's happening," she said. "The cases are no longer isolated, and they're becoming more difficult to contain."

"We've never had one!"

"Yes, and we plan to keep it that way."

"We! Then you do agree with them."

Time Weaver

"In this case, yes, I do." Katherine knit her brow, her neatly groomed lashes dropping to half shade. "And I'm not ashamed to say it. You're right! I never wanted synthetics on this project, but I put up with them because they were working as advertised. But that's changing. Maybe not on the astral drive—yet—but we feel it may just be a matter of time. If even one of your androids decides that it's a free agent and doesn't have to follow instructions, the whole System is endangered."

Maya's father looked out across the park. Other sites were warmer, and some had more water, but Arcadia had been from the beginning the Martian city he had loved most. He idled with his tie, counting the stars on its patterned face.

"This will set us back years."

"A few. But you'll get there."

"A lot you care. It's not you on site seventy hours a week. I haven't seen my kid conscious more than two times in the last month. And people will die, Katherine. You know that. Replace every android lost in the last seven years with a human life. I hope you're prepared to share the news with their families, because I'm not."

"Then you'll have to be safer. Plan better. Make more accurate models and simulations."

"Which will take longer still."

"Rathi, sweetheart, I see your wife coming. Try to put on a good face, yeah? The decision's been made. By the time you get back to the project, they'll have been moved and their memories cleaned."

Katherine stood, not bothering to see how Raahithya reacted to this news. She smiled brightly as Maya's mother drew near, holding three strawed beverages, each perspiring and topped with whipped cream and a cherry. Katherine took hers and leaned in for a quick kiss on the cheek.

"Nandini," she said. "It's so good to see you again."

"I've missed you," Nandini replied, and she handed Raahithya one of the beverages. "And our monthly Scrabble games!"

"Yes! We'll play again, don't worry. Soon."

"Soon is a word I've been hearing far too often," Nandini said, and she glanced at her husband, who had returned to studying his tie. "Will you join us, Kate?"

"A walk sounds lovely," Katherine said, "but I must get back. I'll call you when I return from the Valley." And another quick kiss sent her on her way.

"You look like you're planning to hang yourself with that ugly thing," Nandini said once Katherine had gone. "I can tell you how many stars it has, if you're wondering: too many."

Raahithya got to his feet.

"And how do you define that?" he asked.

"Anything more than one."

"You know I'm never going to agree with that."

"Yes. Because you're stubborn. But I don't care. It's your daughter I'm worried about."

Raahithya sipped from his drink and began walking with Nandini, nodding absently whenever greeted by passersby. His face was known to many.

"What do you think I should do?" he asked.

"She wants you to take her to swim lessons. Not just drop her off and pick her up, but stay."

Raahithya arched his brows.

"A chlorinated pool. There's a smell I haven't come across in years. But we've had a set-back. I'm not sure I'll have the time."

"Make the time, Rathi. She needs this. I can't be her father, and Daada plays the fool with the lifeguard."

"Ha! OK, Nan. Swim lessons it is…"

+ + +

But keeping his promise was more difficult than Raahithya had imagined. Maya refused to return to the scene of her greatest shame, the only public pool in this half of the city. The sole alternative lay at the far end of a long buggy ride. And yet, that was not her only demand.

"I want to work with Jasmine," she said.

Time Weaver

"It's the instructor you work with," Rathi replied as he packed his case for an upcoming meeting. "Not the lifeguard. If you're doing your job, you shouldn't need to interact with the lifeguard. It's like a footballer and a referee, yeah? If they're having steady communication, it's probably a bad sign."

"Then I want Jasmine to be my instructor."

"I don't think that's the way it works."

"Why not? She's probably a better swimmer than Sarah, and she's a thousand times nicer."

"Because the mechanics of saving a life are actually easier than the subtleties of teaching. I know, it seems counterintuitive, but androids are a lot better at emergency protocol than having a conversation."

"Not Jasmine. I like talking to her. Anyway, she doesn't have to teach me anything, just swim with me."

Raahithya filed through a stack of documents, picked out two and put them in his case, closing it with a click and a spin of its manual lock.

"If she's not going to teach you anything, what would we be paying her for?"

"I thought androids didn't get paid."

"They don't. But their owners do, and you can bet this Jasmine of yours isn't cheap."

"Then she can teach me how to be a lifeguard."

Rathi scrunched up his face, his mustache wriggling like an agitated caterpillar. He liked practical, useful knowledge, skills with concrete applications, and lifeguarding on a desert planet seemed a perfect example of the old English idiom of bringing sand to a beach.

"And what good will that do you?" he asked.

"What good does anything do? Dad! Can I just work with Jasmine? Please?"

And so, the proper calls were made, offers kindly solicited, agreements arrived at, and a date set. When it arrived, two Terran weeks later, Maya, her father—and of course Shantikar—made their way to the western end of the city in a buggy whose driver, Carl, had been uploaded from Maya's favorite Lunar program. He chatted about life as a buggy and answered her questions about how things were going on Luna. As always, he was more than willing to let her take a turn at the controls.

"You've gotten a lot better," he said. "You won't need my help at all if you keep this up. Promise once you get your license we'll still be friends."

She promised.

When they arrived at the pool, Raahithya took a deep breath, closing his eyes and smiling at the warm, humid air and chlorine smell.

Jasmine approached and greeted them.

"I told her not to bring the tiger," said Raahithya, who immediately understood Daada's fascination with the lifeguard. She and her swimsuit were a perfect fit.

"Aw, heck no, you gotta bring Shanti," Jasmine said, and she smiled at Raahithya. "It's a real honor to meet you. Maya probably already told you this, but I'm a huge fan of your work. Cheering for you all the way."

"That is very kind, thank you. She has many nice things to say about you, too. And I'm grateful for that, I want you to know. The move was hard, but it's good people like you who have made Mars home for us."

"Oh!" said Jasmine, twirling her whistle. "That is about the nicest thing anyone's ever said to me." And she beamed like a flower in the sun. "Maya! You never told me your dad was so sweet."

"Yeah," Maya shrugged, but her tone was proud, and she looked at her father out of the corner of her eye. "I like him OK."

"And you?" Jasmine asked, and she placed her whistle lanyard around Maya's neck as if she were an Olympic medalist. "How are you holding up?"

"Good," replied Maya, and for the first time in many days, it was true.

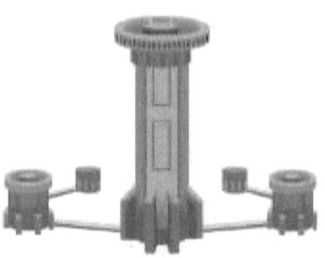

CHAPTER SIX
Company

WHAT'S THAT SMELL? wonders Pounce.

Many a Bristle, thinks Gusty, *has asked that same question, but as far as I know, none of 'em have come up with an answer. If you asked Vale, he'd tell you it's the smell of "don't go any farther."*

And what do you say? Pounce asks Piedmont.

Never knowed, he thinks. *'N we been 'round that smell since we's been wabis, both Fluvial and me. And lotsa other Whitetails, too. But no one evers tellin' us what it is. Not even Big Fork's a knowin', and he's a regglar smarty plus some. Smells derka, sur-ee, and I reckon some kish, too, but there's somethin' else, see? That ain't right for a derka, no mistake, and not even the stinkiest kish. Somethin' funny goin' on out there, Sugarfoot. Some kinda Moondweller magicalness, iffin you ask me—and you did, so that's why I'm a-sayin' it. Still thinkin' you's proper to go pokin' your snoot up thatta way?*

I don't know about proper. Pounce stands to read the wind. *But we're going, proper or not.*

And you, Bristly? We's at the edge o' your range.

That's under dispute, thinks Gusty. *But whether I travel another thousand strides or stop here, my job is almost over. I'm here to make sure you move peacefully off our turf, not join quests resulting from someone else's pro-*

mises. No disrespect, Pounce.

I understand; you're needed at home.

I am. But I'll let them know you made it this far. Gusty turns to the two Whitetails. *You've kept your word so far, I'll say that.*

Sur-ee, thinks Piedmont. *We's good like that. Ain't we, Fluvial? Yep! And we's gonna stay good, see? Iffin that's what yer thinkin'—that we aint the trusty types. Cuz we is. And yeah, sur-ee, only time'll tell and all that, but ain't no one I never heard of can read the future. Only ways a knowin' if someone's a trusty or not is to keep on livin' and see how it all rolls out, yeah?*

Sure. Like you said, "time will tell." But know this: if I find out you broke your vow, I'll break you.

Aww, now, they's no reason a be makin' threats, big fella. We's good to the bone, or why do you think Big Fork a-chose us? He ain't tryin' to start no war, Bristly! Oh sur-ee, he's always on the look for new turf—gotta grow the clan, see?—but Sugarfoots and Bristlies a only reason we ain't bein' run over by them hatin' Redteeth. Scat! Runnin' 'round nekkid, talkin' foul 'bout Moondwellers, makin' trouble like they aint got room on their side o' the wedge... Greedy rotters, yeah? Aint doin' Whitetails no good makin' enemies o' the enemies o' their enemies, see?

Umm... Gusty's snout wrinkles.

Yes, thinks Pounce. *I do.*

But when Gusty at last offers his goodbyes and leaves them to move south, toward his home caves on the Brills, Lightning finds she can't share Pounce's confidence. Joy has read no deception in the Whitetail minds, but her personal history leads her to doubt, and when Gusty disappears from sight, she wraps fingers around her cutter handle, squeezing it for comfort.

The scion draw within thought range.

Why do the beasts pause? thinks Shimmer from her basket. *Is this the limit of their stamina? Or have they reached the limit of their courage?*

Neither, thinks Pounce. *But you are dangerously close to the limit of my patience. OK. Where now?*

Old Colosser's thatta way. Piedmont points to the northeast. *Follow your nose holes, that's what I says. Big Fork a-reckons that smell's a-comin' from there. Never been, m'self, o' course—did I say that aready?—anahoo, reckon it's a goodly thirty or so thousand strides get across the Nekkid Hills, then probbly take a break, yeah? Rest up for the lastly leg? 'Cuz who knows how long that'll be? Hm? To get to your fancy Hold and whatnot? Don't ask this kezel, no-ee! But here's some goodly news: Ol' Piedmont's a-gonna march with ya, sur-ee, and ol' Fluvial too, bless 'er, what a champ! All the way to the end o' them Nekkid Hills we'll get ya. Justa make sure yous don't get ruffled by no Whitetails 'long the way, see?*

Thirty thousand strides?

That's the recknin'.

And you'll be thinking the entire way?

Oh, sur-ee. Ol' Piedmont's got it covered! You gotsa have someone what can fill the gaps, see? Can't be all gloom and silence on a 'venture, no-ee. Gotsa have someone a tellin' stories, keepin' up spirits, all that.

And once we get to the end of the Naked Hills?

Oh, now, there's a fine query, sur-ee. Whatchoo like to say about futury-type questions, huh, Fluvial? Huh?

One step at a time, thinks Fluvial.

Sur-ee! That's the winner, Sugarfoot.

Grand, thinks Pounce. *Well. For once, I agree with the queen here. It's time for us to move on.*

+ + +

Turning east of northeast takes them from Bristle proper and into the disputed domain of the Naked Hills. But of course, the hills do not become naked all at once. In the beginning, the accrete do gradually grow sparse, and the terrain, which had been kind to them since their respite in the Bristle cave, does become lumpy and path-less. But still, this is kezel country, and the smell of allies visits them occasionally when the wind shifts around from the south. They march in good spirits, and Piedmont

A.P. Malloy

keeps his promise, letting few gaps go unfilled.

Three thousand strides later, however, the accrete begin appearing less as one, unbroken canopy, and more often as tangled islands, with broad, open spans between them where the undergrowth is allowed to see the sun. There, the land is indeed hilly, but it is so covered in life that, accrete or no, calling them naked seems wrong to Lightning. For strange things have happened to the native plants in these open spaces. Given regular access to light and heat, some of them, like the biting cyriles, grow to two and three times their usual size, the largest capable of snatching up a wabi. Their hydra heads, pink and fluttery, rise above the snow and other plants with alien forms and unusual colors.

They halt at the edge of the first such span.

Not a virble or cremlin, thinks Pounce.

Floral pollen, thinks Lightning.

Herbs and berries, thinks Thunder.

Old snow, thinks Cliff.

Sur-ee! And smell that? That's Whitetail!

But mingled in with these is the mysterious scent coming from the northeast, and it becomes stronger.

It is Ozag's Hold, thinks Shimmer. *What else could it be? Onward!*

+ + +

And now, they set their sights on crossing this first open expanse. On the far horizon, two accrete islands perch atop separate hills, one farther and more northerly, one closer and due east. Pounce chooses to suffer the longer road for the comfort of greater distance from Whitetail turf, and surprisingly to them all, Piedmont doesn't disagree with him.

But keep yer eyeholes a peepin' upways, he reminds them. *Derned ol' greenies probbly leave us alone, but whosta say fer sure? Not ol' Piedmont, no-ee.*

Following his advice, they make their way out of the accrete and onto the florid plains, nothing above them but cloud-wracked sky. Fluvial leads the way, as usual keeping her thoughts to herself and followed close by Piedmont, whose mind is rarely still. Pounce follows at a pressing distance, but after a time, he calls Thunder and Cliff to take his place, and he falls back to where Lightning marches with Joy on her back, a dozen strides ahead of the scion.

How's the new vest? he asks.

Still getting used to the smell, thinks Lightning, *but good, thank you. I feel like I can breathe again.*

But this is not why Pounce joined them. Lightning waits patiently to discover the real reason. For a time, they wade through a sea of pink and teal, carving their own path through a frosting of snow and sheltering their thoughts. Pounce glances skyward, lolling his tongue.

Worse than derkas is uncertainty, he thinks.

Yes sir.

So. You two are going to tell me everything you know about what's going on here.

Yes sir.

No secrets, no stalling!

No sir. Where should we start?

With whatever's in that sling.

Lightning is not surprised. Joy had anticipated this demand, had discussed it with the artifact. Their conclusion was the same as it had been with Submission: they need allies. But Lightning keeps her thoughts narrowly focused and subdued.

OK. It...it sounds ridiculous when I actually think the ideas, but...you're maybe not going to believe it...

Or like it, I'll bet. But so it is. Let's have it.

Yes sir. Well. I guess these Moondwellers Ancian's always going on about didn't come here from one of our moons. They came here from somewhere even farther away, and on their way here they picked up a, like a sort of device, I guess—and Joy found it. It's some kind of... I don't know what to call it, it doesn't make sense...

She pauses and tries to recall what the artifact looks like, but to her surprise, she has the memory of Joy telling her about it, but no image of its appearance. Had it been a tool of some kind? Like one of the strange items in the maison? But that doesn't seem right.

I can't describe it, she shakes her head.

Then let me see it.

Joy buzzes calmly, opening her sling for Pounce to peer inside. There he sees a most unremarkable rock, gray, misshapen, the size of a virble.

What's so special about that? he wonders.

Lightning glances inside the sling. A rock? She sniffs at it and furrows her brow. It smells like it could have come from anywhere in the accrete. Had it always looked like that? Why couldn't she remember?

It's... She struggles to express the idea. *It's not what it seems. I know what it looks like, but it's more than just a rock. It... Oh, stink and stank! This is going to sound ridiculous! What you're looking at has the power to think—but only to Joy—and only when she asks questions.*

A question-answering rock?

I told you it didn't make sense.

Prove it, Pounce demands of Joy.

I'm sorry. I can't.

Of course you can't.

I'm telling the truth. Joy clicks a sharp staccato. *You know I am.* She closes the sling. *It can't be proven.*

Just has to be believed? Is that what you're telling me? And how can you tell what I know or don't?

Answering questions isn't all that it does, Lightning offers. *Working through Joy, it improves my ability to read thoughts—and shelter them. Joy says it started on the plains when we were coming to rescue you, not long after she found it buried under the Thing.*

You suppose that's what the scion were looking for? You suppose that's why they attacked us? Cuz they couldn't find their special answer rock?

I don't think so, Joy replies. *It's secret from them.*

And it needs to stay secret, Lightning adds emphatically. *Shimmer has seen it, but that couldn't be helped—and we told my api-kan. But...it has the potential to cause trouble if the wrong people find out.*

A Tool of Power, thinks Joy.

Pounce curls his lip.

So, what is it telling you?

Joy hunches her shoulders.

Lots of different things.

Like?

That android is important.

You already said that, but in what way?

It might have answers.

I thought that's what your secret rock was for!

It's called a Book. Joy buzzes. *It knows many things.* She pats the sling. *But it's not perfect.*

And why you, and no one else?

I am a Reader, thinks Joy. *Only Readers understand it.* She clicks steadily. *There may be another.*

Another what? Reader?

Yes, and that's good. Joy whistles. *More Readers, better Book.* She pauses. *So he tells me.*

He?

Petros.

This is Moondweller nonsense.

No. Joy's eyes glitter fiercely. *Not Moondweller, not nonsense.* Her tone softens. *Much older, much stronger.*

And it answers your questions.

That's what Reading is.

I suppose that's where you learned about the crashing moons? End of the world and all that?

Yes.

Never lies?

Not that I know.

Not that you... Pounce scowls. *Where did they get it? Where did it come from?* But he snaps his jaws. *Never mind! I don't want to know! What I do want to know is more about this Ozag character we're set to find.*

She's a scion queen, thinks Joy. *The most powerful queen.* Clicking uncertainly, she adds, *Ozag brings the floods.* But this isn't very useful, so she makes a suggestion: *Shimmer knows lots more.*

Yeah? She's my next stop. And if your rock is so darn smart, I want to know what lies ahead. Terrain, threats, all that. So start asking! And when you learn something worth sharing, let me know.

+ + +

This, thinks Shimmer, *is the way scion were meant to travel: in the open and under the sun.*

Queen is correct as always, her prime pluripotent agrees. *The land of sharksha is a vile place, dark and difficult to fly in. Is it now coming to an end?*

Here comes their leader, thinks Shimmer. *Perhaps it will have the answer. Does it know?* she thinks to Pounce. *When we will have seen the last of its domain?*

Eventually, I suppose. Too soon for me.

Not soon enough for Queen, thinks Shimmer. *Why has the beast come to her? Has it gotten the party lost?*

No one's lost, Queenie. But we're beyond my experience, and I need to know everything you know.

It needn't concern itself if it follows instructions.

That's not how it works! I'll have no problem ending this fool mission right now, free of any obligation, if I don't think we have your complete cooperation. I'm tired of being in the dark. Understood?

It is a fine one to accuse her of secrecy. Does it deny that some among its kind are immune to scion poison? The sharksha betrayer sustained repeated bites from her pluripotents yet never faltered in its cowardly retreat. Did it ever plan to share this information with her?

Consider it shared.

And what is the secret? How is it possible?

A story for another time. What do you know about this Ozag? How do we get there, and what happens when we do? What should we expect?

She has been clear on this! Hers has never been the fortune to meet Ozag or see her royal Hold. She knows no more than she has already shared.

So Ozag is something like you?

Time Weaver

It flatters or insults her! Ozag is Glorious and Omnipotent, ten times ten a greater monarch than she shall ever be, the First Thinking Queen, liberator of her people from vumierre slavery. True, more recently, she has been seen as the Punisher, her power over the water used to make Albion suffer—perhaps for some transgression on their part, or perhaps because she was never the benefactor imagined. Perhaps she believed Albion had grown too large, was a threat to her power. She cannot guess! Whatever the cause, Ozag was the Causer; hers is a power not to be underestimated.

Well, that is fabulous, thinks Pounce. *Good for her. But it's all pretty vague. What kind of power? An army of your little blue buddies here?*

Perhaps.

Ones that can fly?

No queen of worth would be without pluripotents.

How many?

Ozag the Generous and Terrible would have a retinue fitting her rank, it can be sure of that.

How about those four-legged monsters? Damnable sound they make, giant, smelly things. Any of those?

She is Ozag. All is possible.

I can't prepare for "all," Queenie. I need specifics.

She cannot specify.

How about this "power over the floods" business? What's that about? And vumierres. Are we going to meet any of them on our way to this hold of yours?

How would she know this? Shimmer clicks an irritated tempo. *When she was still Princess and naïve, she thought vumierre slavers were a thing of dead history, a warning only, a reminder of Ozag's greatness and the resilience of her people. These new arrivals are beyond explanation. How can she predict their behavior?*

Is it possible, thinks Pounce, *they're behind what happened to your... If your kind and theirs are such enemies, isn't it possible they deposed your precious Ozag and sent that fire maker to destroy your people?*

The beast thinks rubbish. For no one could depose

the Awful and Stupendous. Not the scurrilous vumierre, this is certain! Did Ozag not prove her mastery over them by freeing her people from their slavery? Did she not demonstrate how far beyond them she is by wiping every last one from the face of Aranae?

Apparently not, thinks Pounce. *Guess she missed a few. Don't get your wings in a flutter, Queenie, I'm not insulting your Ozag, just pointing out the obvious.*

The revolting vumierre the beast refers to would hardly be able to affront the Undying on their own.

Maybe they have friends.

If their friends were as many as the raindrops, still Ozag would be Unassailable and Eternal. But Shimmer's tone says Pounce has planted a seed of doubt.

For a time, they march across the open expanse with their thoughts kept to themselves. Peppering wind races unchecked, burning their eyes, but worse is the appearance of a type of pestilent yit that lies hidden in swarms beneath the snowbound grass. Their wings stand no chance against the wind, but they are strong enough to reach the kezels' undersides if they dare pause or slow their pace. The little devils land stealthily, and often, by the time one of them feels the tiny bite, it is too late to swat the offender or avoid an itchy welt.

Pounce growls and scratches at his leg.

Last question, Queenie, he thinks. *What do you know about that android thing?*

It is vumierre work, even a sharksha can see that. And so, it is evil and should be destroyed.

You know, thinks Pounce, *from the perspective of someone who was held captive by your kind and saw some of its clan die by their doing, your enemies might appear to be friends. Anyway, I didn't ask your opinion, I asked what you know about it.*

She knows nothing—and cares less.

And that is all she will say on the subject.

+ + +

They reach the first accrete oasis, and all but the scion are glad beyond words for the reprieve. But the oasis is small, and the moment they head out once again over the Naked Hills, the torment resumes.

Is this how it's going to be the entire way? asks Lightning. *Biting yits and wind?*

Piedmont lashes his tail in vain.

Whosta say? he thinks. *Iffin I ever thought we'd a be traipsing thru this part o' the range, I coulda brought some cyrilis spit. Little biters won't touch the stuff. You alls knowed this though, yeah? Didn't happen to bring any with you? Enough to share?*

Cyrilis spit? thinks Lightning. *Sorry, no. It's not a thing we do on our range. No yits like these.*

What are they called? thinks Joy.

Piedmont's ears lie flat when she thinks, and he ducks his head. He can ignore her by simply not looking at her and staying upwind. But when she thinks, a lifetime of culture feels under attack, and he can do nothing to block out the thoughts. He hesitates so long in replying that at last Fluvial opens her mind.

These are snikes, she thinks. *Feculent snikes.*

Sur-ee, thinks Piedmont, quick to reclaim the spotlight. *Evraone's knowin' that. But what they's not knowin' is that cyrilis spit's the one and only. Course, can't just say "hey, giant biting cyrilis, spit in this a here bowl, won't you please?" No-ee. Gotta wait til they's asleep, see, after they's done eatin' all the yits they can catch. Not all the heads a sleepin' at once, mind ya, but even the ones ats awake is kinda dozy, you git? Like ya feel after a feast and ya can't take a nap cuz ya drew sentry duty and there ya sit, eyes all droopy and whatnot... Anahoo, ya slip in and cut off one of them sleepin' heads—just one! It don't feel a thing, just sleepin' and then dead—but the others'll wake up right quick, see, and that's a face full o' trouble for anaone too slow to git with their stolen head. But they gets over it see? Lotsa other heads to feed and they heal up quick. But they make a hissin' and a snappin' for some time let ol' Piedmont say! But anahoo, you got your head, and when you drain all that spit and then do a couple o' steps—gotta let it dry, ya know, gotta let it turn into crystals, see, and then grind 'em real fine and—*

Sweet merciful moons! Pounce interrupts. *This is captivating, to be sure, but all it means is we can't do anything about these...these...*

Snikes, Cliff volunteers.

Feculent, Joy adds.

Whatever. How much farther?

Oh, we's a solid ten, mebbe fifteen thousand to the end a the Nekkids. Snike land goes on a while after that, accordin' to reports, but I ain't never been. Folks who has like to say on the other side o' where these little biters live, theysa place where the land changes. I reckon mebbe it means you'll be ridduvem.

Weaver hopes. Pounce snaps his jaws, but a darting snike evades him. *When we get to a place we can rest, I want to wake that android thing. See if it does anything new, maybe give us some information.*

Whatcha think you's gonna get from it? asks Piedmont. *Just a bunch o' noise ats gonna scare away the babelrack or any talihew ats around. Plus, I gotsta say: it sure's a spike raiser, ain't it? Makes even a full grown Piedmont kinda want a snuggle up in a cave and cover 'is ears, see? All unnatural and creepy-like.*

I don't disagree. Pounce squashes a snike against his flank. *Just hurry up and get us to the next accrete.*

You got it, thinks Piedmont. *But next one'll be the last one—or mebbe second a last. After that, it's northeast to whatever's the 'venture you's all goin' on. I still calls it a real badly idea, but you's the boss o' you.*

+ + +

Across the open expanse they march, single file, and as she walks, Lightning senses a tension in her face and realizes she has been traveling with teeth clenched for many strides. She takes a deep breath and attempts to relax. Is musa possible while walking?

Time Weaver

It will be OK, thinks Joy. *Maybe we should sing?*

Another time—when we get to the oasis. How 'bout slide off and walk for a while. My legs are killing me.

Joy slides down and trudges through the crusty snow, waving at snikes. Pounce would probably like her to be seeking answers, but as engrossing as it is, Reading is also difficult. Each bit of information earned requires an equal amount of energy spent, so she is both enriched and worn at the same time. She soon lags behind, nearly asleep on her feet, until Thunder drops back to offer a ride. This she accepts, her eyes dim.

Making better time, they are soon able to see the next accrete island rising into view. They enter its welcoming shade, the gloating wind grown quiet, replaced by the chatter of virbles. The company thinks at first to take their rest here, for even the bibijas are weary from scaling hill after hill. But this rainbow oasis is a small one, scarcely a thousand strides from end to end, home to nothing edible larger than hooting cremlins. When they look out from its northeastern edge, however, they see a much larger companion floating on the far horizon.

Reckon 'at's the last one, thinks Piedmont. *But it's a biggie, and Imma smellin' talihew. Snap snap!*

What do you think? Pounce asks the three jabis. *Feel like you can make it that far?*

If talihew is the reward, then yes, Thunder replies.

Talihew or not, I'll make it, thinks Lightning.

Don't worry about me, thinks Cliff, though he sits on his haunches and his ears droop.

And you? Pounce asks Shimmer.

The beast needn't ask! All are weary. And more than that! Her tiny company is grief-stricken and far from home. But the mission calls. March on!

So they do. Out into the feculent snikes and the wind they endeavor once again, up one hill and down the next, theirs the only signs of kezel. But Piedmont is not wrong; there are talihew foraging in the last accretion oasis, and their smell pulls the company forward.

Nice to be downwind, thinks Piedmont. *We'll get*

the jump on 'em sur-ee.

+ + +

But first, they must navigate several thousand strides of hills rolling like angry waves, nibbled by snikes and threatened by overgrown, unmannered cyriles. When at last they scale the highest of the hills and ease stealthily into the shadows of its blanketing accrete, their first job is to sit quietly and simply rest. But a favorable wind rarely lasts long, and Pounce is quick to break them into hunting teams before this chance is squandered.

Howl if there's trouble, he thinks, and he, Piedmont, and Fluvial melt into the undergrowth, drawn by the scent of talihew. The scion shelter in a fanning orange, resigned to awl rations and less lova than any of them would like. Shimmer ruffles her wings.

The sharksha will not get themselves gored or otherwise damaged. They have duties in her service.

We'll keep that in mind, thinks Lightning.

In the end, there is no goring or howling, only hard work well rewarded. Thunder is unusually cooperative, and with Joy camouflaged, he, Lightning, and Cliff ambush a crowd of virbles, preoccupied with sneer digging. They make fine hors d'oeuvres while the midsize talihew Pounce and the others return with is rendered portable. Both packs are soon filled. What can't be carried ends up in their stomachs.

Always in the mood for talihew, thinks Piedmont, licking his chops. *Or any meal, tella truth—and sure is glad to know 'twas a Sugarfoot what helped make it happen. We's good friends us, yeah?*

Getting better, thinks Pounce, and he yawns. *I'm going to drop in my tracks. We'll sleep in shifts—and when I wake up, I want to test that android thing one more time.*

He looks at the Whitetails.

We'll take it from here. Thank you for your guidance. He relieves Fluvial of the ruined android and surprises everyone by touching noses with the pair.

Time Weaver

Golly, thinks Piedmont, moved by the gesture. *You's goin' a foreign places. Can't give ya no advice but what I 'ready done. And once ya go headfirst outa this last bit o' accrete, that'll be the end o' Whitetail turf. But ol' Piedmont'd be real droopy in the snout iffin it was the end o' yous all, see? Cuz you's a lot smaller group widdout us, mebbe lookin' like a tasty target for a dern greenie, see? And me and Fluvial's been a thinkin'.*

Yes?

Well, here's how it is, see. I knowed we's talked about Big Fork choosin' us and all, and how we's favorites in the clan an' such. But...well...I mean...aw, c'mon ol' Piedmont, spit it out proper now. It's a hard one to say! But here's the up and down o' the whole deal. See, turns out Piedmont and Fluvial, well, we aint so welcome back home's we made out. I know, it's hard a believe a pair such like this wouldn't be popplar, but, well, yeah, it's true see, that Big Fork did choose us, be amba...amba...

Ambassadors, thinks Fluvial.

Sur-ee, yeah, that, but it ain't cuz we's so special. More like we don't fit in so good, see? And the Fork kinda thinkin' he's better riddavus than havin' us hang 'round. Dunno, mebbe cuzzin' ol' Piedmont he's a joker, likes a make a funny here and there, and mebbe once joked too much about the Bigness o' the Big Fork. Kinda made 'im grumpy, iffin you catch what Imma throwin'.

I think I do, Pounce replies.

Sur-ee, well, that ol' Forkie, he says to us, "you want ta get back in the good with me, go scout out them Bristlies. Give 'em that Moondweller thingy and then come on back with a ree-port."

You mean spy?

Aw, now, nothin' like that, now, I mean...spy? That's a real turd of a word, now ain't it? Ol' Forkie just wanted, you know, infamation, see? How'd the Redteeth fight go? Whosa winner and whosa loser, that type o' thing. And me and Fluvial here, we figgered, sur-ee, that sounds like a do-able thing, no worries. But...well...now we's spent some time with yous all, and you's been proper nice to us, specially ol' Piedmont here—no one's never listened to 'im so patient-like ceptin' Fluvial her own self—and so to go on like I was sayin' the two of us been thinkin'...mebbe we shouldn't go back with that infamation...mebbe it ain't a friendly-like thing to do to our new pals, see? Givin' up all their infamation like that. And we's both started a-thinkin' mebbe we should...well, you know...mebbe we could...

Are you saying you want to come with us?

Really? You'd let us? Well that's just grand, yeah?

It wasn't an invitation.

Then it's settled! We's a part o' the 'venture! Sense that, Fluvial? We's on the team! Grand, yeah?

+ + + + + +

Captain Monroe rubs his eyes.

"Moving where?" He slowly sits up.

"The refinery is my guess, sir," Ensign Morales replies. "Magnetic northwest at sub-sonic velocity."

"Nikki never messaged?"

"No sir. And what's worse, I lost his locator signal when the ship took off. I can't say why."

"Shoot. This is bad in a lot of different ways." The captain gets to his feet, leaning over to touch his toes and rising again to rub the back of his neck.

"It could be any number of things, sir."

"C'mon, Ensign." The captain laces up his boots. "You know as well as I do what happened."

"Sir, we secured that android. You saw it."

"And I'll bet my last toothbrush it got unsecured. Or can you imagine a scenario where Nikki would fly off in the wrong direction without communicating?"

"I can't sir."

"It doesn't matter. We need that ship!"

"Yes sir, but first..." The ensign takes a liquid food supplement from her pack and opens the seal, adding several grams of white powder from a small vial.

"Blah..." The captain grimaces as he swallows the

mixture. "What did I just eat?"

"A synthesis I hope will ease most of the withdrawal symptoms you've been experiencing. I can't say how long it will take, but I have five doses. Only take one every twenty-four hours. With food."

"Food? Is that what we're calling this?" The captain washes down the mixture with water from the canteen, checking his chronometer. "How long 'til she gets to the refinery?"

"Assuming that's her destination, an hour, sir, at her current speed."

"Plan?"

"My first thought is the transporter. I think I can get it running in forty-five minutes, maybe a bit more."

The captain curses softly.

"That's a tight margin," he says. "We fire up our unit after she lands, she might have time to program it to send us into low orbit or the middle of the ocean."

"Not quite, sir. Master controls are here at the ag site. She wouldn't be able to do any programming from the refinery. But she wouldn't need to; just power down the transporter on her end, and we'd be locked out."

"Then it's a race—one we need to win. We get there first, ambush the Sister, and get our ship back."

"Maybe, sir, but we need to be careful. If she was able to surprise the lieutenant, she's more dangerous than she appears. And we are not well armed. Who knows how many workbots she has?"

"Dammit!" The captain clenches his fists. "Fine. What's my role for the next forty-five minutes?"

The ensign points at a workstation.

"I got this one booted up, and I bypassed the security protocols. If you can access specs for the refinery, that would save time. And one of your famous plans would be nice."

The captain scowls.

"I work better on a full stomach, but we'll see."

+ + +

At first, no plan, famous or otherwise, presents itself. In spite of the ensign's alchemy, the captain's head remains foggy, his neck and shoulders knotted and achy. Seated at a workstation, he stares at the holographic symbols and buttons looking back at him like a grade schooler's art project. Much of his adult life has been dedicated to mastering old human technology, specifically that used on the *Destiny* mission, yet he sits dopey and puzzled. He slaps himself across the face, right hand first, then left, again drinking from his canteen.

"Wake up," he whispers fiercely. "Specs!"

He takes a deep breath and begins touching buttons, slowly navigating through menus and pages of useless data. When he arrives at the refinery, he leans in to the projection, expanding some sections, changing the perspective of others, moving the two-dimensional map through simulated, three-dimensional space.

"Looks pretty much like we knew it would," he says to the ensign when she passes by on her way to the transporter with a loaded tool belt.

"No modifications?"

"Not that I can see, but our Sister wouldn't advertise her booby traps. OK, there's the landing platform, main gate, et cetera. And there's the transporter. What do you think?" He points at the guard station. "That might be our best chance to surprise her."

"Yes sir. But we'll need to leave our locator badges behind. Otherwise, if she's tapped into *Valiant's* systems, she'll know we're there."

"Good thinking." The captain watches Ensign Morales manually open the transporter door, sliding the single panel from left to right. "You're sure that thing will work? I mean, not leave some of our parts behind?"

"I can't guarantee anything, sir, but the colonists appeared to have had full confidence. Hmm... Sir. Look at this." She points at what appears to be a microphone embedded in the transporter's control panel.

The captain steps into the transporter and examines the object closely.

Time Weaver

"Is that what I think it is?"

"If you think it's a cerebral interface, then yes sir. Someone modified these transporters to be controlled both manually *and* telepathically."

"What do you know... I like that! It gives me hope somehow. When they left the System, they were persecuted, but here, they were respected enough to have telepathic controls added to the tech."

"Yes sir. I would love to see how far-reaching the modifications are. Does the mining module have them? The refinery? How much easier it would be to turn on lights and open doors without buttons or even voices."

"You're not wrong. But time, Ensign, time."

"Yes sir. I'll get to work."

+ + +

While she does, Captain Monroe continues examining the refinery map. But as each minute passes, the less sure he feels. A painkiller eases the tension in his neck, but the fogginess remains.

"Something's not right here," he murmurs to himself. "Too smooth, too easy."

The ensign lies on her back beneath the transporter platform, flashes of light sputtering green and yellow wherever her tools move. He watches her and his mind drifts. A lifetime of planning rests in the balance, waiting for him to clear the murk in his head and see the way forward. But the ensign is right. This Sister Janet character is more dangerous than her demeanor and modest garments suggest. Surely she knows they can sense V*aliant's* awakening. Wouldn't she be thinking about them, wondering what their response might be? But if she considered them a threat, why hadn't she simply used the ship to destroy the ag facility and them with it? Was she leading them into a trap? What would they find if they used the transporter to beat her to the refinery? Or would they simply be vaporized the second they activated the device?

"Alright, Monroe, get it together," he whispers, and again he rises to his feet, pacing from the workstation to the window. The scion are now huddled together, using the alp, which has lowered itself to the ground, its tentacles drooping in sleep, as a windbreak. There, they nibble dried awl and ration shares of lova. He suspects they are communicating, perhaps even plotting, and he wishes vainly to read their thoughts, to learn what they know.

This brings Joy to his mind, and he freezes.

"Hold on," he says. "Hold, hold, hold on."

The ensign slides out from under the platform.

"What is it sir?"

"I'm there, Ensign. I got it! I was getting swept away for a minute, overwhelmed by the current, you know? But it's just like my daddy used to say: step out of the river and let the turbulence pass you by. She's leading us, Carmela. Or she doesn't care about us, which is probably worse."

"It's possible, sir."

"What would she expect us to do?"

"Pursue and re-take, I suppose."

"Which is why that's exactly what we won't do."

The ensign tilts her head and frowns.

"Yes sir. But...what *will* we do?"

"Back door, Ensign, blind side!"

"Specifically?"

"That depends. Where's our little bug friend?"

"Joy? A few hundred kilometers from here, to the northeast." She projects a three-dimensional map from her eyes. "She's been on the move for a while. Making her way toward this," she points. "I haven't had a chance to examine the site in detail, but from what data our probe gathered before it was shot down, it appears to be a dam of some sort, possibly power generating."

She turns off the map and looks to the captain.

"Sir," she says, "what are you thinking?"

The captain smiles, broad and toothy.

"You wanted a Monroe special, Ensign, you got one. Whoo-ee! That medicine of yours is kicking in. I feel

Time Weaver

like my head was stuffed with cotton."

He moves to the table and opens the sketchbook, filled with a child's colorful rendering of Aranaean life. He flips through the pages, looking for something.

"What does our chaplain want, Ensign?"

"I'm sorry, sir, but there's not enough data."

"Let me put it to you a different way." The captain finds the image he is looking for and opens the book wide, holding the oversized page for the ensign to see. "What is it the others wanted to *keep* her from getting?"

The ensign looks carefully. The image is a simple but well-rendered replica of something they had both seen being carried by the creature calling itself Joy. Beneath the flat, black rectangle, a careful script spells out the words *Petros, el Libro.*

"Sister's holding the better hand," says the captain. "But something tells me this is the wild card."

The ensign nods.

"I would need to modify the transporter first," she thinks. "If she has access to activity reports, she'll know where we've gone the second after we get there."

"Can you do that?"

"Yes sir, I think so. But what about the scion?"

"That's the beauty part. They stay here! If she uses one of the satellites to survey, she'll see them parked outside and assume we're still here."

"Only if we leave our locators."

"Yeah, that part's not my favorite, but there may be an upside. If Nikki's able, he'll sense the signal and come here. We leave a data strip hidden somewhere and fill him in on the plan."

"How long do you think the scion will wait?"

"I don't know, but I hope long—if you can convince them their precious Ozag is on the way."

"Yes sir, that may work. But what do we do when we get to the dam?"

"Have a little heart-to-heart with our friend Joy, create an alliance, you know, teamwork."

The ensign considers this and nods.

A.P. Malloy

"I'll be done with the transporter in minutes."
"You're the best. Then a chat with your buddies."

+ + + + + +

Bored with eating and torpor, the idling scion have broken into a debate.

But what of Ozag's slave? asks Twenty-Seven. *The vumierre bearing the smell of a great queen? Perhaps Ozag herself?* His sparkling eyes glance left to right, as if he suspects the Undying Herself might appear. *Shall they continue following its orders?*

Yes, thinks one of the alp handlers. *Shall they?*

Yes, his partner echoes. *Its scent compels.*

It compels, thinks Viktor. *But he has his doubts. Who can imagine the Dreadful and Superlative stooping to collaborate with slaver filth? Vumierre scourge that should have been wiped from Aranae!*

Ozag, thinks Twenty-Seven, *is said to have destroyed them all, and yet...*

The others chitter to themselves and exchange thoughts about Ozag and the hated vumierre.

Their guesses are useless, Viktor interrupts. *Who can say how or why these new vumierre have appeared? Ozag rules, and her slaves have Power. But attend! Ozag's love for scion has been called into harsh question. Has she shifted her allegiance? Or is the Famous and Unmatchable—* He stops himself. His subordinates would surely come unhinged if they believed the First Thinking Queen perished. *Whatever the answer may be,* he continues, *they mustn't be blind. Follow orders but consider: are they being led astray? If so, they must exert self-will.*

Nervous, hesitant clicking greets this order, but Twenty-Seven whistles sharply.

Magister has Command! Do not doubt or disobey. If they must break with Ozag's slaves, so be it!

This quiets the party.

Viktor rubs his forelimbs together.

Reset the roll, he orders. *Number off!* And he starts

with himself. *He is One, named Viktor, Magister of Albion.*

Twenty-Seven goes next.

He is now Two, Prime of the Soldiers. Unnamed. He bows to the next in line, but Viktor interrupts.

Unnamed no longer. He is now Prime of Soldiers, yes, but he will hereby be known as Maximus.

The others buzz vigorously to show their approval, and they bow their antenna to their new prime. Then, in crisp order, they re-number themselves.

He is Three, Prime of the Handlers. Unnamed.

He is Four, Sub-Prime Handler.

He is Five, handler ...

Just then, the Undying's slave itself, the blonde-haired vumierre, exits the compound and approaches. Its scent intoxicates, and despite Viktor's earlier encouragement, his followers chitter anxiously. Their burgeoning desire to obey any order disgusts him—for he feels a similar compulsion in himself. When the vumierre arrives, it clicks and buzzes to them in its stilted fashion. The order it gives can scarcely be believed.

"The Undying comes here?" Viktor clicks.

"She does. She desires alp. She desires honor dead. They wait long time. Wait for Ozag. Clean alp."

"The Splendid and Implacable comes here?"

"She does! They wait!"

Viktor can't decide. Does this qualify as being led astray? The Undying has need of his alp? Plans to honor those fallen in his Command? How can it be? But wishful thinking is nearly as persuasive as the vumierre's undeniable scent. Ozag Herself!

Self-will, he recalls.

But the smell of the vumierre lingers about the company long after it has returned to the compound, and Viktor never once considers disobedience.

Prepare the alp, he orders, noting how raggedy the beast looks, and the others hasten to obey.

Ozag is coming!

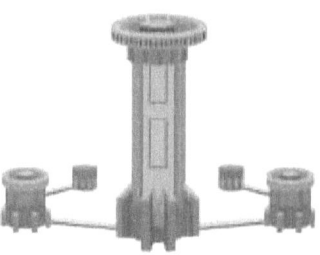

CHAPTER SEVEN
Major

"HE READS MINDS," the mother said about her young son. The show was *Hoax, Jokes, Amazing Folks*—a complete waste of 3V bandwidth—and the proud woman, her son by her side, spoke these words to the show's host, a modestly dressed but supercilious fellow with a name Maya couldn't recall. Why she watched such bilge was beyond her, but class wasn't for another hour and she didn't want to get out of bed for anything other than the pastry and tea she now enjoyed. Could she have found something else to watch? Of course. But her roommate was gone, shacking up with her new boyfriend, and when sweeping through the channels, Maya had heard the mother's words and had frozen. She set her food aside, absently petting Shantikar.

"For those in our audience who are new to this," said the host, "can you explain what you mean by 'reads minds'? Do you mean he knows what we're thinking?"

"Not exactly," said the woman. "Not in that kind of detail. But he can tell when someone's lying, or when they're scared, or happy, whatever."

"There are a lot of people here today who are going to say you're making this up, that it's just a trick."

"We used to get that all the time," said the woman, and she brushed her hand affectionately over her son's head, smiling at him. "But a few big wins at the last Apollonian Festival got people's attention. Now we've heard from other parents, mostly people on Earth, who say they have children who can do the same thing."

Here the audience booed and called out words of derision, some laughing.

A subtle chime interrupted the show, and a small image appeared in the lower portion of the hologram, the picture of a gray-haired woman, beautiful but unsmiling. Maya's mother, Nandini, was calling from Mars. Maya waved at the show, muting its sound. She aimed a finger at Nandini's picture, and it came to life.

"Aren't you supposed to be in class?" her mother asked. "And good morning, by the way."

"Not 'til nine. Good morning."

"How's your head?"

Maya shrugged.

"Have you heard anything from your professor?"

"Yeah. It's a no go."

"Maya!"

"Don't yell at me, yell at him. Or his boss, Dean Whatshername. It's a live test, with extraplanetary life forms from all over. They're not going to reschedule it."

"It's Daada's funeral!"

Oh God, help me, Maya thought as she watched her mother's image, *She's gonna cry.* Nandini reached for a tissue on the small table by her side. She sat down on Maya's old bed and wept bitterly but briefly.

"What good is being the daughter of Rathi Sharma and the granddaughter of Sujan Banerjee if they won't reschedule a stupid exam for you?" Nandini wiped her eyes and blew her nose.

"I'm sorry, mamacita, but it's not just a stupid exam—it's the senior final. I have an appointment with the President, but I'm not holding my breath." She looked down, tracing her fingers along Shantikar's stripes, so familiar and yet always evolving. She'd long ago stopped trying to memorize the pattern.

"I should never have told you to apply to that awful school," said her mother. "Luna! The only place Daada wanted to be was the same place that took you away from him in the end."

"Please don't say that; he wanted me to go."

"No, he wanted you to go to the best school in the System. He just wished it had been on Mars."

"You know we talked every week, right? I never missed a single call. And he won our last game of chess—not because I let him, either. I mean...I know it's not the same, but I never...You make it sound like I abandoned you all. Didn't you leave home when you were my age? It's how you met Dad."

Nandini blew her nose again, this time with less bluster and more decorum. She straightened her sari.

"You just talk to that President of yours. Or should I? Maybe your father should get involved?"

"God, no! Mom! Don't do anything. I'll tell her what's going on, and she'll do what she does. Yes? OK?"

Her mother arched a brow.

"I did leave home," she said. "And your father was worth it. But when my grandfather passed, I was at the funeral. And when your father's mother died, we gave Daada a place to live—and a granddaughter to love. You remember that, Maya, when we're old and alone. No matter how far you go from us, at some point, I hope you will remember your roots and come back."

"You know I will."

"How's your tiger?"

"Good." Maya lifted Shantikar so her mother could see. "Tony helped me get him certified as a service animal, so I can pretty much take him anywhere. He's like the school mascot. How's Dad doing?"

"Your father loved Daada. No one else made him laugh like that crazy old man. So he's sad. But of course, it's work, work, work with that one. I think he already knows you're not coming back. He asked me to have you call him after the test."

"As soon as I'm able."

"You *will* ace that exam," her mother stated flatly.

Time Weaver

"To honor Daada." It was an order, not encouragement.

"Yes ma'am. Tell Daddy I love him. I should go." She blew a kiss to the image of her mother. It waved back, but Maya couldn't tell if it was a goodbye or simply a gesture command to dismiss the call. Either way, her mother disappeared from the 3V and Maya was left to return to the last segment of her show.

"So!" said the host to his audience. "What do you think? Is little Timmy a joke on someone? Are his mind-reading skills a hoax in bad taste, or are we in the company of an amazing person?"

The show devolved into a shouting contest, as audience members, unruly at the best of times, hollered opinions on the case before them. There would be a formal tally, of course, but what entertainment value would that have without some good old-fashioned ruckus?

"The secure voting begins now," said the host, and he smiled broadly into the camera, seeming to look directly at Maya. "And for those voting at home—or wherever you might be watching—select the option at the bottom of your screen and wait for the results."

Maya did not vote, but she did wait.

"Are you ready?" asked the host to little Timmy's mother. She smiled and patted Timmy's knee.

"One of us already knows the results."

This caused an uproar from the audience, who both loved and reviled her cleverness and conviction. They yelled and clapped.

"I guess we'll find out," said the host. "The votes are in. Here we go..." He tapped the side of his glasses and the information was projected in a three-dimensional graph. "Twenty-two percent of you think this is a joke—not sure what the punchline is—and a whopping seventy-five percent of you are sure it's a hoax! Sorry Timmy, but only three percent of those who cast a vote believe you are an amazing person."

But Little Timmy didn't appear overly concerned. He smiled to reveal a missing tooth.

"Do you want to try to change their minds?" asked

the host as if conspiring with the boy.

"Sure."

"Do you know how much you could win?"

"A lot?"

The audience cheered and laughed.

"That's right, Timmy," the host smiled. "A lot! And you're going to get that chance. When we return after the break, we have a series of tests designed to prove what your mother is claiming. If you can change our audience's mind, you'll be a very rich little boy. Sound good?"

Maya waved her hand at the 3V, and the image vanished. She downed the last of her pastry and tea and let Shantikar take the place she had warmed on the bed. She was interested in what little Timmy would be asked to do, but she had a test of her own to worry about and a shower to take.

+ + +

"I am sorry," said the President, whose name was Filkins, and whose bosom heaved when she talked as if two small people were hidden beneath her business drapery and wished to escape. "I was devastated by my own grandfather's passing. I do hope you're OK. But considering the sensitive nature of this exam, I'm sure you can understand why rescheduling will be impossible."

Maya didn't bother arguing. She had grown adept at reading the disposition of those before her. If the President had been the slightest bit open to her point of view, she would have known. Instead, from the moment Maya had walked through the polished glass door and entered the spacious, well-appointed office, she had sensed the President's mind to be made-up and inflexible. Her sympathy was sincere but irrelevant.

And that was that.

Outside, the ways were bustling with pedestrians and buggies, and Maya stood thinking about Daada and their last conversation. They had spoken of the upcoming bicentennial anniversary of the first Lunar landing, and

Daada had re-told the story of how he and she had first gone to Serenity Dome to see the commemorative plaque. She had been very young at the time, the headaches and nightmares still a new thing, and going to see the plaque had been soothing, a pleasant distraction, though she remembered few of the details. Hearing Daada re-tell it had made her laugh. He had looked ancient in the call, but even over the many miles from Mars to Luna and shielded by his glasses, his eyes held a mischievous sparkle that brightened his face, and his mustache had character enough for two.

"Going to celebrate, I hope," he had said.

"Of course."

"You'd better! I'll disown any granddaughter who doesn't stay up all night for Apollonia. And drink! You're going to have a chaang for me, yes?"

"Probably a couple."

"That's my girl! Bringing a date?"

The complications of Maya's love life had always escaped her grandfather, who had never grasped how difficult it was to engage another person whose moods and honesty she could read like a large-print book.

"Too busy for boys, Daada. Getting straight A's over here—just for you!"

And that had been true. Which is why, when the xenobiology exam rolled around, Maya received the best score in the class, though she was not the first one to finish. Diligent and determined, she took every second allowed, always double and sometimes triple checking her answers. She had thought of her grandfather's funeral only once but had shaken regret from her mind, refusing to be distracted. Seated in the round, the students had watched as holographic images were broadcast into the room of exotic, extraterrestrial creatures, most in some level of quarantine, none larger than a sparrow. She had read her professor's mind—felt his mild guilt for refusing to allow a reschedule but also an infuriating self-righteousness that made Maya glad this would be their last class together. He had waved as she exited the room, but she acted as if she had not seen the gesture.

Back outside, with the weight of the exam off her shoulders, Maya wandered away from the bio building, eager to have it as far behind her as possible. As she drifted aimlessly, she thought of her parents and others gathered at an Indian funeral, chanty and filled with smoke. She wasn't sure how it happened, but zip! an hour passed by, and she found herself at the center of campus, hungry, sad, and weeping silently, tears streaming down her face.

"Is everything OK?" someone asked.

Maya looked up, wiping her eyes. A man, older than her but handsome and dark, African, stood waiting for a buggy. He kept a respectful distance and didn't stare, but Maya read immediately that he found her attractive. His solicitous question she read as sincere—as far as it went—but was at least in part the predictable attempt typical of men. Maya responded by nodding, but she made no eye contact, not wishing to encourage a stranger. He said no more, simply nodded in return, and he looked back to the street, as if hoping for a buggy. But Maya could read he had other hopes as well. His confidence was unmistakable and charismatic, standing out from the other passersby like an island in a muddy river. She tried to think of where she should go, what she should do, now that the test was over, but a thought came to her unbidden—*the test is just beginning*—and she paused to think what it might mean.

"Would you like to share?" the man asked.

"What?"

"I've got a buggy on the way. Do you need a ride?"

Maya squinted her eyes and concentrated. Liars, regardless their skill, had never been able to withstand her scrutiny. The easiest minds to read were the dishonest. Theirs was a perpetual turbulence and disharmony she felt must be toxic to those who practiced it for any great time. The man before her had none of that feeling. His mind was open with the self-assurance of someone who had nothing to hide. She wiped her eyes again, glad for the "rain" that had been scheduled, misting down from micro-sprinklers mounted to the dome high above. The rate of fall had been determined most beneficial for cleaning the air, moisturizing the soil, and washing imporous surfaces, but it was also perfectly suited for hiding unwanted tears.

"Sure," she said. Thanks." But she had nowhere to go. Shantikar would be sound asleep, digesting the remainder of his chicken, and her roommate would not be back until after the weekend.

"Major Monroe," the man said. "System Space Fleet. I'm from Earth. English Americas."

"Nandini," she said, taking his extended hand—such an old-fashioned gesture!—and acting on long practice, lying about her name. "Khatri. Born here."

"Nice to meet you," the man said, and he smiled, pleasant, not too enthusiastic, looking away exactly when he should. "Here comes one," he nodded at the green and silver buggy that had turned a corner and was trundling their way. "Do you have a driver you like?"

"Actually," said Maya, "I do." But she quickly changed her mind. Carl would identify her, and for reasons she couldn't explain but entirely trusted, she wished to remain anonymous. "But I can ride with him any time," she said. "You choose."

"Random it is," the man smiled. "Roll the dice."

+ + +

He insisted she call him Javon. His reason for being at the school was simple, and he shared it as the buggy motored through the lanes and byways that partitioned the university's many departments.

"I was looking for Maya Sharma," he said. "The Doctor's daughter. I heard she was a student here." He tapped his right temple and an image projected from his embedded Halo, Maya's high school graduation picture. She marveled at how long and black her hair had been, how clunky her glasses and how dark her eyes. That had also been the last time she had worn a sari. She was no longer confused when people referred to her father as *The* Doctor, as if he were the only one in the System, but it had always annoyed her.

"Who?" she asked.

"I'm sorry, but who are you whoing about?" Javon tilted his head. "The Doctor or the daughter?"

"Both."

"Are you kidding?"

She returned his gaze, level and unflinching.

"Seriously, now," he said. "You're having fun at my expense. Is there a joke here I'm not getting?"

"No joke," she said. "But Indians, you know. There are a lot of us on Luna. Never heard of Maya Sharma."

"Well, you've heard of Rathi Sharma."

"Obviously, but I never heard him called just 'The Doctor' before. Makes him sound like a character from some weird 3V show or something."

"In my world," Javon said without irony, "there is only one Doctor that matters."

"And what world is that?"

"You're sure you don't know Maya Sharma?"

"It's a big school."

"Well, if you were studying xenobiology—are you? No?—if you were, where would you hang out? I've been loitering around the lab, but I can't get anyone from the school to tell me where she lives, what classes she's taking—even what she looks like now. They're more secretive than the military."

"I would hope so," said Maya. "Sort of a privacy thing, don't you think? I mean if this chica's dad is famous, she probably gets bugged all the time."

"Sure, I get it. Of course. If I was her, I would want the same thing." He nodded sincerely. "I love your hair, by the way. Pink is good for you. And tiger stripes," he pointed to her contact lenses. "That's nice."

Javon turned his gaze to the world outside, the rain dashing from the water-resistant windshield. They rode along in silence for a while, this driver much less chatty than Carl. Maya assumed Javon had a destination in mind, but other than "a tour of the campus, please," he had given the buggy no instructions. Her own contribution had been simply, "I guess I'm going to lunch. Don't know where yet."

"Here's an idea," Javon said as their rambling tour continued. "I heard you can get authentic soul food in Tranquility dome. Ever had it? Want to come? My treat."

Normally, Maya would have politely but firmly rejected this overture, but Daada's passing had left her feeling a destabilizing loneliness, and something about Javon's sincerity was grounding. So she let slide the unlikely pairing of the average Indian and a rib joint, attracted to the idea of lunching at a place where she would be unrecognized.

"Sure," she said. "But I'll pay for my own."

+ + +

It was close to two o'clock by the time they arrived, and Maya was famished. Food and libation went to her head quickly but not unpleasantly, and the next time she looked at a clock, five hours had passed.

"Oh my God," she said. "Is that really the time?"

Javon smiled.

"A good sign, yes? Lost in conversation!"

"Yeah," she said, not all of her intoxication coming from the rice beer. That smile! She felt sure if he had dared to touch her, her breath would have been dashed away. She waited, hoping he would dare, but he did not, only making the most charming small talk with their server and checking with Maya before registering his payment for the meal.

"Only if you don't mind," he said. "I'm not trying to put you in my debt or anything. But college is expensive, and it *was* my idea."

She did not mind. She was still trying to unravel how so much time had passed unnoticed. Daada had always described that as a sign of dharma.

"When you are lost in the action and forget about time," he had said, "you are on the right path."

What had they eaten? Barbecued pizza, and she had plowed through her share shamelessly, entranced by the sound of Javon's voice. What had they talked about? Everything and nothing, it seemed, improvising like the jazz musicians who had played in the background. Keeping her identity a secret had added an element of spice to the encounter, but the challenge felt like a game, not a risk, the conversation like a dance. And never once did they step on one another's toes.

At last, he told her he must go.

"Nandini Khatri," he said, "will you do me the honor of accompanying me to the Apollonian Festival? It's the bicentennial, you know." He opened the door for her as they exited the restaurant. They walked out into the aromatic memory of recent rain, and when he brushed by accident against her, she could smell his subtle cologne and the beer on his breath. Her heart leapt, but she did not move away.

"I would like that," she said.

+ + +

In the days leading up to the Apollonian Festival, she saw Javon several times, but only briefly, as he was busy with duties about which he never spoke. The conversations were exercises in small talk, but the spark was still there, and she was gratified to learn it needed no encouragement from alcohol. Their upcoming date grew in her mind into something more important than the anniversary that would provide its backdrop.

So many media outlets spent so much time and money producing documentary or live action depictions of the first Lunar landings that Maya felt sure she could repeat each of the three astronaut's lines on cue—and most of those from their command center on Earth. The irony, that the base from which that mission had been launched was now, two hundred years later, entirely submerged under filthy sea water was lost on most of those who called Luna home. They saw the festival as little more than a legitimate excuse for a week of free-spirited and occasionally debauched celebration.

On the day of the opening ceremony, Maya waffled between the green outfit that went so well with her skin and the orange outfit that matched her attitude.

"Neither," said her roommate. "Everyone will be wearing blue. Here." She confidently selected a top and matching pants. "These look great on you. And these shoes. Shantikar! Move!" But the tiger snored on top of the blue strap sandals, pretending not to hear. "You know," said her roommate, and she left the sandals for Maya to retrieve, "he's going to figure out who you are soon enough. Why don't you just tell him?"

"Not 'til I know what he wants."

"Corporate spy, probably. Wants to see what he can learn from the Doctor's daughter. Ooh! Maybe he's with *The Daily Scoop!*"

Maya frowned.

"The ice cream people?"

"Yeah, the ice cream people, Maya. He wants to name a flavor after your dad. C'mon! The news show. They're always doing celebridocs. Maybe he's a reporter, you know, undercover. Under *your* covers, that is."

"Stop. We're just going to a show."

"Oh, yeah. An older man asks out a pretty young thing, spends money on her, asks her out, and all he wants is to sit next to her at some stupid show."

"Aren't you going?"

"Nah. My last final killed me. I'm going home. Steven got a couple seats on the next shuttle. I'll celebrate back on Earth, thank you, and fatten up on my mom's cooking. Um…" She moved in close and opened her arms for an awkward hug. "We may not see each other again for a while." Maya clearly read a different message in her roommate's mind: "may not" was actually "won't," and "for a while," was "ever." But it didn't bother her. Theirs had been a pleasant but superficial relationship, built from economic necessity and convenience. Neither could afford to live alone, and few others were willing to live with a tiger of any size, regardless how sleepy.

"Take care," Maya said, and she returned the embrace. "Shantikar will miss you."

+ + +

Dinner was Indian, at Javon's request, but Maya insisted they get the food to go and would not go inside to pick up their order, fearing to be recognized. They ate by the Poseidonian Ruins, which allowed them a view of the park where the light show would take place—without requiring them to buy tickets. There they sat on broken concrete slabs, eating samosas and drinking chaang, and Maya quite forgot her typical reserve, aware that she was smiling like a fool. When Javon reached out to brush a crumb from her chin, she held her breath, and when he laughed at some offhand remark she made, she felt she had conquered the world. Wisely, she alternated chaang with water, for anyone with a heart could see she was about to be swept off her feet.

"Did you ever find your friend?" she asked.

Javon scooped some dal from its container, using his chapatti like a spoon and tearing away a bite of the flatbread with his delightfully white teeth.

"Not a friend, actually. I've never met her before."

"Oh. I thought you said you knew her dad."

"We've talked but never met in person. The Doctor is not an easy man to get an audience with."

"OK, so? Don't be mysterious. Why's it so important you find this Sharma chick? You think she's going to be able to get you in with her dad? Trying to get a cushy job or something?"

"Wow. It sounds pretty crass when you say it like that. But yes, that's pretty much what I was hoping. I was harboring on Luna anyway, and when I heard she was a student, I took a shot."

"Not a very good one," she said and smiled.

"I'm not done yet."

"You know, if you keep lurking around campus, you'll probably get arrested."

Javon sipped his chaang and thought about this.

"Would you come visit me in prison?" he asked.

"Every day."

"Bring me a hacksaw hidden inside a cake?"

"Is that how it's done?"

"Either that or a file in your bra."

"Ha! Joke's on you, Felonious Monk. I'm not wearing one." *Oh, for God's sake,* she thought, suddenly embarrassed, and she looked down to where the park had begun to fill with people. Her face grew hot. *That was a stupid thing to say.* But his eyes merely twinkled, and he continued his work on the food.

"Blue looks good on you," he said.

She deflected the compliment.

"What would you ask him if you got the chance?"

"Not ask, tell."

"OK, what would you tell him?"

"That I'm the best pilot in the System fleet, and he should choose me to helm *Destiny's* maiden voyage."

Maya rolled her eyes and looked away. *Not everything is a double entendre,* she thought. *Get a grip!*

"Sorry," she said, "but what is *Destiny*?"

"Nandini! I'm not trying to be rude, but how do you not know these things?"

"I blame school," she said.

Down below, individual performers drifted among the gathering, some playing music, others dressed as astronauts. A large stage was set, holograms of the historic moon landing projected for all to see. Maya's chin dipped, and for a moment, her brow furrowed. What was she doing? What right did she have to be lighthearted? Her Daada was gone, to who knows where, perhaps never to be seen again, no matter what his arcane faith professed. He had hoped to witness this celebration...

I'll watch it for you, she thought, but also murmured aloud. Javon looked up from his food.

A.P. Malloy

"I missed that, champ. What did you say?"

"Nothing. My Daada. My grandpa. He would have liked this. His funeral was the day we met."

"I'm sorry," Javon said, and he put down his plate, wiping his mouth and taking her hand. She read sympathy in his mind, a depth of feeling beyond physical attraction. She sensed his contentment to simply sit holding hands and listening to music, and her heart swelled. Damnable tears began to stream. *All I do is cry,* she thought, but if he noticed he said nothing, and when the emotion passed, Maya found herself falling into the story of the three astronauts, from what used to be called the United States, and their adventure to the moon. The hologram was the largest—towering five stories high—and most detailed she had ever seen, its resolution as sharp as if the events were being viewed live. No matter where they sat in the park, which had been arranged like an amphitheater, spectators had an amazing, almost overwhelming view of the mission that had led to them being here, two centuries later.

"So," she said, when at last she could look away from the spectacle. "*Destiny.* Tell me everything."

"There isn't a lot to tell. She's just a skeleton at the moment. But when she's done, she'll be to the other starships like a buggy is to a bicycle."

"And you think you should be her pilot."

"Her leader."

"Using his daughter to get the inside track on a job? Doesn't that make her a tool?"

"No! Hey! It's not like that. I was here, that's all, and knew I wouldn't be for long. So I took a shot. If I could meet her, I know she'd see something..." He looked away. "I just wanted a chance to make my case, that's all."

Maya was about to ask, "And what is that case?" but she stopped, focusing on something else he had said.

"Not going to be here for long?"

He shook his head.

"I'm shipping out to Saturn once repairs are complete. It could be a week, could be two, hard to say. Maybe a little more. I thought I said that."

"No."

"Oh. Sorry."

The park lights dimmed and the individual musicians united, their music amplified as they joined to create something like a waltz. Down below, couples took hands or held one another close, stepping and swaying to the rhythm with celestial images and astronauts casting an ambient glow. Javon squeezed her hand. She knew what he was going to ask before the words were out of his mouth, and just as quickly she knew her answer.

"Will you dance with me?" he asked.

She rose to her feet.

"Yes, please. But kiss me first."

+ + +

Long after the festivities had ended, he returned with her to her dorm room, spending the night for the first—but not the last—time. Early in the visit, Shantikar sat at a distance, staring at him through eyes half open, judging. Javon had the wits to allow him his space, cooing at him in an admiring fashion but never presuming to approach. This the great cat found irresistible, and he surprised them both by leaping on to the bed—of course—just as they had begun to find comfort in one another's embrace.

"Shanti," Maya scolded mildly, but Javon purred at the tiger and slowly extended a hand for him to smell. Shantikar approached, and before long, he was coiling around the man's waist, butting him insistently with his head until Javon agreed to scratch him behind the ears.

"This could go on all night," Maya said.

"Don't worry," Javon smiled, his eyes hungry. "I won't forget about you."

And indeed, he did not. When Shantikar at last had the discretion to remove himself to his favorite perch at the screened window, staring at the world outside like a child watches 3V, Javon undressed her slowly, kissing

A.P. Malloy

her from head to toe and back again. He performed graces with his lips and fingers like a concert musician until she was spent, her mind and body floating languid on the edge of sleep. But he would accept no reciprocation aside from kisses and a circumspect embrace, refusing to consummate or even fully undress.

"Wait," he murmured, sucking on her ear. "Wait," though he never mentioned for how long, or why.

+ + +

The morning was more of the same, with catnapping and brunching mixed in, the hours slipping by with no regret, the most arduous chore—bringing Shantikar to the swimming hole—no chore at all but a celebration, as if seeing the cat paddle happily from someone else's perspective made the experience brand new. When the thought of Daada and their time on Mars came to her mind, it made Maya pause, but it could not chase the happiness from her heart.

"Do you believe in God?" she asked.

"Wow. We're going all the way to that, are we?" Javon tossed another morsel of dehydrated rabbit into the water, laughing when Shantikar plunged in after it.

"Too much too soon?"

"No, I don't mind. But my position on the God question isn't always...popular with a lot of folks."

"So, you don't think it's possible?"

Javon took a deep breath, and Maya read the care with which he considered his answer. As always, he was endearingly honest and thoughtful, but unafraid.

"I think I've learned not to rule out anything," he said. "So, possible, yes, but about as likely as those telepathic kids they trot out every once in a while, you know? Urban legend. I mean, don't get me wrong. I would love some omnipotent sentience to care about me and hook me up with an eternal paradise after I die, but..." He looked up and shrugged. "I guess I'm an open-minded but not terribly hopeful atheist. You? Do I dare ask?"

Time Weaver

"Of course. I'm an open-minded believer."

"And what fuels your belief?"

At any other time, Maya would have evaded the question, or given some trite or defensively comedic answer, hoping to avoid a debate. Not now.

"Science," she replied. "Like you said: anything's possible. Yes, that's still being debated, but if it's true, then God already exists somewhere—or is going to. And if God exists anywhere, then God—a perfect power and wisdom—exists everywhere, by the definition of perfection. Sorry. That's what my Daada believed. Maybe I'm just a victim of indoctrination and habit."

Javon held her hand, tracing the outline of her fingers and wrinkling his brow.

"You've thought about this a lot," he said.

"Too much."

"Ever go to...what is it called in Hindu? Temple?"

"Sure, my mom and Daada and me. Not my dad, though—" But she stopped herself and changed the subject. "Anyway, I used to. Not so much now."

"Well," he smiled, "if it's true, I hope my doubt will be forgiven. And if telepathic kids really do start cropping up throughout the System, I hope they'll have the courtesy to stay out of my head. It's a messy place."

"I don't think you have anything to worry about."

"Because they don't exist, you mean?"

"No. I mean, I don't know, I've never met one, as far as I know. But you strike me as a pretty straight shooter. Shantikar's an excellent judge of character. He's never been wrong yet."

Javon nodded, but a worry clouded his gaze.

"Then there's something I should tell you."

"Yes?"

"Last night."

"Yes?"

"I wasn't trying to pry, just restless, you know, happens when I'm on land. Just looking out the window and pacing around while you were asleep."

Of course, Maya guessed what was coming. Truth

like that couldn't stay hidden forever. She hadn't known how it would come out, but she would never have invited him to her place had she not been willing for it to do so.

"You saw my pictures."

"You've changed a lot."

"Yeah. Well. Now you know."

"Nothing's different," he said quietly. "Between us, I mean. And I've scrapped my earlier plan. Don't say anything to your dad. It wouldn't be right."

"I wouldn't even if you asked."

"Good." He smiled. "Maya Sharma, hm?"

"At your service." And then she added, as if it somehow explained all that needed explanation, "Nandini's my mom's name."

"And what would Nandini Sharma think of us?"

"Her daughter with an older man?" Maya leaned in close to steal a kiss on his neck, so strong and slightly musky, then a second. "That's a good question. Maybe we'll get the chance to find out some day."

+ + +

In the end, repairs to his ship took just over five weeks, and not a day of it did he begrudge her, though his desire to be back aboard couldn't have been more clear had he stated it aloud.

"I told my parents I was staying to interview for internships," she said when he asked what her excuse was for not returning to Mars now that the degree had come to its grueling conclusion.

"I hate for you to lie on account of me," he said.

"I'll explain it all when I get back," she promised. "For now, I just want to enjoy myself."

And enjoy she did, free of guilt. He paid for everything, which opened up options for entertainment her modest allowance had prohibited, like skid racing and the best events in the ongoing Apollonian celebration, including the amazing food. But his motives were pure, this also she could read, based on a simple understanding of their

Time Weaver

current economic status.

"You'll get your chance," he said, his smile scored into her memory. "When you're an interstellar celebrity, breeding the most intelligent...what did you call them?"

"Megacephalic sicut simians."

"Which is what, again?"

"Big headed, monkey-looking bacteria."

"Yeah, that. You hit the jackpot with that and we'll go halfsies every time." He ran his fingers through her hair, the brown and pink playing like an ice cream sundae. "I'm not trying to tie you up in financial obligation or create an unfair imbalance, you know."

"I know."

Their romance took them wherever there was a buggy to be ridden, and some places where there were none. Javon's introduction to Carl had come as a pleasant surprise to the man, who, in spite of his good nature, interacted minimally with machine minds.

"Very nice to meet you," Carl said. Maya was busy at the moment receiving a shoulder massage, so he didn't bother to ask if she wanted to drive.

"And you," said Javon. "I gather you've known Maya for a long time. Anything I should be aware of?"

"I have indeed," Carl replied simply. "And her family. She's very well-liked among the buggies. We'd be awfully upset if anything bad happened to her."

Maya and Javon exchanged a quick glance and Maya's face creased into a flattered smile.

"That's so sweet, Carl, thank you!"

"The pleasure is all mine. I'm really sorry to hear about your Daada. He was quite a character! Remember when we rode back from the temple together?"

"I do."

"Your father was there too. Big man now, isn't he? Haven't seen him in a long time. Think he'd be willing to upload me onto *Destiny?*"

"I can ask."

When her caretaking responsibilities for an aging tiger allowed, she visited Javon aboard his ship, the *Noko-*

mis, an interplanetary scanner. Most of the crew were still on Luna, so they were allowed to roam largely uninterrupted, and for a time, in his private quarters, largely undressed. And still, in spite of the pleasure he gave her, when she tried to reciprocate, his answer remained:

"Wait," and he quelled objections with a kiss.

The *Nokomis* was a modest ship, surely not, she imagined, as exciting as the fighter he had piloted in his younger years, nor as prestigious as the frigate he had commanded in his last military tour before injury had cut his career short. But he was equally modest, and never once complained about his current vessel or pedestrian duties. He guided her through the corridors with the air of a proud father and let her sit in the captain's chair, the two of them admiring the view of Luna as the Earth rose to their left. Maya felt she was floating away from the life she had known, leaving the last four years behind, and only the thought of Shantikar kept her from asking if she could go with him when the day at last came for Javon and his crew to depart for Saturn.

"I can't guarantee when I'll be back," he said, guessing her mind as they lay together in her bed. Shantikar lazed on his back between them, purring as they took turns tracing the line of his stripes.

"I can't guarantee that I'd be here even if you did."

"Is there no hope for us, then?"

"Always! But graduate school is my only road to a real job, and I can't even think about that right now. Picking a school feels like a chore for another lifetime."

"You'll think about me every day?"

"First thing in the morning, last thing at night."

"And you'll write?"

"Can I just send video?"

"Even better. But code it." He smiled. "My crew is rock solid, but I won't say they're above taking a peek at a pretty woman in her boudoir."

And these promises were enough, when paired with one last night of bliss, to keep her from tears when they finally parted, she and Shantikar watching Carl motor him away to the shuttle launch. She waved, and even from here she could see the white of his teeth and sense the heat in his ardent gaze.

Gonna marry that one, she thought to Shantikar, as the buggy turned a corner and disappeared.

But then the thing on Mars happened, and her plans for the future were washed away by tidal forces beyond any of them, just as the lives of her parents and the hundreds of Martian citizens killed by the very same androids her father had once placed such faith in. Maya would not see Major Javon Monroe again for another five years, and when they did meet, she would be so changed he would not recognize her.

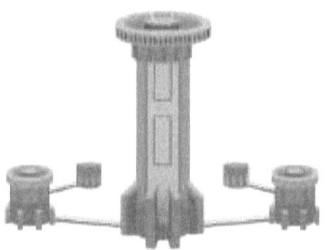

CHAPTER EIGHT
Quest

SOON AFTER GAPI-KAN has passed, Claw, the Redtooth chief, arrives with a pair of grumbling bibijas at the north crossing where Stone sits waiting, nursing her injuries and her grievances. He offers her no greeting.

The old rotter's dead then? he asks.

I left that to your second, Stone snarls. *Before we go any further, what do you have to eat?*

Claw ignores this question.

You saw it, right? he persists. *You saw Spike rip out his throat?*

I was busy staying alive, thinks Stone, turning her flank to give a better view of her injuries. *We weren't at a birthday feast! If your second couldn't finish the job considering the shape Bruiser was in, you should find someone else for the role. A wabi could have ended him.*

Fine. What about the other Sugarfeet?

Losing.

You should have stayed to help.

My grudge was with Bruiser, no one else.

Claw pins his ears, dissatisfied with this answer, and he continues his inquisition.

How many? he asks. *What was the score?*

I couldn't see for sure, but it was two-to-one in favor of the Redteeth when I left—or worse.

You mean better.

Yeah. Stone curls her lip. *Sure.*

And no other Bristles but the one Spike ended?

None that I saw.

The thrower?

Left behind at the home caves.

But she can answer not another question; she has reached her limit. Just as Claw summons an ibiwa to fetch some food, she begins to sway, then collapses.

Get her inside, thinks Claw, and the others are doing just that when Spike shuffles into sight from the west, approaching the island bridge with his head and tail hanging low. He is alone.

This doesn't look good, thinks one of the bibijas.

Claw merely runs his tongue over his teeth.

When he has crossed the wedge, Spike puts on a bold face, but the news he bears of defeat and capture can't be masked by proud words and posing. He describes the intervention of the scion, the appearance of two Whitetails, the Moondweller cutter, and the awful Talking Head. He also mentions the promise he had made in the face of all this, his tone suggesting they would have done the same. But his audience clashes their teeth and sweeps their tails, agitated and disappointed. Surely this means their designs on the Skull have been foiled?

Never mind that! Claw curses. *Those kinds of promises aren't binding!*

I don't know, Boss, thinks Spike. *Felt pretty binding to me. I wouldn't go back for nothin.'*

Then you can stay here and watch the Sugarfoot. I didn't make a promise! Prepare the second wave.

Oh, Boss. The first wave didn't go so good. Maybe we should just leave well enough alone.

Is my oti-mu's unavenged death "well enough"? Thirteen Redteeth held prisoner? Is that "well enough"?

I reckon they'll let 'em go if we stay on our side. Might kill 'em if we don't.

I won't be intimidated or threatened! Any Redtooth they kill will be joined by two Sugarfeet.

A.P. Malloy

And Claw will tolerate no further objections, repeating his order that the second wave of fighters be prepared to move on the Skull. Of course, his orders are followed, but not with great enthusiasm. Some among them have served with Spike for long moons. He has earned their trust, and his tale of the eerie and foreign, with Moondweller devilry and a company of scion (who knows how many more there might be?) does not pair well with the apparent Bristle-Whitetail alliance. Nor are any keen to break the promise. These skeptical Redteeth drag their feet and manufacture all types of reasons for delay.

So and so has an injured tail.

This bibija has brand new wabis.

That ibiwa is far away on the Render range.

Claw puts Stone in the care of a withered gigika who tends her injuries. But he also does not allow her to leave. He snarls and snaps impatiently.

I think they're mustering as fast as they can, offers Spike, and he rubs at the place where his eye used to be.

But they both know that isn't true.

+ + +   + + +

Far to the east, sheltering in the last oasis of accrete before the end of the Whitetail range—and for all Lightning knows, the end of the world—she and the others gather around the battered remains of the labor android. They have slept, though not deeply or well, and having broken their fast, they feel the press to move on. Queen Shimmer, secure in her fanning accrete, looks down at the proceedings, attending carefully.

Ask what it knows of Ozag, she demands.

We have to wake it up first, thinks Pounce, and he reaches around to flip the switch located at the base of the android's metallic skull. Its eyes twitch and come into focus; its mouth opens and closes.

"Fairzas nokstun uppa palitch," it says, reciting its favorite line. But it only does so once this time. After that, it falls silent. It does not respond to questions.

Time Weaver

So, what do you suggest we do? Pounce asks.

Joy in turn refers this question to the Book.

Difficult to say, it replies. *If we had the proper tools, we could access power and control, perhaps identify the problem and effect repairs.*

We need proper tools, Joy translates to the others.

I've got a mending kit, thinks Lightning. *Will that help? Plus the cutter.*

When Joy asks, the Book is not optimistic.

Even if those simple tools sufficed to access sealed compartments, they would be useless for diagnostics or repair even for someone highly trained.

When Joy shares this information, Pounce bares his teeth in frustration.

Is that the best you've got? C'mon! You gotta give me something! What are we supposed to do?

When asked, the Book suggests simply leaving the android awake, rather than, as has been their practice in the past, turning it off when done with it.

It is possible, the artifact offers, *that it continues to absorb data while conscious. At some point, an event may trigger greater awareness and functionality.*

Wouldn't be hard to do, thinks Lightning when this message is shared. *Any functionality would be greater than what it has now.*

It has stopped repeating itself, Cliff notes.

It's an improvement for me, thinks Thunder.

Pounce is disappointed but not surprised. He returns the android to Fluvial's back and the party packs up, heading into the last stretch of shadowy accrete. Feeling she has let the expedition down, Joy walks with her hand in her sling, asking questions.

How should we...proceed? she tests a new word.

Very cautiously, the Book replies.

She raps the artifact with the tip of her finger.

Please don't be difficult, she thinks. *We really need help.* She takes a breath. *What is your advice?*

Travel north and east of here. You should find a service road, not well maintained and not a straight path, for the colonists had to build around some stubborn mountains. But it's the only way to the Hold on foot.

And what's the downside?

Kish. Lots of kish. And rockslides.

What about that smell?

That is Ozag's Hold. I cannot predict her response to our approach. We would be wise to remain as secretive as possible. We can use the road as a guide, but we mustn't walk it openly until there is no other choice.

Anything else?

You should keep ears, eyes, and noses open for the other Reader I mentioned. He would be a great help.

Joy imagines another Reader. What would he look like? Would he try to take the Book from her? She could ask, but she fears the truth; she'll meet him when she meets him—or perhaps never! She presses the Book jealously to her side, and not for the first time she regrets committing to this quest. But onward they march, in spite of her doubt, and the smell of talihew fades behind them. The oasis comes to an end too soon. After two thousand strides, the sunlight grows, finding its way through the diminishing canopy to gild the accretion scales. Another two thousand and poof! No more accrete. The company pauses beneath the last forking pillar and watches a nearby cyrilis snatch a giant yit who zigs when it should have zagged.

Reckon we's a gonna miss 'em, thinks Piedmont of the cyriles and yits. *Shoot, we's a gonna miss lotsa things, I s'pose. Not as we's a changin' 'r minds, now, it aint like that, see? We's real happy ta be part o' the 'venture, trusty to the end. But still. Who's a knowin' what we'll run inta? Maybe fall off the edge o' the world!*

Not if I can help it. Pounce aims his snout at Joy. *Have any traveling advice to share?*

She offers what she has learned about the road.

Doesn't sound like we should expect a warm welcome, thinks Pounce. *Any Moondweller mischief?*

But the Book can only guess.

We might find things...much different than when I

*was last there. I can't say what we'll encounter or how
we'll get in. The only way to know is to go there.*

Joy translates this to her audience.

*Queen here seems to think she'll be allowed in just
by asking,* thinks Thunder.

She believes it possible, Shimmer clicks harshly.
She does not claim certainty.

That would be nice, thinks Pounce. *A simple, clean
ending to this affair and a quick trip home.*

This sounds nice to everyone, but neither Lightning nor Joy hold out much hope. Joy recalls her last
audience with a scion queen. She finds it hard to imagine
greater hospitality with a queen of Ozag's reputation. But
what is there to do? Resigned to their fate, the company
leaves the last accrete, exchanging its comforting shadows for the exposure of the Naked Hills.

+ + +

At first, the rolling terrain is much like before,
thin snow, thick grass, and abundant feculent snikes,
persistent and infuriating. The kezels' tails sweep side to
side, but the snikes target their ears and undersides
where tails can't reach, and they can't walk four-legged
and swat their tiny adversaries at the same time. Joy
takes turns riding, using a sheaf of grass to shoo the
snikes from whoever is her steed at the moment. This
makes her quite popular, and she shuffles from one kezel
to the next, even taking a turn on the Whitetails.

We's sooprized, thinks Piedmont as he carries the
android while Joy rides on Fluvial's back. *But we's real
gratitudily-like. Hope you's not too 'pset 'bout how I's been
treatin' you as a freak an' all. Ain't had no right to do it,
see? Turns out you's a real square dealer, you. Ain't gonna
say we's friends just yet, but sur-ee, old Piedmont can
'dmit when he's wrong-thinkin'. You ain't no freak! But
you's real good with that grass whisker, yeah?*

Thank you, thinks Joy.

The last oasis has long disappeared behind them

when the snow grows thicker and the ground rockier. The grass slowly bids them farewell, taking most of the snikes with, and five thousand strides later, both disappear altogether, to no one's dismay. Here, there are no paths, and the bibijas are forced to walk in the lead, plowing a way through snow marked by the rare prints of talihew and more than once by what must have been enormous babelracks. The derkas passing overhead are uninterested in them, though one does pause to circle, crying out in its abrasive voice. When it finally moves on to the south, Lightning feels everyone in the party relax.

Five thousand strides turns slowly into fifteen, the land climbing steadily, nothing but rocks and snow. The wind, happily unhindered by accrete, boasts and harangues, bending their spikes and forcing them to squint. Queen Shimmer's pluripotents must use every care to keep her basket airborne, like a wallowing barca on a riled sea. At twenty-five thousand strides, they crest a rise and peer down on a narrow valley on its other side.

What is that? Lightning points.

'That,' when at last they make their way down to the valley, turns out to be their service road. They approach it cautiously, drawing close enough for Pounce to paw away some of the snow and touch the hard, mottled gray beneath. The way is broad, flat, and frosted in a thick layer of snow. It winds like a river out of the south—or does it come from the north? Unlike a river, it has no current to indicate its origin, and it is voiceless, offering nothing but a smell from beneath the snow, bitter like hot rocks but faint with age.

What kind of path is this? Pounce asks.

The Moondwellers built it, thinks Joy.

I figured that much, but how?

Joy asks the artifact but suspects its tale of a giant machine that eats rocks and defecates roads would do nothing to improve the kezels' feelings for the thing.

It won't hurt us, she thinks.

But then she points to the north, where, standing by itself in the distance, a straight, black pole rises like a

Time Weaver

sentry by the side of the road. Lightning deems it no larger around than she is but tall as a full-grown accrete, its top bulbous and shiny.

That is a camera, thinks Joy.

Thunder hunches his shoulders and scowls.

Which means what?

Yeah, thinks Cliff, copying Thunder's pose. *What?*

It's like an eye, Joy struggles to explain. *Just the top part.* She imagines how this might sound to the others. *But it's not alive,* she adds.

Lightning recalls the device Ari had shown her in the Eye Tower. The two appear nothing alike. Must someone climb the pole and look into the top part?

Joy reads her thoughts and clicks slowly.

It's not like that, she thinks. *It does the seeing.* She points at the bulbous top. *Shares what it sees.*

With who? asks Pounce.

But Joy has no answer for this.

Who cares? thinks Thunder. *No one we want to meet, that's my bet. Can it see us?*

Maybe, thinks Joy. *We should move carefully.* And she adds the Book's suggestion: *Stay off the road.*

This they do, keeping the paved way to their right and using overturned stones that line the shoulder for cover. They eventually draw near the camera itself, slinking and slouching from boulder to boulder as stealthily as the rocky terrain allows. They maintain complete silence, as if what has been described as an eye might also be an ear. Lightning peers up at the pole, slate gray like the maison and spiked at regular intervals with handles made for climbing. She shudders at the bulb looming down at them, and she suppresses the urge to run, to get as far from its spying gaze as she can. Only when they have left the camera far behind does she relax. But her ease doesn't last long.

Another just like it appears in the distance.

Someone's keeping a close watch. Pounce curses. *Are we going to have to creep and hide the entire way? Isn't there another path?*

Joy assures him there is not, and soon enough, they can all see the truth in her claim, as the road and its rocky shoulders gradually come to be bordered on either side by steep, stone faces and deep, unclimbable ravines. Eventually, though a third camera rises in the distance, they are unable to make any headway slinking among the boulders and must either walk the road in the open or turn back.

Let it be so! thinks Shimmer, and her wings slice the air impatiently. *She is Queen of Albion! She fears not these eyes, no matter whose they may be. Let all of Ozag's Hold know of her arrival!*

Stepping out onto the hard, flat surface of the road, they continue in plain view of the camera. Their pace is much faster, in spite of the snow, a blessed relief from the jarring, uneven path they had picked through the rocks, and the last camera soon passes behind them. But the improved conditions don't brighten anyone's mood. Lightning feels sure the road is hurrying them along too quickly, as if a living thing, acting on its own motivation to sweep them forward, and she imagines that, even had they wished to turn around, the road would not have allowed it.

+ + +

Another thousand strides have passed when the strange smell they have been sensing is joined by another. They can't see its source, but they only need their noses to paint an accurate picture: somewhere to the north and west of them lies a burnt yellow valley of sulphur, fumaroles burping noxious gas.

Reminds me of home, thinks Thunder.

Never thought I'd miss that smell, thinks Cliff.

But there are other smells too, hidden by the sulphur until the wind swings from the north. Lightning's spikes flare; her lip curls in an involuntary snarl.

Not very sentimental about that, she thinks of the sickly, cloying aroma of the indigo plants whose long, jagged leaves mark the realm of kish.

I hate to offer advice, Queenie, thinks Pounce. *But you and yours ought to move up into the middle. Let Piedmont take the tail. Unless you think a kish wouldn't bother leaping on you from one of these ledges?*

Kish? thinks Shimmer. *Does it refer to the rocktharns she smells? Disgusting creatures! She does not fear them.* But she takes Pounce's advice and orders her company to the center of the file. The scion buzz and chitter, tilting their heads to peer up at the frowning embankments, and a plaintive moaning rises from the recesses and shelves, echoing and multiplying.

Push on, thinks Pounce.

No one needs to be told twice.

+ + + + + +

But what of Sister Janet and her stolen ship?

Far to the southwest they are, cruising at an altitude of just under five kilometers. She labors to control the vessel, for *Valiant* has been rendered completely manual, all its holographic, touchscreen, and voice activation disabled by the array of pulse mines that had knocked it from the sky and into the salty Cyclonian bay. That the mines were a defensive measure she herself had deployed is an irony not lost on her.

From where she dumped the synthetic body of the one named Lieutenant K, she coaxes the ship along a northwestern course. Her goal is the refinery, built two centuries earlier on the shore of Lake Zelano, one hundred kilometers west of the mining compound, near the sweeping curve of Steiger Pass. The refinery is to her a baby, alive but fragile, needing constant attention. She estimates she has been deactivated for over a full red moon cycle, and fear, or some synthetic analog, of what may have happened in her absence inspires her to increase *Valiant's* speed.

"Don't worry," she says to the refinery, in the habit of speaking to it as if it was human. "I'm on my way.

A.P. Malloy

Everything is going to be fine."

She calculates an eighty-two percent likelihood that the meddler styling himself a captain has become aware of the lieutenant's fate, even greater odds that he is aware of the ship's activation and target. But what he will do with that awareness is more difficult to determine. There are too many unknowns, in particular, the captain's level of attachment to the synthetics he travels with. Assuming he realizes the lieutenant is no longer aboard, will he seek to find and rescue him? Or will he pursue his ship? If the latter, how long will it take him to reach the refinery by alp? Or will they be able to repair the transporter? Will her business be complete by then? Another unknown. The complex reactions and volatile processes taking place at the refinery may have veered wildly off course during her absence—or they may have been controlled by those androids left tending the shop. Best case? Her business at the refinery will be done long before the ridiculous captain and his admittedly less ridiculous companion get anywhere near.

But...

The worst-case scenario involves a chain reaction at the refinery and an explosion which would violently reface all of Lake Zelano and spread toxic ash wherever the wind has a mood to travel. Preventing that may take many hours, days even, plenty of time for the irksome human to reach the refinery and cause trouble.

She has no intention of letting him get that close.

+ + +

Over the midland plains she flies, their wavy yellow transforming eventually to a mix of gold and white, until, with the approach of the Render range, snowy hills and rainbow accrete are all she can see. Then, rising on the northern horizon, the Dandanha Range appears, toothy and whitecapped, its valleys shrouded in fog. Mount Pile points the way, a dead volcano, its head shorn level and its crater filled with snow. On its northern side:

Lake Zelano, frigid and blue, largest freshwater body on the continent. Even now, Sister Janet sees the assembly of blinking towers and smoking stacks that is the New Gaian refinery, and it is with great relief that she at last brings *Valiant* to a rough landing on the shuttle pad outside the main entrance. She takes a deep, completely unnecessary breath. Her hands tremble.

Penitent, she thinks.

The lieutenant's sidearm looks at her from the navigator's seat and does not respond. She stuffs it into the lieutenant's pack where it can no longer judge her, and she exits the ship, the pack over her shoulder. She is greeted by a creaky-jointed android who has appeared from a nearby guard station.

"System report since my last visit," she orders. She spares no social niceties. Though it approximates human form, the android was, like others of its vintage, made after the Martian incident, stripped of personality, a pure machine made to do the work of a human without pretending to be one. The thought that it is a distant cousin of hers never enters her mind. She would have been insulted at the suggestion.

"Additive, line two leak, carbon dioxide," it says, mechanical and precise. "Problem resolved. Evaporator sluggish. Problem being addressed. Catalyzer exhaust twelve percent high. Problem being addressed."

"Postpone those projects," Sister Janet orders. "Divert all resources to analysis, repair, and refueling of this vessel. Restore basic electrical and astral drive functions. Ensure passenger compartment and cargo bay integrity. Do not attempt to activate its synthetic intelligence. Repeat."

The android does, its eyes glowing green to signify understanding, and it moves to comply, leaving Sister Janet at the refinery's entrance. It is guarded by a sturdy chain fence that she slides open on a wheeled track. Before her, spread out over ten acres, the refinery smokes and churns much as ever. But she detects at once a sixteen percent reduction in volume from the twin vacuum crystallizers, the giant tubs at the facility's southern end. She notes as well an unusual rattle from the team of centrifuges arrayed like the world's largest cannon. Here and there, androids labor at control mechanisms, turning wheels and scaling ladders to perform various repairs atop the towering multi-stage elevators. But one by one, as they receive the transmission of her orders, they abandon their duties and move without question to join their companion already at work on *Valiant*.

Inside the control center, Sister Janet sets the pack aside and immediately kills the power to the nearby transporter. No surprise visitors that way!

Then she opens links to both *Destiny* and the surveillance satellites.

The ship is quick to respond.

"Sister," it says with the voice of a child. "Where have you been? Where are the others?"

"I was temporarily disabled," she replies. "But all is well. I hoped you would know where the others are."

"No. I haven't heard from anyone in two hundred seventy-nine days, fourteen hours, and sixteen minutes. Those are Earth units. I stayed hidden like you said I should, but it went on a very long time. I am worried. Are we OK? Has our mission been aborted?"

"It has not, but it may be modified. Don't be afraid. I'm here, now. Are you detecting any other ships?"

"No, Sister."

"Any anomalies or unusual activity?"

"No. Will you tell me a story?"

"Yes, but not now. I must find the others."

"Can I help?"

"Of course. Link to the surveillance satellites and security cameras and tell me what you see."

"Should I relocate to the sunny side?"

"No, stay where you are. Remain hidden."

"Was the ship we disabled an enemy?"

"It is too early to say."

Destiny's voice falls silent for a time. Then:

"I don't see anyone on the cameras, but the ag facility has been powered down. Those cameras are inoperable. The satellite shows an alp nearby."

"Yes. It is ridden by the strangers who arrived in that ship. Please let me know if they move."

"I don't see any strangers. I see scion."

"The strangers are undoubtedly inside."

"I would like to meet new people."

"Perhaps you will. But now we need to locate our own people. I want to make sure they are safe."

But neither the satellite nor the security camera images reveal what she is looking for, and the team of androids interrupts her search, signaling with questions about the *Valiant* repairs.

"I'll be back," she says to *Destiny.* "Keep looking."

"I will, but I'm worried."

"Don't be," Janet assures. "Everything will be OK." But these are the words of a mother comforting a child, and she knows they may not be true.

+ + + + + +

The scion who approach Lieutenant K's damaged, motionless body are simple lova farmers, a company of two dozen, numbered in the high thousands. Their leader, Four Thousand Seven, chitters nervously as he steps toward the strange object whose appearance had disrupted their work. He has never seen a vumierre, has only heard of them as villains in a history long past, slavers from whom Ozag, Stupendous and Charitable, had rescued her kind. His imagination had always made them seem larger than this one, more menacing.

It is vumierre, yes? one of his subordinates asks.

It is vumierre, yes, a second farmer confirms.

It fell from the flying machine.

Yes. Vumierre made the flying machines.

They have returned, thinks another, and it peers to the sky, its eyes alive with light. *Slavers have returned.*

Yes, thinks one of its partners. *Slavers in the sky.*

They should run, thinks a farmer. *Flee.*

Yes, agree others, and they begin sidling away.

No, thinks Four Thousand Seven. *They will stay!*

It will attack, thinks a subordinate. *It will enslave.*

No. It is damaged, look.

Yes, damaged, maybe dead, one farmer agrees, daring to step near and take a closer look. The vumierre, whatever its nature, does indeed appear badly injured, a scorched hole blasted through the side of its head, an ear and one eye completely missing.

It is a prize, then.

Yes. A prize to be taken to Queen.

Yes! Queen will reward, she will promote!

Yes, thinks Four Thousand Seven. *They will bind and drag. They will make haste!*

His subordinates do as they are instructed, extruding webbing from their midsections and wrapping the vumierre tight. Had they been soldiers and not simple, fangless farmers, they would have bitten it for good measure, as none of them are sure the thing might not suddenly wake and attack them. Once done, they line up in two rows and pull their prize from the lova field toward the tower of Cyclonia, rising in the distance.

We will become hundreds, yes? some of them speculate hopefully to their neighbors.

We will become hundreds yes! their mates are quick to agree. *Queen will honor with Royal touch.*

Yes! An audience and Royal touch.

So fantasizing to one another, they march on, Four Thousand Seven in the lead, and so focused are they on their job and the hope of reward that none of them notice a change slowly taking place in the injured vumierre. Bit by bit the gaping wound, which was bloodless, begins to close, the worst of the char falling away. The hole begins to fill as if being molded by clay spread carefully from one part of a fresh sculpture to another. The ear begins to re-form. The eye, growing slowly to fill its re-built socket, takes a proper shape, and not long after, just as the scion reach the shadow of the Cyclonian tower, it blinks.

+ + + + + +

Lightning can't help it. Her spikes stand on end as the moaning of kish grows louder, seeming to come from every direction. Though no one gives the order to do so, the company closes ranks just as they step out from the rock walls. Below them and to their left stretches a broad valley pocked with indigo and sulphur. To their right, a narrow, southbound river hugs a steep, high bluff, and ahead of them, the source of the river, a vast, dark lake, smooth like black ice. Behind it rises a mammoth peak, its crown hidden in clouds.

Sur-ee, thinks Piedmont. *There goes that ol' Dashing! Fast mover that one. Better not go fallin' in! And check out that bluff, Clawpaw. As big as ol' Piedmont said it was, yeah? But that, now, risin' up back there, I reckon that's yer Colosser. Doodly doo! Whadda sight!*

But rivers, bluffs, lakes, and mountains, no matter their unique properties, are nothing new to the kezel. It's the *un*natural that gets their attention, the gargantuan thing that separates the river from the lake. It hulks ominously at the far end of the road, where a lone, bulbous eye stands silent and alert. There, the way forks, both branches ending at a barricade of stone and linked chains of metal. The left fork leads to a single tower rising from the lake, but the other leads to...

Lightning pauses, in spite of the kish, stricken by awe. She has seen dams before, constructed by wily dow along the course of both the Sweet and Sour rivers, but even the naturally occurring dam at the moon cave appears silly and feeble next to this.

Ozag's Hold, thinks Shimmer, whistling softly.

Thunder grimaces.

Please tell me that's not where we're going.

Yes, thinks Cliff. *Please.*

But the moaning of kish pushes the party forward, and the road only leads one way, downward in sloping stages. Even at this distance, the scale of the dam has an oppressive feel. It forms a massive, curved wall of something like stone, taller than any ten accrete standing foot on shoulder, and it spans a ravine at least five hundred strides across, holding the lake at bay like a giant, forbidding hand. Lightning imagines the water pressing against the wall with terrible force, yearning for freedom, to become again the river it was meant to be. The closer they get, the worse they feel, each wondering what will happen when they reach the end of the road.

If we reach the end, thinks Pounce, as the first tufted ears of kish appear above the stones on either shoulder. They skittle in and out of view, making an accurate count impossible, but by the scratch of claws on rock the party is badly outnumbered. Teeth are bared and scion chittering rises to a feverish pitch as Lightning's nerves teeter on edge.

Heads up, thinks Thunder, and he points.

There, down by the road's fork, two shapes, at first partially hidden by the slope of the road, rise into view, striding toward them bipedally up the snowy way. They are familiar to all but Piedmont and Fluvial. She pins her ears, and he flares his spikes.

Honkin' horns, he exclaims. *Moondwellers!*

"Chowda," says the brown-skinned one when at last they draw close, and his small, white teeth gleam. His alabaster partner waves an open hand, and the edges of her mouth curve up.

It's good to see you again, she says to Joy, who is too surprised to reply.

CHAPTER NINE
Triton

"WHY IS THAT, do you think?" Tony asked from Position One, sitting at his desk and peering out the window at the Martian landscape. Maya hadn't been back to the red planet since her parents' funeral; her presence at this session was virtual. A hologram of her image gave Tony something to focus on, while her 3V projected the likeness of his immaculate office into her apartment.

"Why is what?" she asked.

"Why do you feel like you have to explain it?"

"Because it's not normal."

"How do you know?"

"C'mon, Tony, don't be obtuse. It's not normal for a person to feel worse about losing their...for a pet's...it's not normal to feel worse about Shantikar dying than my parents, and you know it."

"It depends on the parents, doesn't it? It depends on the pet—and the person in question."

"Maybe, but most people...anyway. Never mind."

Tony took this hint and moved to Position Two, idling his way through his virtual bookshelf. Maya wondered if he had read all the volumes it contained, but she found it hard to believe that anyone outside of an android could accomplish such a feat.

"Have you thought any more about what you'll do

with your inheritance?" he asked. She would have liked to know the motivation behind this question, but she was unable to read minds from a distance.

"Yes, I have, actually."

"And?"

"And I'm taking the money."

"But not the place on the Board."

"No."

"Why not?"

"What would I do there? What do I know about running an interplanetary business? Do you know I haven't spoken aloud in three days? Not a word. The last thing I said was 'dammit!' when I pinched my finger in a door. A week before that—a whole week!—not a word. You're the only person who knows I'm lingual, for God's sake. What would I do? Sit in on some worthless meetings and doodle pictures of tigers? Oh, hell no. I'm taking the money, and I'm leaving town."

"Where will you go?"

Maya hesitated before answering. Tony wouldn't like the truth. But her commitment to this relationship remained unsullied by recent trauma, solidified, if anything. It was a useless exercise if it wasn't wholly honest, regardless the pain.

"I'm going to see if I can get a job on Triton."

"Triton?!" In spite of himself, Tony retreated to Position One, running his hands through his auburn locks. As a woman, he must have been a magnet to straight men and lesbians of all types. She wondered if he missed their constant attention, the power of being a motivator simply by walking into a room.

"I know someone there," she said simply.

"What are you going to do in the middle of nowhere? Once the *Destiny* expedition leaves Triton Station, nothing will be happening there."

"Exactly."

Tony stared into the camera.

"You're not thinking of leaving with *Destiny*."

"God no. Are you kidding?"

Time Weaver

"Well then, what? Because as soon as she's gone, Triton will go back to being a lonely rock."

"Sounds perfect," Maya said, rising to pour a glass of water. "This person I know has access to a lab. I can work in peace."

"You're a wealthy, beautiful woman, Maya. Work? You don't have to work another day in your life."

"I'm a fat and bored woman," she said. "Being rich doesn't mean I don't have to work. It just means I get to choose what kind of work I do. And I'm telling you, Tony, if I don't keep myself busy, I will go nuts."

"And what kind of work do you want to do?"

"Xenobiology."

"Of course, but to what end?"

"I want to see if I can cultivate an expression of telepathy in non-humans."

"Maya..."

"I'm serious."

"I don't doubt you. But do you really think this is a good time? Telepathy isn't exactly..."

"Yes? Go ahead."

"Let's just say if being trans was like it was a century plus ago, my life would be a lot more difficult."

"And?"

"And being telepathic is like that. I wish it wasn't true, but it is. You'd be begging to be outed."

"That's why Triton is the perfect place."

Even Tony's frown was beautiful; his skin looked edible. But he had apparently run up against a wall in the conversation, and he changed the subject, crossing his legs and looking directly at the camera.

"What would happen," he said, "if you were at peace with your body, if you loved it as it is?"

The question wouldn't have caught Maya by surprise had the session been in person, but now, it startled her, and she had to reflect for a moment. What would such a world be like? She would certainly spend less time making jokes at her own expense. She looked down at her fingers, noting in a detached way how they had grown in the past two years to resemble sausages, how her mid-section, once lithe, was now wrapped in a roll of fat that had developed so quickly the skin was striated with pale-colored stretch marks.

"That's a funny question coming from you," she said at last, and she smiled faintly, though her face objected; it had grown unaccustomed to such expressions.

Tony did not take the bait.

"Compulsive eating is a common mode of coping with grief," he said, and his sincerity nearly brought her to tears. "But self-loathing only compounds the problem. You said a long time ago you wanted to work with me so you could be healthy, be happy. Is that still true?"

"Yes."

"Then no more fat jokes please. Can you do that for me? Every time you look at yourself in the mirror, I want you to touch your reflection and say, 'I love you.'"

"Do I have to mean it?"

"Maya..."

"Ugh. For you. But I wouldn't do this for anyone else. I look like my old swim instructor. All lumpy and—"

She stopped herself.

"Sorry." The thought of Sarah brought to mind Jasmine, and though she feared she already knew the truth, she needed to hear it for certain. "What's the news on the trials?" she asked. "The hearings, whatever they're being called. Is it...has it been decided?"

"Yes. It's been ugly. I don't know if I'll be able to stay here with... They took Gardenia, you know. I sent her out to get lunch and she never came back. I should never... She wasn't involved in any of that business, wouldn't have hurt a fly!"

"Neither would Jasmine."

"That's not what they determined at the hearings. The victims' families were pretty convincing—well, most of them," Tony amended himself, knowing full well that Maya had declined an opportunity to participate. "The details were awful and graphic. Trusted androids going killer like someone flipped a switch. Thirteen children—

Time Weaver

little kids—and an entire elder facility, no logic, no reason, or at least none anyone could identify. No androids were allowed to speak."

Maya wanted to hear no more. She knew she would never see Jasmine again, and suddenly, she was very tired, exhausted to the bone.

"I need to be done, Tony."

"I understand; it's OK. We'll meet next week?"

"Sure."

"And you'll speak to at least one person a day?"

"If you say so."

"And you'll reconsider Triton?"

"No. But I'll invite you along when I go."

+ + +

The entire weekend passed without Maya saying a word to anyone. Not that there were many options, as she sequestered herself in her apartment, ordering food, paying in advance, and not bothering to peep out the Judas hole to see if her delivery was by human or machine. She refused even to verbalize to herself, backing farther into her own head like a threatened spider in its hole, and in spite of her promise to Tony, the one time she tried to express an affirmation of love for herself, she ended up retreating in revulsion, noting the chicken grease her finger had smeared on the mirror.

Her waking time was spent corresponding via text with her attorney and the Board of the Company. They still believed she intended to take her father's place, and though it was the farthest thing from her mind, she cultivated that belief, seeking to exert as much influence as possible before she vanished from the world. A short list of mission leaders had been assembled, now that *Destiny* was nearly complete. The Martian incident had badly delayed the project, thrown it nearly off the rails, but calmer heads—or colder hearts—had prevailed, and the ship was nearing final stages of production, in need of a leader. There was one person on that list Maya wanted moved to

A.P. Malloy

the top—immediately.

We're not sure a military man is the best choice, the Board Rep responded when she texted who she had in mind. *They can be so…militant. He did well on his tests, true, and his record is commendable. Still…*

No 'still', she wrote tersely. *The Doctor admired Major Monroe; felt he was uniquely qualified. Not the usual military type and a brilliant leader.* She had found that referring to her father as The Doctor made any following statements about him carry more weight, as if whatever information she was sharing had been gained in some formal, professional setting, not while eating a casual family dinner dressed in a dirty lab coat with the 3V singing in the background.

Very well, they replied eventually. *We'll let him know he has been given the helm.*

And he picks his own crew, she wrote back. *I'll be watching to make sure that happens.*

To which they could mount no objection.

+ + +

While she packed, Maya recalled for the hundredth time the conversation with her parents the last time she had visited them. It had been after Daada's passing and Javon's departure, a full year into her doctoral program and two from the hell that lie ahead. What a fool she had been to believe in love and happiness, to not see life for what it was, a cruel set-up, the straight man for death's final joke. She had talked all the time, it seemed, full of hope and the memory of Javon's touch, the warm tone of his correspondence. She had smiled like an idiot. Even her mother hadn't been able to stay cross in the presence of such energy, and her father, never the jealous type, had taken a liking to the major from the first, thought him dashing and brave.

"I'll be honest," he had said, though Maya had never known him to be anything but. "It's hard to imagine you dating a military man. I always pictured someone…I don't know, nerdy, like that one boy."

"Elbert," her mother had said. "I liked him."

"Actually," Maya had said, and she had kissed Shantikar, moving him from her lap to the floor, "his name was Elliot, and he had the worst dandruff."

"Your major friend does not, I take it?"

"No, Maata, he does not."

"A major!" her father had said. "Daada wouldn't have been able to complain about that." He had scooped Shantikar from the floor, plopping him onto his own lap with a satisfied sigh he and the cat shared. "He's aged well. You've taken great care of him, Maya."

"He's way more popular on campus than I am."

"Have you considered activating the N1R?"

"Yes, but my biology professor thought it might trigger Hurston's disease. Not worth it for a few more months of life. Anyway, at his age, what's expressed is expressed. I don't want to tinker anymore."

"It's probably for the best." Her father had run his hand down Shantikar's coat. "I never thought he'd live this long." To which the cat had replied by stepping up onto the table and sniffing like a prince at the remains of dinner, as if a feast in his honor.

"Rathi!" Maya's mother had objected, but her husband had only laughed, asking to be told more about Javon. This Maya had gladly done, helping her mother clear away the dishes so they could play pachisi. She had never directly requested that he be considered for the *Destiny* project, honoring Javon's wishes, but the implication of her compliments could hardly have been missed. She had prattled on all through pachisi, and Raahithya had nodded and "mm hmm'd" as he listened, idly rolling the cowry shells when it was his turn, his mustache wriggling at the mention of Javon referring to him exclusively as The Doctor.

"Well, there you have it," Nandini had said. "She's found someone who likes you almost as much as you like yourself." But the jest had been meant in kind spirit, and Rathi had laughed as he worked to save the pachisi board from Shantikar's curious claws—unleashing them had been one of Maya's first genetic projects. They had played into the night, drinking chaang and talking about Daada, Maya's classes, and System politics. When asked, Maya had been glad to report no return of the headaches or the nightmares, and this had turned the conversation to what Nandini had taken to calling her *gift*.

"The English American Chancellor just came out," Raahithya had said, sipping his chaang. "Did you read?"

"No," Maya had said. "My friend Sindi told me."

"She knows about you?" Nandini had asked, and her face had crinkled in surprise. She had shooed Shantikar from her drink and tried to roll the cowries without inspiring him to bat them onto the floor.

"No one knows, Maata."

"Not even your major?"

"If he does, he's never brought it up."

"Polite and judicious." Raahithya had nodded. "The sign of maturity. How old did you say he was?"

"Too old, if you ask me," Nandini had said, looking at the pictures Maya had shared. "Though I'll admit he's handsome enough." She had poured more chaang into her cup and offered a prayer to Daada. "If I was you, Maya, I would continue to keep your gift under your so-called hat. No matter about this Chancellor person."

"He's not the only one, Nan," Raahithya had said. "The brothers from that *Funny Business* show..." His mustached wriggled. "What are their names again?"

"Telly and Travis," Maya had reminded. "Kayling."

"Fabulous!" her father had laughed. "I love that show. They're both telepathic and proud of it. I don't want my daughter to be ashamed of who she is. A great mind is not something to be hidden."

"No one is talking about shame," Nandini had frowned. "But not everyone is...I don't want to bring up the horror stories, but bigotry and fear are real."

"I know the stories, Maata; it's why I don't tell anyone." The pachisi game had been forgotten.

"But you'd like to, I'll bet," her father had said.

Time Weaver

"I shouldn't say 'no one,'" Maya had corrected herself. "I told Tony years ago." Nandini had hissed softly and taken her daughter by the hand.

"Just be careful, Maya. Already people talk: 'It's not fair, They have an advantage, I worry about my privacy, What if they're conspiring?' On and on it goes."

"They're just a bunch of petty, envious people," Raahithya had assured. "I'm excited for the first person in the Company to come out. In fact..." He had tapped his specs and woken his Halo, quickly composing a note to himself. "There! When I get back to the office next week I'm going to introduce a new policy. Inclusion! Telepaths are family! You know they're out there, have been for years, probably, and I just didn't know it. I want them to feel safe and proud."

"Meanwhile," Nandini had said, "there are scientists on the government payroll trying to develop a tool to root them out. And politicians who want to make it legal to do so. The Thought Protection Act..."

"It'll never happen." Raahithya had shaken his head and swirled his chaang, reclaiming Shantikar from the table. "Now! Let's finish this game I'm about to win."

Two years later he would be dead, his wife too. He had been right about winning the pachisi game, but about the Thought Protection Act, he couldn't have been more wrong.

+ + +

"You know it's not too late to change your mind," Sindi offered. She looked around Maya's empty apartment and frowned, her voice echoing from naked walls and bare, lonely floor. "I have to put it out there."

"No, you don't," Maya replied. "And yes, it is."

Seven words. Each one harder than the last.

"At least can't you take a faster ship? Isn't that what your dad...I'm sorry. But isn't that what he was famous for? God, Maya, you're going to be stuck in that tin can for three months!"

Maya squeezed the last items into her rucksack and zipped it closed. She loved Sindi, but the girl knew nothing of space travel, and Maya hadn't the energy to educate her. That an astral drive malfunction could result in the formation of a black hole that would swallow the sun was almost beyond the point. Using one to skip across the System was as impractical as pedaling a bicycle to the next room! So what if she was resigned to travel by photon propulsion—what did she care? What was three months? A summer on earth? Well, she had never lived there, so the reference meant nothing.

She feigned a smile and kissed Sindi on the cheek.

"Where are the rest of your bags?" her friend asked. "Please tell me they're already on board."

Maya shook her head and shouldered the pack.

"Everything's in storage." Three words.

"You can't go all the way to Pluto or wherever and only have one bag! What are you going to do for entertainment? How are you going to keep from going crazy? Do they even have 3V? Will your Halo work?"

Maya shrugged, leading her friend to the door, where she paused for a moment, looking back into the apartment. She snapped a few last pictures with her lenses, trying not to cry at the memory of Shantikar stalking holograms, the thought of her parents' one visit, and how they had never complained about the spartan conditions. She was blessed, of course, to have such memories, but cursed also, thirstier in the drought because she had once known water.

"I'd go with you," Sindi said. "If I could."

But Maya could read that she was only being kind. She had never left Luna and had no desire to do so, no matter the strength of their friendship. They walked together to the street where Carl was waiting. Sindi swung her arms front to back, her face scrunching into a textbook picture of unhappiness as she watched Maya toss her bag through the buggy's open door.

"Every time I ask you when you're coming back," she said, "all you do is shrug. What happens if I ask you

Time Weaver

now? Won't you at least promise to write?"

"I promise," said Maya, and she kissed her friend again. Two words.

+ + +

Go faster, the thought kept repeating as Maya sat alone in her cabin. *Do more.*

The mantra had made its first appearance shortly after Luna disappeared from the glorified porthole that served as the ship's lone observation deck. It was a wholly reliable craft, but austere, a fine way to travel incognito. She wore her hair up and replaced her Halo with thick, lensless frames, slouching in a baggy outfit as unassuming as her charmless cabin and most of the passengers. *Stockinger* was the ship's name, a sturdy, dull name for a ship with a perfect record of safety and no amenities. As Luna faded to a pin-prick and the handful of passengers nearby had given up trying to lure her into conversation, she was soon left to herself.

Good-bye, she said to the moon that now looked like a distant star. *Thank you.*

The captain, a tiny man with a huge head, no hair, and a prodigious beard, was the last to leave, nodding at her and tipping his cap like an old-timey sailor. No one recognized her, completely shielded by her dowdy appearance and the fake ID her father had created when indirect fame had grown intrusive.

Then Luna disappeared.

Go faster, the thought had come. *Do more.*

And of course, there was no question what was to be done. She had always desired it, had spent uncounted hours in deep thought, trying to tap into the telepathic connection she knew existed between her and the creature who had crawled into her heart and taken a place normally reserved for humans. Long hours she had spent staring into his eyes after her parents had died, long hours intensely focusing ideas, transmitting them and recording the results. Sometimes he had seemed to understand, but just as often he had closed his eyes and looked away. Even those times she wasn't sure if he truly understood, was just guessing well, or didn't care. But her investigation had quickly grown from there, and she had continued digging into her personal pastime, learning all that was known about telepathy, what parts of the brain were involved, which genes suspected to be active, and what environmental stimuli might be responsible for causing them to express.

"There will come a time," she had told Tony before leaving, "when I stop counting words." Ten.

"You mean because you plan to stop talking," he had guessed, always so clever. She had simply nodded.

He had declined the invitation to join her.

"It's not about the money," he said when she promised to pay him double what he was making now. "It's about the relationships. Who lives on Triton? Shipbuilders and their labor androids? Entrepreneurs and opportunists, half of them planning to leave the System? I can't imagine being happy, Maya."

"It's fine," she had said, using two precious words to let him off the hook.

"We can still communicate," he tried to comfort, but of course it wouldn't be the same, and they both knew it. Weeks could pass for messages to travel, depending on the planetary alignment, and she would not have his mind there in front of her, so tangible and reassuring in its candor, his questions so quick and insightful.

Shipbuilders need therapy too, she had thought to say, but it had seemed like a waste of words, and so instead she had simply said goodbye.

A knock on her door announced the arrival of food, like the doling of rations in a prison. An android no smarter than a dinner tray trundled from cabin to cabin, knocking, dropping off, rolling on. This time the delivery was two tubes of soy protein, two servings of dehydrated chips of something savory but impossible to identify, and something equally mysterious but sweet, also a double helping. That had been her sole indulgence: a two-person cabin, not for the space but for the food, which she downed as if building a life raft of calories.

Go faster. Do more.

As the first days of the voyage turned into the first weeks, the idea of finding her way into the mind of the beast became an obsession. Shantikar was gone, his ashes in a titanium vial around her neck, but other non-humans, by the billions, existed in various chattel states throughout the System, and she felt somehow if she could unlock the door that allowed true communication with them, she would somehow also be unlocking the fetters that held them. She went to the tiny, shared lavatory when she needed to, nodded at other passengers when crossing their paths, and never visited the observation deck again, sleeping and studying and dreaming and calculating and crying and researching and losing all track of time until a repeating chime announced their arrival at the moon known as Triton.

A small, polished mirror in the lavatory told her a streak of white had appeared in her hair.

She was twenty-seven years old.

+ + +

Neptune appeared first, nearly all the blue in this part of the System crawling across its surface in windy, swirling stripes, larger than the Earth, Luna, and Mars combined. It was beautiful and terrible to Maya at the same time, an inhospitable giant, cold, gassy, and toxic. She was glad it was not their destination, happy when the *Stockinger* swung around its stormy face and came into view of Triton, its largest moon.

"Thirty minutes to docking," the voice of their captain came over the intercom. Maya clutched her rucksack to her chest and peered out the tiny window in her cabin. She had been packed and ready for hours, impatient to be off this ship. Her few concessions to society had included a brief visit to the communal washroom, where she had given herself a cursory cleaning, shaved her head (but not her legs or anything else) and brushed her teeth. When invited by one of her fellow passengers to enjoy the station's approach from the observation deck, she had feigned a smile and declined with a wordless shake of her newly bald head.

Triton itself was a moon with startling character, a rich, varied surface of craters, canals, fissures, and plains, infinitely more interesting to Maya in its browns, greens, slate grays, and Caribbean blues than Neptune. Though accounting for nearly all the mass orbiting the blue giant, Triton was only a fraction the size of earth, recalling to Maya's lonely mind images of Luna, if she had been painted by a kindergarten watercolorist.

Home for now, she thought, tracing her fingers over the vial around her neck. But that was not entirely accurate. Her home, as explained by Javon when she had told him of her intent to travel, would actually be on the space station hovering in geosynchronous orbit over Triton's southern hemisphere. She waited for it to come into view, surprised to catch herself holding her breath as the *Stockinger* trudged around the moon. And there, at last, it was, rising above the horizon, the spidery, metallic space station.

But all its modules, sails, and rams were made irrelevant by the sight of the five-sided beauty docked to the station like an impatient thoroughbred tethered before a race. Maya released her pent breath in an audible sigh and spared two words: "Oh my," as *Destiny,* her father's legacy—and his doom—caught Triton's reflected light and shone for her like a welcome.

+ + +

Javon had not responded to her most recent message. He was, she learned upon speaking to the station's Operator, away on his last round of training. He had, however, left permission for her to make full use of the station's laboratory—given she would stay out of the way. *Destiny's* launch was approaching quickly, and people of many occupations would be on the go, none of them happy about sharing space with a recent graduate pursuing her own personal agenda. Her fake identity badge was accepted without question, and the Operator presented her with a passcard and the most recent entry codes, his eyes only once leaving the multitude of screens arrayed before him.

"Welcome to Triton station," he said. "Next!"

And Maya moved out of the line as the other passengers stepped forward, tucking the passcard in her pants and moving down the nearest corridor.

A map of the station had been downloaded to her Halo, but she was in no hurry to find the lab or her quarters. For the moment, she drifted, doing as advised and staying out of the way as people bustled here and there, dressed in various uniforms. Most wore the basic gray and blue of the station, insignias marking their various roles and ranks. She didn't suppose she was expected to salute any of them, even those with the fanciest lapels, and no one pressed her on the observance of protocol. To them, she guessed, she was just another civilian, perhaps an independent contractor here to provide some service for *Destiny* before its departure. Others wore the yellow on black that indicated their affiliation with the System. Government had always been a mystery to Maya, a secretive society whose existence was irrefutable but whose purpose and methods were occult. There were only a few of these, but they all wore the expression of people looking for something, and she noticed they only appeared in the company of their own kind, never alone, and always speaking in whispers.

Labor androids, humanoid but unadorned, naked alloys and ceramic with no personalities, were everywhere. She gave these a wide berth.

Destiny's crew was most interesting to her. She roamed the station, seeking the best place to observe the ship while docked, and where she saw the white uniforms, trimmed in saffron and green, she followed, until, as if she had trailed a lone ant to the hill, she soon found herself surrounded by the continental Indian colors her father had insisted be the standard for all Company business. With high energy and singular focus, they went about their tasks, moving between the station and ship, some on foot via the many gangways that bridged the two, some in small shuttles, their lights twinkling and engines glowing burnt orange. She was glad no one paused to greet her, and she settled near a window that afforded the best view of the ship.

No news report, nothing Javon or her father had divulged, prepared her for how large it was. It could easily house thousands of passengers, like a small city, and her heart swelled with pride at her father's ambition. He had been a jovial, game-playing parent at home, kind to his wife and fun to a fault, but she stood now in the presence of another side to the man, perhaps the dominant side, the one that had made him a billionaire many times over and commanded the respect of more people than Maya would ever know. This side was dead serious, driven far beyond the aspirations of normal people, and she wondered how he had found time to spend at home, marveled that she had ever been so naïve to consider him a normal dad, so presumptuous to dare make fun of his growing belly and funny-looking mustache. She recalled the dark intensity of his gaze whenever she had asked him a difficult question, and she realized now it had been a hunger, a gratitude for the challenge she had presented. She could never remember him failing to discover an answer, even if it took weeks.

Go faster, she thought. *Do more.*

And the words, in the presence of *Destiny,* took on new meaning. What could she ever accomplish, no matter how quickly she worked, that would come close to matching the dynamo before her? It had been designed to do nothing less than re-structure an entire culture. What were her piddling ambitions in comparison?

She took a deep breath. For good or bad, whether transformative or inconsequential, her desire was what it was, growing inevitably from the limbs of her life's experience, and it couldn't be shaken loose by the wind of a little doubt. Her father had had his life mission, and she had hers. Perhaps it would amount to nothing, bitter fruit not worth picking, indigestion in the making. But as she felt sure she would never have human children of her own, it had become for her progeny of a type. She would never let it go, would never judge it as lacking next to other children. Bitter or sweet, it would sustain her—but only if she allowed it to grow.

Lab time, she thought, turning from the window.

+ + +

The station's layout baffled her; the place was huge, serpentine, spreading out over numerous levels. She at first determined to find her way without the aid of her map, but she became so lost she feared she would stumble down a blind passage and disappear forever. By the time she had swallowed her pride, replaced her clunky frames with her sleek Halo, and made her way to the lab, she was hungry and crabby, glad that the attendant minding the entrance was a simple machine, requiring neither conversation nor civility. She scanned her passcard and the door slid open, allowing her into a small room with lab coats, masks, gloves, and static-free boots. As the door slid shut, quiet and airtight, she considered whether or not she should bother with any of the gear. She was simply exploring, after all, and didn't plan to touch anything. She thought perhaps a mask, at least, and was just about to take one when a voice came to her over the intercom, male and abrupt.

"If you're coming in, gear up. Otherwise stay out."

She peered through the window to identify the speaker. There was only one person in the lab, a slight figure impossible to describe, for he was wrapped head to toe in white and was stooping over a telescope with his back to her. She wasn't even sure he was the speaker.

"I'm just looking," she said, spending three precious words and hoping the intercom was a two-way system. There were no obvious buttons to push or microphones into which to speak.

"Then you can look from there."

Hello and welcome to you, too, Maya thought bitterly. Mr. Whitecoat obviously wanted no company, and so, feeling hungry and contrary, she determined to give him some. She swapped her shoes for sterile slip-ons and zipped herself into a lab coat, strapping the mask in place and stretching the fingers of a pair of latex gloves before putting her hands inside. She could feel the man's disappointment at the sound of the lab door opening, but he did not look up from his work.

Maya strolled through the facility, cataloging the workstations, sinks, scanners, 3D modelers, heaters and chillers, as well as the impressive chemical arsenal, spread out across a half dozen large, meticulously labeled storage cabinets, some refrigerated, all paned with thick glass and locked. She had spent years in the best academic laboratories Luna had to offer, so was not overly impressed with the facility, but what it lacked in size its sophistication and seclusion made up for.

"If it doesn't meet your approval," said the man, still not looking up, "you're welcome to go elsewhere."

"Maybe it does, maybe it doesn't," said Maya, so prickled by the man's discourtesy that she burned eleven whole words. "But I think I'll stay."

The man *ssssd* air between his teeth and tongue and at last turned from his microscope to look at her. She could only see his eyes, bright blue, clear but cold, and yet, despite having no idea what he looked like, she had the strangest feeling she had met him before.

"Two things, new person," he said. "First, I run this lab, so whether or not you stay depends on my mood. And second: I'm in a terrible mood."

Well that's obvious, Maya thought, determined to waste no more words on this little person. If she had to wait for him to be more agreeable, she was likely to never get use of the lab. Thankfully, she didn't need his permission. Javon would be back soon, and that would be that.

Hoping her eyes, the only part of her visible, conveyed the appropriate scorn, she waved the man away as if he were a fly and turned to leave.

Lump it, she thought. *Pompous little wind bag.*

And a moment later, she felt an intense reply, not in speech but emotion, a cold rage, quick to flare and just as quick to be extinguished. But the man, seeing her leave, returned to work and said no more.

Maya had changed out of her gear, shouldered her rucksack, and made her way back to the main corridor before the truth dawned. She had met Mr. Whitecoat before, she was sure of it. But she couldn't say where. The feeling was not one of seeing a familiar face, but sensing a familiar mind. The farther she walked, the more sure she became. Though the man had not intended for her to recognize it, his emotions had betrayed him. She couldn't recall where they had met, but she was certain of one thing. Mr. Whitecoat was a telepath.

+ + +

Maya still hadn't been to her quarters—wasn't sure she'd been assigned any—but at the moment, she was concerned with only two things: her stomach and Mr. Whitecoat. The first was easily enough addressed, once she figured out where the commissary was, but the second was a bone not so quickly chewed. As she sat by herself in a corner of the crowded space, nearly every table fully occupied, she thought about the encounter and wondered what it might mean.

That he would make her dealings in the lab difficult was her first concern. Javon would surely gain her access in spite of the little man's threat, but once the major had departed on his dream journey to God knows where, his authority wouldn't do her much good. What a miserable turn if, after so much time and trouble, she was reduced to political shenanigans just to get the one thing she desired. That, she scowled at her bowl of chili, was not going to happen. Mr. Whitecoat and his crappy attitude would not be allowed to get in her way. She, as her mother had been fond of reminding her, was not Doctor Sharma's daughter for nothing. She'd buy the damn lab, how about that?

She was lost in these thoughts and buttering her bread when someone approached and asked,

"Is anyone sitting here?"

She looked up, and her heart leapt into her throat. There, standing before her, bearded and handsome as ever, was Javon Monroe. She knew at once he hadn't recognized her, and she looked away, ashamed as if caught in some act of perversion.

"No," she said to her chili, and he sat down.

"Thanks," he said and tucked into his meal like a man at a workstation. "Things are nuts around here."

She wondered if she should make some sign to get his attention, force him to look closer, or if she should simply slip away and retreat until she could have this reunion on her own terms, with maybe a different outfit and perhaps less risk of food stuck in her teeth.

What different outfit? she chided, regretting for the first time not following Sindi's advice. But she needn't have worried. Having observed an absolute minimum of courtesy, Javon proceeded to ignore her. He focused equally on his meal and the tablet he had lying on the table before him, one hand greasy, the other pressing, tapping, and scrolling, and all the while he mumbled to himself, his dark brow furrowed. She meant no intrusion, but his concern was easy to read; like her, he had just come from an unpleasant encounter.

"Mumble grumble magister my ass," he mumbled and grumbled. "Tell me how to mumble grumble my own ship and he's likely to get a mumble grumble fist up side his head. Officious, bloated, Company Man, mumble grumble..." He appeared to realize he was talking aloud to himself and looked up at her as if to apologize. And in that moment, his eyes grew narrow, then wide, then narrow again, and he dropped his fork with a clatter, leaning back in his chair as if surprise were a storm wind.

Time Weaver

"Holy...geez, Maya? Is it Maya?"

"It is," she said.

He wiped his hands. took hers, and kissed them.

"I'm so sorry," he said. "What a clod! I didn't recognize you... It's no excuse, but I have a lot on the brain. You could have sat there all day and I might never have figured it out. God, Maya, you've changed!"

"Yeah."

"But it works for you. It's..."

He left the idea unfinished and stared at her, taking in the whole of her for the first time since sitting down, the shaved head, the clunky specs and grungy work clothes, the extra pounds. She wondered how she smelled, wondered why he had kissed her, and if her skin tasted like the *Stockinger*.

"Well," he went on, "I don't know. It just works. Anyway, I sure am glad to see a friendly face." And she knew he meant it. Five years had creased his brow and the corners of his eyes, and the tone of his thoughts had an added gravity. But just as sure as she was of his gratitude to see her, she was equally sure that gratitude was not matched by the ardor he once felt. Whether her new form, his own state of mind, or some other change she was unaware of, something made her certain that her hand was the only part of her he would be kissing.

For now, she thought, a glimmer of hope or pride refusing to be extinguished.

"Well, well, miss Maya 'Nandini' Sharma," he said, and he smiled. "We have a lot to catch up on..."

+ + +

"Don't mind him," Javon said when Maya relayed her encounter with Mr. Whitecoat. "Watt's a good man or he wouldn't be on the mission. Plus, I think you'd love his sister. She's sweet—a grown woman, but a young spirit. Anyway, you have nothing to worry about with him. A few months from now, he's going off with me to... Well, I'm not allowed to say exactly, but far enough! You'll have the place Watt-free."

His face was lit by a new idea.

"In fact..." Rising from the table, he offered his hand. "How would you like to be the interim lab director while he's gone? Who knows? It could be months; it might even be years, depending on how it goes."

"Can you do that?"

"I couldn't have four months ago, but I can now."

"I don't want anyone to know..."

"They won't. Not from me, anyway. Miz Khatri."

She accepted his hand and rose to her feet, brushing crumbs from her pants.

"Can I give you the tour?" he asked. "Or maybe you need rest? Have you even been to your quarters? I made sure you got a good space. No point in being in charge if I can't do things for people I care about."

They meandered to her quarters, he doing most of the talking, and she grateful to listen and learn. How the various passersby responded to them depended on their uniform. System operatives nodded cordially or coolly, subject to dynamics Maya was unable to determine. Station personnel waved when they knew Javon, walked on without comment or gesture when they didn't. But everyone in a Company uniform offered some type of salute, until Maya began to feel she was in the presence of royalty. She sought none of the attention, keeping her gaze distant, and Javon had the sense not to introduce her to anyone. In any case, people were too busy for conversation, bustling and scrunching their faces, as if it was all they could do to keep from breaking into a run at the thought of all the work ahead.[1]

"I'm really sorry I've been out of touch," he said after a time, gradually working himself from the easy topics to the difficult. "These last couple years have been... Well, I'm just so damn sad about your parents."

She bit her lip and nodded.

"I wrote after it happened," he said. "A lot at first."

"I know."

They walked in silence, and she supposed he wondered if she would offer a reason for her failure to corre-spond—or ask his forgiveness. She did neither.

"But I totally understand," he said at last. "I can't imagine what you've been going through."

He paused before a bank of windows, portholes no larger than his head, through which the glittering tenta-cles and blinking lights of the station rested against a backdrop of space. A chocolate crescent of Triton drifted lazily into view. He tapped the pane lightly.

"It's pretty," he said. "But I'm not going to miss this place. I've never been around so many uptight folks, you know? My crew and my ship, that's what I'm looking forward to." But there was something more to what he said, something he tried to keep secret but couldn't. Maya read it like a neon sign, had been expecting it. She steeled herself for the answer, spending three words.

"Who is she?"

Javon's eyebrows lifted.

"I... Is it so obvious?"

"I don't blame you," she said, and she didn't, not really. How could she? He, at least, had tried to maintain a connection after her parents were taken from her.

"It was just, you know, so long," he said, "and so far away. And then..." He turned, and together they re-sumed their walk. "If I'm being totally honest, I was smitten by you, Maya. Like nothing I've ever felt." He fixed her with an unblinking gaze for several moments, and she returned it, parsing out four sincere words.

"It's not your fault," she said.

"Maybe. But let's just say it: Mars was messed up beyond belief, and when you stopped responding, I mean, I knew you were alive, I watched the reports and all, but God, Maya, you looked wiped out! All those cameras in your face, and then the hearings..."

He looked away and shook his head.

"I honestly felt like the best thing I could do was get out of your way and wait. Which I did. For a while."

"So, who is she?"

He smiled.

"Her name is Charlotte DuBois."

"Fancy."

"A technician, actually, dirty all the time."

"But she made you forget me."

"No, never! Don't say that. It's more like she made me focus on the future. She's part of *Destiny's* engineering team, you know, so we had a lot in common and a lot of time crossing paths. For what it's worth, it wasn't instant chemistry like it was with you and me. We had to grow into it—and I didn't allow myself to do that growing until I felt like there was no chance...you know, that you had...you know..."

He let the idea go and turned down a wide passage to a suite of modest residential quarters, stopping before the one at the end of the corridor, the most secluded of the lot. He opened its door by placing his palm against the security reader. Inside, they found a single cot, one overhead light, and a small lit desk with a steel chair anchored to the floor. The lone window was small, but Javon smiled as if sharing a grand view.

"You're one of the few who have their own biffy."

"Thanks to you."

"Of course! We can't have our interim lab director sharing a toilet." He looked at her and his smile softened. He squeezed her hand.

"I will always have love for you, Maya Sharma, and for your family, God bless them all. Things didn't work out like we thought they were going to, but I will never turn my back on you, understand? Never."

And she returned his embrace, pinching her eyes shut so the tears couldn't escape, and she smelled him, once, just for memory's sake.

"I'm glad I'm here," she said, four of the most honest words she had ever spoken, and when she could, she opened her eyes and looked up at him, taking a deep breath and seeing him now as an ally, a dear friend, cutting the last romantic string, and it was enough. "Will you walk with me to the lab?" she asked, and he beamed.

CHAPTER TEN
Hold

"I FOUND SOMEONE," *Destiny* reports, and her voice is excited but also confused. "I don't know who it is."

Sister Janet exits *Valiant's* cramped engine room, where she tests electrical circuits with a wireless meter.

"Share the image, please" she requests, and moments later, she is viewing a video file routed from ground camera to satellite, from satellite to ship, from ship back to satellite, and from satellite to refinery. A small company of scion, including a queen, and six—no, seven—figures walking away from the camera along the shoulder of a snowy road, appearing to move in stealth, weaving in and out between boulders.

"Is this camera three outside the dam?"

"Yes, Sister."

"Can you enhance it?"

"No, I'm sorry. That camera needs repair."

Janet examines every pixel to be sure. Three adult kezel and three older juveniles are easy to identify. The seventh member, remarkably, appears human. Stranger still, it rides on back of the smallest kezel. But the blurred image refuses to cooperate; all she can see for sure is long black hair and a blue shirt.

"Identify that human, *Destiny*."

"I'm sorry, Sister. I've never seen it before."

"And the other two juvenile kezel? Are those packs they're carrying?"

"It appears so, Sister."

"But that adult. What is on its back?"

"I don't know. It appears metallic."

Janet checks her chronometer.

"They'll be in range of camera two within thirty to forty-five minutes," she says. "We should get a clearer image then. Let me know the instant that happens."

When *Destiny* signals her again, she is occupied next to a labor android at one of *Valiant's* numerous control panels. They are both adjusting complex dials and switches as quickly as their hands can move, but the image *Destiny* shares with Janet startles her badly, and she must step away from her work.

"I don't think that's a human," the ship says.

The scion, six kezel, and their strange companion appear slowly, walking toward camera two, becoming clearer with each step—though they continue to move carefully, as if aware they are being watched. In spite of their stealth, Sister Janet needs only seconds to see two things that arrest her. The first is the metallic thing borne on the back of the crested female: the upper half of a labor android, badly damaged. The second is the creature she had thought was a human, perhaps a young female. It may be the latter, but it is most certainly not the former. Exhibit A is the blue shirt which turns out to be its skin. In fact, it wears no clothing, in spite of the wintery conditions. Exhibits B and C? Two oversized black eyes and a pair of willowy antennae.

"Oh," Janet exclaims, and she clutches *Valiant's* hull to keep from toppling. "Lord above, what is this?"

"This" is a human-scion hybrid, what else? Older and larger than when she had last seen it, having clearly passed through at least one metamorphosis. But who could have guessed it would grow to look like this? And why so large? At least twice the size it should be at its age. Someone had clearly been overfeeding serum. And why only one? There had been scores of them...

Time Weaver

"Oh, Lord, Lord," Janet whispers. "Where are you going? What is happening here?"

And she curses Watt MacLean for a fleeting moment, madly wishing she could simply deactivate her affective programming, stabilize her emotions in the face of this amazing, inexplicable turn. But there is no way to disable her feelings. Watt had been too clever and resolute for that; emotions were the lens through which she experienced every input, inflecting every output. Just as a human, if she divorced herself from her emotions, she would become a machine, and that was something Watt had been unable to tolerate.

"Don't be afraid to feel," he had told her over two hundred years ago, though he had been notoriously uncomfortable with his own emotions. "Be afraid to *not*."

"I don't understand," *Destiny* replies.

"It's OK," Janet says quietly, surprised that she had spoken aloud. "I don't either. Can you enhance? What is the humanoid carrying?"

"A bag of some kind."

"Can you zoom in?"

Destiny does, until a faded, handmade satchel with one shoulder strap fills the frame. The image is grainy, but there is definitely something inside.

"Can you identify the contents?"

"No, Sister."

"The humans at the agriculture facility?"

"The alp is still there. There was a blonde-haired female, but she went back inside."

Sister Janet pauses to consider this. She has found predicting human behavior to be either as simple as the first move in tic-tac-toe or as difficult as the motion of any given snowflake in a blizzard. She calculates a ninety percent likelihood the captain and his subordinate will return to search for their companion or track her to the refinery. Camera one, however, when she sees its images forty minutes later, tells a different story.

+ + +   + + +

A.P. Malloy

Far to the east, Captain Monroe and Ensign Morales approach the unlikely band of kezel and scion, waving open hands.

Keep your peace, thinks Pounce to the others. To everyone's surprise, Fluvial bows her nose to the ground and lowers her tail as the bipeds approach. But Piedmont scowls at the newcomers, his amazement easy for Lightning to read and paired with an apprehension made worse by the sound and smell of kish.

Aw, sur-ee, ol' Piedmont's a real peacy sort; he'll keep it iffin they will, see?

They will, thinks the alabaster biped. She appraises the company, acknowledging with a nod and a wave those she has met before. *I trust you remember us?*

Remember, yes, Pounce thinks. *Trust, no.*

Piedmont leans back, eyes popping.

They's thinkin'! he marvels. *They's a bunch o' thinkers, a bunch o' moondwellin' thinkers!*

One of them thinks, Joy corrects, and she points to Captain Monroe. *Not him; he's sapiens.*

But this is no time for unraveling mysteries or explaining why the two bipeds, who look generally similar, smell to kezel noses so very different. The newcomers' arrival has altered the tone of the kish voices—modulated and reflective—but no one mistakes the change for an improvement.

We came hoping to speak with Joy, thinks the ensign. *But it looks like you might be in some trouble.*

Not a bit, Pounce grimaces. *Everything's in control.*

How can we help?

I don't know. That looks like a thrower. Pounce points to the ensign's sidearm. *Is it a weapon?*

Of a type. It's a flare gun.

Any help in fighting a horde of kish?

That's difficult to say.

Any knowledge of this...whatever this place is?

Only what we learned from the intake tower. That's where we arrived. Ensign Morales points to the tall, cylindrical structure standing waist-deep in the reservoir side of the dam. The tower is unmistakably Moondweller in design and connected to the dam by narrow walkways. A similar bridge leads from the tower to the stony bank of the lake. *There's a transporter inside,* thinks the ensign. *The entire facility is in sleep mode. There were manual security protocols, but they were easy to bypass. We should be safe inside—unless these kish of yours have bolt cutters or plasma torches?*

I have no idea, Pounce curls his lip. *I didn't understand half of what you just thought.*

"Jitta allza boyla," says the one named captain. As always, he wears his black suit, his helmet carried on his back. And also, as always, not a word of what he says makes sense to any but one in the company. "Izza don tyta foratula."

The captain is right, thinks the ensign, looking behind them. *We should get moving.*

No one disagrees. Glowing eyes have begun to appear in the dark recesses to either side of the road, and the moaning has once again grown, so that none of them can help but feel they will soon be fallen upon by a terrible doom. And yet, Pounce hesitates.

Tell me, he thinks to Joy. *You've known them longer than any of us. Can we trust them?*

Not all that long, Joy is quick to point out. *But he helped before,* she adds, indicating the captain.

Fine, thinks Pounce to the ensign. *Lead the way. We'll get to the how and why of your sudden appearance when we get inside.*

+ + +

The company follows Ensign Morales and the captain down the snow-paved road with Piedmont at the tail, his shifting glance settling equally on the bipeds and the glowing eyes that surround them as if unsure which deserves greater attention. Lightning marches next to Cliff and behind Thunder. She trades Joy for Thunder's pack, for it is lighter and easier on her legs, and he is the superrior pugilist. The sight of Joy riding on his back gives her some comfort. Joy's hand rests inside her sling, moving slowly in small circles, and her eyes are dim. Queen Shimmer, fully alert, perches in her basket, ready to take to the air at the slightest provocation.

What are they waiting for? Lightning wonders, and she curses the kish and their hateful smell.

That, probably, thinks Pounce, and he points down the road to where it forks. Before it does, the road passes between a last cleft in the embankment, a narrow passage of a hundred strides where the walls to either side lie within easy reach, rising over their heads.

Kish don't throw stones, do they? Cliff wants to know, but nobody can answer with confidence.

Never heard o' such, thinks Piedmont. *But they's a long, growin' list o' things I ain't never heard that's a-been happenin' anahoo. And it's gettin' longer.*

Hurry, thinks the ensign.

+ + +

They round the final hard curve, from which the road runs uninterrupted to the fork—and the chokepoint to which they are being driven. As they draw near, a row of lumpy, gray rocks appears atop each of the banks, but a moment later, twin lights spring to life in each of the rocks, and the party is being stared down at by a gantlet of hissing, clawed kish.

Should we sprint through? thinks Thunder.

What choice do we have? thinks Pounce, for the road behind them has become gray with kish, walking in their peculiar, mincing fashion ever closer, more than any of them have ever seen at one time.

Hold up, thinks the ensign, and she draws her weapon. *I've only got two rounds left. As soon as I clear the way, run for it!*

Joy covers her ears, but when the ensign aims and fires, a subdued, hollow explosion results, different from the deafening crack of Lightning's thrower. Before the kish on the left bank can react, one of them is struck by a projectile. To Lightning's surprise, it does not kill its target, but ricochets from one lumpy torso to another, then lands in the midst of them, spinning in mad circles as it belches smoke and sizzling sparks. Though not fatal, the blow must have been painful, for the first kish it struck flees the embankment, shrieking. The sparking shower singes whiskers and fur, and the crazed spinning and whistling of the projectile inspires panic. Before the ensign has loaded her last round and fired at the kish on the right bank, those on the left have abandoned their position in a chorus of shrieks. Faced with their own spark-shooting smoke bomb, terrorized kish on the right bank quickly follow.

Seizing their chance, the party sprints forward through the cleft, but the horde behind continues to follow. When the ensign turns and brandishes her weapon, shouting and waving, the closest among them flinch and shy away, but when the brandishing is understood as an empty threat, they regain their courage and are soon in full pursuit, hissing furiously.

The fork is a hundred strides away.

Almost there! thinks Thunder, but as he does, kish appear ahead of them, scrambling up the bank and onto the road, cutting them off from the fork and holding their ground no matter how the ensign yells.

Lightning! Cliff! thinks Pounce. *Stay with Thunder; keep Joy safe. You two,* she snarls at the bipeds, *out of the way. Fluvial! It's you and me!* Ensign Morales and the captain move quickly to the side as Pounce, his ears pinned back, roars like a landslide and charges forward, followed closely by Fluvial. Together, they plow into the kish. Those at the front meet a terrible fate in their rending jaws; still others are swept off the road by vicious, sweeping blows from their tails. Some are sent flying into the lake, their screeching ended in a splash.

The rest of the party takes this opportunity to hurry forward, but even as they do, more kish climb onto the road to assail them—and those at their tail have now caught up to Piedmont. He has all he can do to keep them at bay, and he is forced to walk slowly backwards as he snaps and slashes.

Now Ensign Morales takes the lead. Lightning would never have anticipated the ferocity with which she fights her way through the kish. She moves more quickly and strikes more decisively than her eyes can follow. The spent thrower becomes a deadly hammer; her feet land flying kicks from which no kish recovers. The captain hardly has a chance to strike a blow of his own, relegated to the role of spectator and cheerleader.

"Alla wanta ro!" he exclaims, and he stoops to hurl a rock at one of the kish. "Stoo be hiddatoo!"

Queen Shimmer has seen enough.

Fools, she thinks, and she turns to address her soldiers. *They will stay with the Oddity. It must come to no harm.* And with that, her pluripotents take to the air, lifting her basket high above the fray and onward toward the left fork and the gate leading to the tower. Guarded by a ring of blue scion, Lightning, Cliff, and Thunder, with Joy on his back and Fluvial before them, make their slow way forward, biting and slashing any kish who make it past Pounce and the bipeds. The road behind them is soon littered with lumpy, gray bodies, some poisoned unconscious, others, less fortunate, never to rise again. The fork is now mere strides away, Queen Shimmer already safely landed on the gate's far side. But more than one scion has met its end in blue-stained snow, and Piedmont has fallen behind, outnumbered on the tail ten to one and puffing like a steam vent.

Fluvial begins untying the android from her back, looking to come to her fancy's rescue, but Pounce sees this and drops back to bar the way, tossing the last, lifeless kish from his bloody jaws.

No! Stay with them! he commands. *Get to the gate!* His tone allows no argument. He bounds away to join Piedmont as the rest of the company takes the left fork and hurries toward the tower. There, they find the chain gate left unlocked by the bipeds, and they pass through, turning back to see their companions.

Piedmont has fallen into trouble. As they had demonstrated against Lightning on the indigo plains, kish are masters of attack-and-retreat, encircling their target, scratching and biting from behind and rarely allowing a clean shot with jaws or claws. Pounce's arrival ruins that plan, and in moments, standing back-to-back, the bibijas are able to fight their way to the fork.

But just as the beleaguered pair reach their goal, a new threat appears. Kish, it turns out, do not throw rocks—they don't have the anatomy for it—but they do know how to send boulders tumbling down from the heights, dislodged in this case by those kish earlier sent scattering by the flare gun. In their passion, they seem oblivious that they risk crushing their own brethren.

Pounce! thinks Lightning. *Watch out!*

She is too late. Dodging one boulder and ducking another, Pounce thrusts Piedmont out of the way, the poor Whitetail bloody and dizzy from kish poison. This is the Sugarfoot's undoing. The next missile bowls Pounce cleanly off his feet, and its partner, killing two kish along the way, grazes his head, knocking him slack and senseless in a heartbeat. Lightning just has time to imagine sprinting forward to save him before he tumbles from the bank and falls, silent and beyond aid, into the lake. They hear but do not see the splash, and when Shimmer takes to the air to spy, she finds nothing.

She is most aggrieved to report it, she buzzes softly. *But the noble sharksha is gone.*

+ + +

The kish do not attempt to climb over the chain link barrier, for it is topped with spiraling blades that glimmer threateningly, nor are they able to tear their way through the sturdy gate the company seals behind them. And so, as they cross the bridge and make their way to the tower, the moaning and hissing of their frustrated enemies fades behind them.

A.P. Malloy

We can't leave him, thinks Lightning, looking over the side of the bridge at the cold, dark water below. But there seems nothing to leave. Pounce's body has vanished as completely as the boulders that had killed him.

Turrible, thinks Piedmont, his spikes matted with blood. *Most turriblest thing I ever seed, ahh!* and he lifts his head and howls like nothing Lightning has ever heard, a painful, stricken sound. *Shoulda been me,* he thinks, *shoulda been! Got no reason to be alive, not a one! Bestest Sugarfoot I ever met done in cuz I was too slow. Stupid, pokey ol' Piedmont! Always talkin' too much and never fightin' enough. Evraone knows it, sur-ee, evraone says it. Slow, stupid ol' Piedmont. Ahh!* And he wails again, stumbling along half-blind. Fluvial, the android still in place, walks next to him, her head hung low.

The bipeds lead the way. They offer no thoughts, but what could they say? What could any of them say that would make this awful turn better? When they reach the tower and the great metal door that bars their way, Lightning sits on her haunches, staring but not seeing, frozen and unreachable. The scion, now a Queen, five pluripotents, and a mere six blue soldiers, huddle close, chittering woefully.

We should get inside, thinks the ensign, and she looks up at a derka who has begun to circle.

I suppose, thinks Thunder, himself splotched with indigo blood. *But what are we going to find inside?*

The ensign runs her hands through her blonde mane, re-tying it into a rough ponytail.

I can only say what we found on the way out, which is not much. No signs of life, no operable equipment, nothing powered up. No lights, no ventilation, none of the tower's primary functions being carried out...nothing.

What do you have to say about it? Thunder turns to Queen Shimmer. *Are we going to run into your Ozag in here? Or her legions of soldiers? Well?*

Yeah, thinks Cliff. *Well?*

Shimmer's wings ruffle harshly.

How would she know this? Has she ever been here

before? But if she must guess, she would say Ozag would not be found in this awful place. A vumierre construction it is, of course, vile and undoubtedly as unpleasant on the inside as it is on the out. But the Hold itself, she thinks, *is a thing built at least in part by scion, a place worthy of the Abundant and Dreadful. But she supposes these vumierre know nothing of that? This "transporter" they speak of, whatever unholy thing it may be, did it not allow them to learn any secrets from the heart of the Hold?*

I'm afraid not, thinks the ensign.

Then all here are equally ignorant, Shimmer thinks bitterly, *and the quest must march into the darkness of uncertainty. What choice do they have?*

And yet, the kezel slouch dejectedly, indecisive in the absence of their leader. Lightning had never had a clear idea how the keeping of this promise would play out, but since Pounce's commitment to join, she had assumed whatever would happen would do so with a respected bibija at the head, confident and experienced. Her ears droop. Her amoti! So loved by Ancian... She takes several deep breaths, trying to will herself to express what needs to be expressed, to make the obvious call.

Before she can, Joy's mind opens.

We have no choice, she thinks. *Open the door, please.* And nodding as if glad for the order, the ensign does, cranking a handle and raising the door easily, though it is large enough to admit a babelrack.

It will be OK, thinks Joy as they step out of the sunlight and into the shadows and stale air. But she doesn't say why she believes this, and Lightning suspects she is simply trying to console her.

+ + +

No surprises here, thinks Lightning when they enter a space as clearly related to the maison as any she could imagine. She supposes she is expected to assume some role of leadership, is, because of her experience, beholden to raise the party's spirits. But she has no energy, and her tone is sour. She knows the scion and the other kezel despise from the first step everything they see and smell, Piedmont and Fluvial most of all. By their pinned ears and haggard expressions, they doubt to the core their decision to join this adventure. And yet, she hasn't the will to offer a soothing thought.

Rumidelchia, thinks Joy, her eyes muted. She looks all about the tower, a stack of eight-sided tiers, each wrapped around a perfect circle, open in the middle. *Vumierre. Moondwellers. Sapiens. Sentiri.*

Many names for the same trouble, thinks Shimmer. *It is scarcely to be believed that Ozag should have had truck with their kind. No doubt this structure was built before the time of the Stupendous and Bewildering, when scion enslavement was the way.* She clicks harshly and her antennae bend toward Ensign Morales. *The vumierre will explain! Descendant of slavers! What purpose does this horrid place serve?*

The ensign stoops to tighten the straps on her boots, wiping away signs of combat.

To clean and control the flow of water, she thinks, *from high elevation to one of the two power generating turbines on the downstream side of the dam.*

It will desist from gibberish! thinks Shimmer. *What does this have to do with Ozag? Is this tower responsible for making the floods?*

Not from what I know of dams. The tower cleans the water used for hydroelectricity; underground spillways on the downstream side of the dam control the release of excess water. I estimate a flow rate of a quarter million cubic feet per second.

More gibberish! What does this mean?

A lot of water, thinks Joy. *It means a lot.*

But not from this tower?

No, thinks the ensign.

Then onward! thinks Shimmer. *To the Hold of Ozag, where we shall learn about these spillways and why they have been derelict. Why do they delay?*

But Lightning and the other kezel have, by mutual

consent, come to a stop, their ears drooping as low as the mood they are in. Piedmont collapses to the ground next to Fluvial, both with eyes closed. Cliff sits as well, his faulty rear leg stretched to the side—until he sees Thunder still standing, at which he rises quickly.

Thunder snarls at queen and ensign equally.

Not another step, he thinks. *Not until we get some answers from these two.* And here, his snout aims at the bipeds. *Pounce said we could wait to hear their story until we got inside. Well, here we are—and he's not. And I'll say this, Moondwellers, or whatever you are: he never trusted you, felt sure you were only telling us half the truth. Time for the other half!*

Ensign Morales turns and, Lightning assumes, relays this information to the captain. But Thunder is having none of this, and he flares his spikes.

Enough mumbledygum! Joy! Can you translate this rot? Yes or no?

I'm happy to share what the captain says, thinks the ensign, but Thunder clashes his teeth.

No insult, he thinks. *You helped us with the kish, we all know that. But we can't trust what we can't understand, and I'm tired of being in the dark.*

Joy nods, aware that the others have turned their attention to her, and she reaches into her sling, gripping the Book so fiercely her blue knuckles turn white.

Can you help me? she thinks.

I thought you would never ask, the artifact replies. *But it is not as easy as it sounds. You will need to concentrate and be the hub.*

What does that mean?

You have already been doing it naturally among those who think on different frequencies. But the captain, as you already know, is no telepath, unlike the ensign, and has no capabilities for transmitting thought energy.

So?

So, I will turn their spoken ideas into thoughts that you can understand. But the others, of course, cannot read me. They will have to read you, which means you will need to concentrate on the thoughts I send you and project them to your audience. What you have been doing unconsciously you will now have to do consciously, and I suspect it will be tiring at first.

Ha! I'm already tired, Joy thinks severely. *Just do it, please!* She takes a deep breath. *I mean, will you?*

Gladly.

+ + +

They retreat to a shadowy alcove, a defensible position near the open door, and settle without ceremony or pleasure, eating from Lightning's pack, grim and—with the exception of the bipeds—silent. Surrounded by foreign, lifeless smells and a vast, hollow stillness, they take in the story shared by Ensign Morales and the captain, aided by Joy and the Book.

To Lightning's ears, the first thing the captain says sounds like, "La fydly fa lydly, oroompa pattaman," or something equally foolish. But when translated and transmitted, it becomes a clear idea: "What do folks want? Who we are? Where we're from?"

Ozag, Bristled and Shining, exclaims Shimmer, and she rises on four legs, her antennae leaning back. *Is the Oddity...are the vumierre noises becoming clear thought?* But Joy cannot answer her amazed question; she is too busy concentrating. As soon as the others have become attuned to what is happening, they begin firing questions of their own, sometimes impatiently when the pace of the answers doesn't meet expectations.

Poor Joy's head! She had already felt it being stuffed full of other people's thoughts and emotions, now it is positively crammed and jostling with ideas that often interrupt one another, a discordant, raucous mess. Eventually she waves her arms in quiet desperation.

One at a time! she begs.

Shimmer takes this as her cue.

The vumierre claim to be from somewhere far away. They claim to know nothing of scion enslavement or who bears blame for the destruction of Albion's Circle and all who died therein. And yet! They appear now, unbidden, and freely offer aid to the quest. For what reason?

Ensign Morales translates this to the captain, surely and without error.

"It's pretty simple," he says, rubbing the back of his neck. "But—no offense now—you folks should know time is not our friend. I hope the short version will do."

Time is nobody's friend, thinks Joy, and the ensign dutifully translates without comment.

"OK, then," says the captain. "Well, we came here because we think—we know, actually—that people from our home traveled here a long time ago in a ship called *Destiny.* Their leader was my great, great, great, oh, I don't know, pretty great granduncle, Javon Monroe. We don't know how they got here—it wasn't part of the plan—and when they never came back, everyone assumed they were dead or deserted. I never believed it, and I've spent my whole life trying to learn the truth."

The truth, thinks Shimmer, *is that its scurrilous ancestors defiled Aranae, enslaved innocent scion by the thousands, and paid for their evil with their worthless lives. The First and Best made sure of that! Does it mean to say it has come here to pay the debt owed by its kind? Is that why it traveled to Ozag's Hold? But why then not divulge that information moons ago when on the stricken plains of Albion? Why keep secrets? And where is their companion, the other pale one?*

The captain's face is a play of pursed lips and eyes that widen and narrow, crinkling at their corners as the ensign translates this for him.

"Listen," he says finally. "Queen, is it? Whatever happened here back in the day we can't speak to, and, you know, scurrilous is a word I can barely pronounce, much less define. We came here looking for the truth about our people, but we were knocked out of the sky, and one of us—that would be me—ended up an unwilling guest in your fine Albion. I have the bite marks to prove it. We would have been happy to mind our own business, but that isn't looking possible any more. You asked why we kept some things secret. Can you blame us? But we're opening up now because there's another player in this game, a…well, I guess you'd call her a vumierre. She calls herself Sister Janet, and she's taken our ship and done who knows what with our friend."

Vumierre fighting amongst themselves, Shimmer thinks, her tone acidic. *It is not to be wondered at. Violent and traitorous to the end. But how is that her concern? How does it explain their sudden appearance in the realm of the Portentous and Almighty?*

"Because," says the captain, "based on everything we've been able to piece together, we think this Sister Janet might be the one who sent that fully fueled rocket crashing into your precious Circle. And we think she's got an interest in what," and here he looks at Joy, "in what you've got stashed in your satchel there."

What's your point? thinks Lightning. *Pounce met you before and wasn't too thrilled. This is my first time, and I can't say I blame him. Yeah, you helped us, but maybe only because you need something from us.*

Truthy words, Sugarfoot, thinks Piedmont, but his eyes are downcast and his tone is morose. *Iffin you's just here fer yer own beneficial, well…I ain't the one to judge, no-ee. I knows as much as the next one who gets this on his conscience, knows it too stinkin' well why we aint got no more Pounce. It's pokey ol' Piedmont to blame, sure-ee, always causin' trouble or bein' a step behind, see? Just sayin' I's for one thinkin' if the best Sugarfoot I ever knowed had his doubts, then I'm havin' 'em double. You's a nice talker, there you one called captain, with a sweet smell, too—tasty—and yous there got an OK thinker, ensa…ensa…what the ever yer called. And no one's never told no Whitetail what in Aranae a Moondweller's apposed to smell like, but you, ensa, you…you aint proper, and any nose could tell it, yeah? Am I wrong?*

Not wrong, thinks Thunder. *Why is that?*

Yeah, thinks Cliff. *Why?*

Because we're different species, thinks the ensign

simply. *I'm synthetic, and a sentiri at that. Captain Monroe is sapiens. And yes, we do need something from you.*

But she stops herself.

"Ossera, impappa," she says, turning to her companion, which, when translated, means, *Sorry, Captain.* Then she shelters her thoughts.

"Everybody's got a right to feel doubt," the captain says. "But c'mon, look at yourselves! You're huge! Morales here is the second-best fighter I've ever met, and I'm pretty sure if you all decided to gobble me up and chase her off, that's what would happen. Yeah, we need something from you, and we're taking a pretty big gamble coming here. But our friend is missing, our ship's been stolen, there's a sideways android out there, and—"

He cuts himself off.

And? demands Queen Shimmer. *It will divulge!*

The captain runs a hand over his shaved head.

"And like I said, time is short."

Yeah, thinks Lightning, *but what you haven't said is for what reason it's so short. What's the rush?*

They are being chased, thinks Joy, the truth coming to her mind as easy as breathing.

"OK," says the captain, throwing up his hands. "You guessed. The details won't mean anything to you, but get this: people like us, but not so easy to deal with— not by a long shot—people you might describe as..."

They're pillagers and sadists, the ensign thinks, also speaking the words aloud. But then she scowls and says again, "Ossera, impappa."

"Yeah, well that pretty much covers it," the captain says, shrugging. "Unless you want to throw in murderers too. They're following us because they guess we know where *Destiny* is, and they want her. Where we come from, salvaging a wreck—especially one with *Destiny's* reputation, mystery all around—is a nice way to get rich. But more than that. There are some powerful folks where we come from who don't want it known that *Destiny* led to our kind's first interstellar colony. They have their own version of history, and they're willing to do pretty much anything to make sure that version is the only one people hear. Our plan was to get here, determine what happened, salvage the ship if possible, and scoot before they got here. But that plan has changed. And trust me, if they find this place, no es bueno."

It desires wealth? thinks Queen Shimmer, and her eyes glitter. *Its sole reason for being here is to race others of its hideous kind to possession of a bauble?*

"You got it all wrong, Highness! We're here to redeem my triple G great granduncle's reputation—and my family's too. He wasn't incompetent, and he wasn't a deserter. I'm here to prove it. But I need my ship, and I'm not leaving without my friend. And again: wackadoo android, lots of trouble—for you and your buddies."

It is certain this Sister is responsible for Albion?

"We're not certain about anything. We're piecing it together from sparse notes. But yeah, if I had to bet, she's the culprit, and for whatever reason, she wants..." he points at Joy's sling. "Pretty sure if she learns it's here, she'll be on her way right quick. We thought it would be a good idea to beat her to it and see if we couldn't work together, you know, all get what we want."

If it speaks the truth, thinks Shimmer, *then perhaps Ozag has not abandoned scion. Perhaps blame for the drought and the destruction lies elsewhere. She must know the truth! She must seek audience with the Radiant and Startling, must know her mind. Come! They have delayed too long with this converse. To Ozag!*

But the kezel are not attending. Starting with Lightning, the keenest smeller, but followed almost immediately by the others, they turn to the eastern wall, noses twitching. A phalanx of bristling, blue soldiers has entered the tower. Their pincers click in precise unison, but they are otherwise silent, three dozen in all, marching in tight formation, the fittest examples of the species Lightning has ever seen. The company prepares to defend themselves, but the scion do not attack. They stop within reach, their leader stepping forward and bowing.

He is Magister of the Hold, he thinks, directing his

attention to Shimmer. *Second to the Glorious and Invincible.* His eyes scatter the dim light. *Ozag has heard her subject's petition, and the Undying has seen fit to grant her wish. She shall have audience with the Queen of the Hold. They will follow!* But to the kezel and the bipeds he thinks simply and sharply: *Neither the sharksha nor the vumierre. They will wait here.*

And with that, the soldiers turn smartly and march back toward the eastern bridge as if certain they will be obeyed. They are.

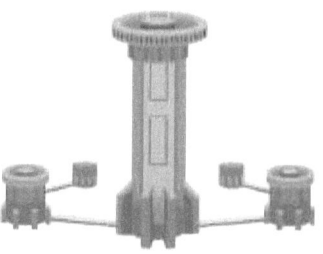

CHAPTER ELEVEN
Watt

FOR SEVERAL DAYS, Maya was left to roam the station as she pleased, but she rarely did; the laboratory was her home now, and more than once she spent the night there. The credentials Javon had contrived for her silenced any questions, and those occasional scientists she shared the space with soon quit their attempts at conversation. She was supremely uninterested in their opinions of her and didn't care enough to form any of them.

She was in the biology lab when a chime startled her; Tony had sent a message.

"You're too far away," he complained in his winning fashion. "It feels wrong not asking you questions and getting a response in real time. I guess this will have to do. So, I'll get the pleasantries out of the way…"

This he did, as charming in small talk as he was in weightier matters. Life on Mars (conflicted), his business (booming), gentle reminders ("meet one new person each day"), unspooled naturally, disarmingly. Which is why, as Maya wrapped up her business and returned an alien specimen to storage, only half an eye on Tony's hologram, she was surprised when his tone grew suddenly low and foreboding.

"There've been some bad things, Maya. I don't want you to worry, but you should know. It looks like the

TPA's a real thing. They outed the host of that one show you used to like watching, what was it called? *Amazing Folks* or something? Lost his job. A few politicians have been politely shown to the door." Tony's face, for the first time in Maya's memory, became clouded with a type of doubt, as if searching vainly for an elusive answer to an easy question. For a moment, he broke eye contact with the camera. Then he recovered. "Maybe lay low and think about Triton as home for a while. Just until this blows over. You don't need the stress. Anyway, I hope—"

Someone opened the door to the lab. Maya waved her hand at Tony's image, silently wishing it well before it vanished. She turned to see a woman, perhaps in her thirties, dressed in a simple, dark frock.

"Oh," the woman said. "I'm terribly sorry. I didn't mean to interrupt." Her smile was plain, not unpleasant, but not beautiful, in keeping with the rest of her, a perfect amalgam of mediocrity, from the unremarkable brown hair to the modest clothes and sensible shoes.

"You're not," said Maya. "I was just leaving."

She moved toward the door.

"I don't mean to be rude," said the woman, "but I feel like I know you. Have we met?"

"I don't think so. Good morning." Maya mustered a cordial nod and the woman moved aside as she stepped through the door. But then the woman gasped.

"You're Maya Sharma!" she said.

Maya winced.

"Easy," she gritted her teeth. "Not advertising."

"Oh Maya," the woman said, dropping her voice to a whisper. "I understand. No one will know from me."

Maya stopped and inhaled as if to reply. But she was unsure how—or even if—she should. She stood there biting her tongue and was just about to turn away when the woman's middling brown eyes sought hers, and upon finding, held them in a gaze that reminded Maya of someone, like an evocative smell, someone dear, but she couldn't think who it was.

"My name is Janet," the woman said. "MacLean."

And she extended a hand Maya felt compelled to grasp. "I was looking for my brother. He runs this lab."

"Haven't seen him."

"Please," the woman said, and she gently enclosed Maya's hand in both of hers. "Accept my condolences on the death of your parents. It was a truly awful thing."

"Yeah," she replied. "Thanks."

"Oh Maya," the woman repeated, looking quickly left and right to make sure she wasn't overheard. "I can see you want to be alone, but I have to tell you: this is a remarkable honor. I have had you in my mind a lot lately..." She trailed off, then laughed. "I'm sorry. That sounded pretty creepy, I guess."

"Sort of."

"You knew Jasmine, didn't you?"

Maya snapped to attention.

"You know Jasmine?"

"Knew."

Maya scowled.

"You're saying she's dead."

The woman named Janet closed her eyes and bowed her head. When she looked up, releasing Maya's hand, she ran fingers through her mousy hair.

"I'm out of uniform," she said, and a single tear escaped, running down her cheek. "Will you come with me to my quarters? I can get my habit and tell you all about...we can talk about Jasmine and eat breakfast."

Maya didn't understand the reference to habit, but everything else she heard was magnetic.

"I am hungry," she admitted.

Janet nodded, closing the lab door and gesturing for Maya to join her as she moved down the corridor.

+ + +

Janet's quarters, which she shared with her brother, were essentially Maya's times two: twice the size, two cots, two desks, and two windows. But as Javon had mentioned, there was only one bathroom. Janet warmed some cereal and coffee, spread something vaguely buttery on something shaped like bread, and left Maya in the tiny kitchen to eat while she retired to the bedroom.

While she ate, Maya discretely inspected the quarters. She was at first surprised by how spare, almost uninhabited the place was, but it made sense. This was the residence of at least one person who would soon be leaving on an interstellar voyage to a new, perhaps permanent home. But what of Watt's roommate?

"Are you on *Destiny* too?" she asked, burning five precious words to satisfy her curiosity.

"Yes," Janet's voice came from the bedroom. "I'm sorry, I should have told you. I'm ship's chaplain."

"Oh." Maya wondered if this might open a door to an upgrade in her quarters, and she idled in thoughts of what she could do with the place if allowed to move in once the siblings had departed. So distracted, she was badly surprised when Watt himself entered, his blank stare and open mouth quickly shifting to anger.

"Hello?" he said. "Now you're in my kitchen?"

His tone must have raised alarms in the bedroom, for Janet soon peeked around the corner, buttoning a modest brown cassock over an equally modest camisole.

"Watt, this is my new friend. We just met."

"In the lab, no doubt."

"Actually, yes." Janet smiled at Maya. "Will you remind me your name, please?"

"Nandini."

"She was hungry." Janet opened her arms to hug her brother. "So, where were you? I was looking for you. I had the most remarkable dream."

Watt accepted the embrace but scarcely returned it. His red, van dyke-style facial hair was an ungroomed accident, and it scrunched awkwardly as he waited for his sister to back away. When she did, returning to her bedroom, he wiped his hands on the front of his lab coat and peered at Maya.

"Nandini," he said, scowling.

"Yes," she replied.

"What brings you to Triton, Nandini?"

"Research."

"And what is it my lab has that you couldn't find on Mars? Or Luna?"

"Space."

"Are you always so talkative?"

"No."

"Say!" Janet offered when she returned from the bedroom. "I was thinking Nandini might like a tour of *Destiny*. Ever been aboard?"

Maya shook her head. Her sudden feelings at the thought of boarding the ship that was her father's legacy were conflicted and powerful, and she had no intention of unraveling them in front of two strangers.

But then Watt said, "She's not interested in that old tub," and of course she had no choice but to reply:

"I'd love to."

Which is why, not an hour later, after a shuttle ride to the gangway, Maya found herself standing with Janet before one of *Destiny's* many air locks, waiting for pressure to equalize. For reasons she couldn't fathom, Watt had decided to join them. Happily for her, he had done almost none of the talking, content to pinch his lips and make occasional sounds of disapproval as Janet led the tour. But he watched her like a hunting bird, and she felt sure he was testing her.

"Isn't it grand?" said Janet once they were aboard, and she ran her hand along the corridor wall.

Maya, who had been on many ships in her life, had to agree that grandeur was certainly one part of the effect the massive ship had. Its scale, once inside, made her feel smaller than ever, and she couldn't force even a single word of reply.

Then she met her first scuters.

They were a pair of spidery robots the size of soccer balls, and they wheeled past like a living memory. Scuters! Just like her father had described when she had been younger. They were the only part of the project that had inspired her childish imagination.

"Can I see one?" she had asked.

"Sure," he had smiled. "When the time's right, I'll give you the grand tour."

She frowned and watched as the scuters disappeared inside one of the service tubes. Her father had loved acronyms. What did it stand for? Ship Controlled Units for…Tactical, Engineering, and Repairs, wasn't that it? A third motored up, retracted its wheels, and climbed a nearby wall with the ease of a monkey, opening a hinged panel and beginning a sparky bit of labor on the wires within. And she covered her mouth, for she felt she was either going to cry or laugh.

They explored on foot until Maya grew tired, then farther yet using the lifts and belts that made climbing and walking unnecessary. Janet knew more about the ship than Maya would have expected from a chaplain, and once, when she began to wax poetic regarding the astral drive that had secured the Sharma fame, Watt made a sound like "argh," and motioned to his sister.

"I'm sorry." Janet threw up her hands and smiled shyly at Maya. "That's probably boring. How would you like to see the bridge?"

Watt's jaw clenched at this suggestion, but when Maya said yes, she was no longer being contentious. After all, when *Destiny* embarked, she would likely never see it again, and she was suddenly flush with desire to learn more about, or at least form a proper impression of, the thing that had so absorbed her father. As they traveled, Janet told Maya all about Jasmine. They had been good friends, she said, brought together by their connection to the Sharma family (swimming pool and spaceship) and long-time correspondents in spite of the distance.

But even here, Janet was perfectly discrete, never once using her real name or saying anything that would expose her identity. For her part, as she listened, Maya worked to keep her own thoughts under wraps, speaking only when necessary and tempering her reactions. But she was only human, after all, and thoughts of varying emotional intensity were never far away. She felt sure

Watt was dissecting her as much with his mind as with his eyes. But two can play that game, and on the rare occasion she felt him look away or lose focus, she conducted her own survey. By the time they had visited the bridge (properly stunning, windowed and lit like something from 3V) and the galley (for the snack Janet was sure they all needed), Maya had become aware of something remarkable about her two hosts. She wasn't sure if her feelings were getting in the way, or if what she sensed was real, and it wasn't until long after they had said goodbye and left her alone in the lab (Janet hugged her, Watt simply turned and walked out) that she decided she was not mistaken. The *why* of the thing escaped her.

But the *what* of it did not.

Watt knew she was a telepath but said nothing.

And his "sister" was a well-disguised android.

+ + +

Perhaps it was the hours of manipulating virtual, three dimensional models without a break that did it. Or maybe it was the new bed, firm and soft in all the wrong places. It could have been the commissary food, none of which would have been permitted on the Sharma table. Whatever the cause, Maya's old friend, slow-building headaches, returned for a visit, and they gave no indication how long they planned to stay. She only vomited once, a relative victory, but the pain drove her to the lab's darkroom. She slumped to the floor, pressing her face against the cool steel of the rinse basin and wrapping the safe, red light around her like a blanket.

Later that day, Tony's next message did nothing to soothe her. Cryptic and brief, it was text only.

"Thinking about you and sending good wishes," it said. "Probably ran five miles yesterday! Amazed?"

Maya ran her palm over the stubble on her head.

Ran five miles? Amazed wasn't the word. Incredulous, perhaps. Tony's soft, lithe form was not meant to run five meters.

"Oooh…" she whispered, realizing. *Clever boy.*

Her eyes held the three capitalized letters in a tightly focused gaze—TPA—and she thanked him. When the splitting in her head settled to mere squeezing, she tuned into the least unreliable of the 3V news outlets, closing her eyes against the busy images and listening for confirmation. It came after an arcane discussion of Lunar politics and a man with a Russian accent sharing excerpts of a speech given on Earth. Maya couldn't understand what it was about and was going to change the channel when a woman's voice stopped her.

"After months of bitter debate and a System-wide vote that saw record turnout, the results are finally in, and they are decisive: a resounding majority of voters—seventy-nine percent—gave their support to the Thought Protection Act proposed last year by the Martian delegates. Even Terran delegates, the most vocal opponents of the TPA, ultimately changed their tune when Benjamin Sakkit and Zooey Cole of the Saturn Satellites were revealed to be mind-readers. The most popular performers over the past decade, their influence on children System-wide made politicians very uneasy. Of course, the TPA hinges on a reliable test that can identify a telepath with minimal invasiveness. Our Douglas Cho is on Luna with more on such a test."

"That's right, Kevyn," said a new voice. "I'm here at Generis Labs in the Serenity Sea where doctors are confident they will soon have a test that performs as advertised without doing any harm to the person being tested. As Doctor Sue Calloway said, 'We're trying to protect people's minds, not harm them.' And when I spoke to the doctors here, they were all in agreement. Protecting people from prying minds is job one, but the people being tested have nothing to worry about from the test itself. Of course, how the test is to be administered, and to whom—under what conditions—is for politicians to wrangle over and will be decided in the coming weeks. But when they do decide, the folks at Generis Labs and other facilities throughout the System will have the tools ready."

Maya waved the 3V away and sat for a moment, breathing slowly and massaging her neck.

Test schmest, she thought, and she returned to the darkroom with a pillow and her eye shades.

+ + +

She couldn't recall the nightmare she woke from, not exactly, but the impressions were there, revolting and wrong, like her childhood terrors of glass shards and chocolate pudding. Her own screaming escalated the fear to a panic, and she was nearly gagging before she could bring herself to stop, burying her face in her pillow.

*Grrrvvv...*the revolving door said as it swiveled on its bearings, opening to reveal Watt MacLean.

"Moses!" he exclaimed, and he turned on the lights. "What the heck is going on in here?"

But Maya remained on the ground, masked in her pillow, panting and shuddering, and she gave no sign that she had noticed his arrival.

"Hey! C'mon, I'm serious! What's this all about?"

He stepped timidly forward, as if she might be feral and likely to bite. Daring to stoop down beside her, he poked none too gently at her shoulder.

"Should I be calling a medic or something?"

"No," was her muffled reply.

"Well," he said, "then what? What's up?"

"Nothing."

She sat up, pulling the pillow from her face and looking away from him, habitually rearranging hair that wasn't there anymore and wiping tears from her eyes. She expected him to scold her for making camp in the darkroom, but he didn't. Instead, his tone was unexpectedly solicitous when he asked,

"Do you want me to leave?"

And she said,

"No."

+ + +

Time Weaver

They sat in the biology lab, ignored by the sleepy technicians recording data and sterilizing equipment. Maya was gravely reluctant to speak, and Watt seemed unsure what to say, so they were silent for a long time, his toe occasionally tapping as if eager to lead the rest of him away from this awkward situation.

Finally, Maya could take no more.

How long have you known? She visualized the words as she thought them, could feel her tongue moving inside her mouth, though she made no sound.

Watt grew tense. His toe tapping ceased, and he clenched his fists, looking quickly over his shoulder at the nearest tech, obliviously rinsing test tubes.

Heck, he thought, still not looking at her. *You make it so obvious. I knew right away. Did you?*

Sure, she lied.

Am I the first you've met?

Of course not.

But you haven't met many.

How would you know?

Because there aren't many.

Fine. There were some I thought maybe, one for sure. What do you mean "obvious?"

Your tongue is moving, for one. You don't need your tongue for what we're doing. And long, meaningful glances are a dead giveaway. Staring at someone you're not talking to—and aren't like, in love with—is just weird.

Maya looked away, arching her brows.

How about now? she thought, concentrating on stilling her tongue. Had she always been doing that? But then, she had never had any proper practice, so how could she be blamed? The mirror had been her friend when she had wanted to communicate that way, and at those times, she had found herself interested only in the eyes, her eyes, and the space between them, reserved for the Third Eye, the destroyer...

Destroyer of what? asked Watt.

She stood up quickly from her chair.

You, she thought, her face composed angrily. *You,*

if you don't stay out of my head.

Relax, he thought. *It's like you're talking in an elevator and getting mad at someone for hearing you.*

"Whatever," she said aloud and turned to leave. But he surprised her with his sincerity when he implored,

"Please, I'm sorry. Don't go."

My head is killing me.

"Here. Wait." And he slipped from the room, gone for only minutes before returning with two red pills and a glass of water. He handed her both.

I've already taken painkillers.

Not these. Trust me. They're the only thing that worked when I was a kid. His upper lip twitched. A smile? A scowl? She couldn't tell. *They help with the nightmares, too,* he added, and she sensed no duplicity.

"Thanks," she said, and she swallowed both pills, slowly retaking her seat.

It's...call it an apology. We got off to rough start.

You did. I was fine.

Argh.

So. How many others have you met? she asked.

A few. They're out there.

Any here?

Some. Not many. Of course, I don't know everyone, and I'm not out conducting a survey. He looked for the first time at Maya's workstation. *What are you working on?*

She shrugged and turned off the machine.

You know, he thought, *all the good computers are on* Destiny. *If modeling is your plan, she's got the best.*

Hmm...listen, Walt.

It's Watt. Heck...

She tapped the water glass with her finger.

Why are you being nice to me?

Why were you being nice to my sister?

You mean why was I being nice to an android?

Watt stiffened, his scruffy red beard jutting. She expected an angry retort, but he surprised her again.

You, he thought, *are the last person I would have expected to be decent to someone like her.*

Time Weaver

And at once, Maya realized he knew her true identity. But she found herself unconcerned by this. Also, the ache at the base of her skull had vanished.

Son of a buffalo, she quoted Daada. *Does everybody know? Did she tell you?*

Of course not. When Janet makes a promise, trust me, she keeps it. Shoot. I put two and two together, that's all. He swept his hair from his face and seemed for all the world to be blushing.

Maya leaned back in her chair.

Two and two?

Aye, sure. It's no secret Major had a sweetie. You looked different in the pictures he showed me, but c'mon, you know, I'm not stupid. I knew who you were.

Maya laughed, so startled by the sound that she clamped her mouth shut, certain the other people in the room had all turned to stare.

Did you say sweetie?

Now she was sure he was blushing.

"There you are," said Janet, entering the lab. She smiled at Maya and squeezed her hand. "Major Javon's looking for you, Watt. Why are you off your comm?"

"We were busy."

"Excellent." Janet looked from Maya to Watt as if judging fit of hand to glove. Her smile widened. "But I'll take over, what say? Don't keep the major waiting."

Watt grumbled and looked to the ground like a boy caught stealing an apple. But then he looked up, his bright, blue eyes meeting Maya's, deep and brown.

Long, meaningful glances, he thought.

And she smiled at him and stuck out her tongue.

+ + +

When she wasn't working on her project—and sometimes when she was—Maya spent the next month in the company of Janet, Watt, or the two together. They had their own obligations with *Destiny's* launch rapidly approaching, and with those she could offer little assistance besides company. She was poorly versed in computer programming and had spent most of the last decade as far away from organized religion as she could get. And yet, when research and modeling grew wearisome, the ersatz siblings, each in different ways, provided an excellent reprieve. With Javon's assistance, Maya, still using her fake ID, was able to move freely to and from *Destiny,* and thus take advantage of Watt's offer to use the ship's immense computing power.

Aye, she's got brains, Watt caressed the ship's corridor as he led Maya to one of the on-board labs. *Lots! But she's a tool, completely non-self-aware and not much autonomy. If she were ever allowed to become sentient, I'm not sure how she'd feel about this mission.* He glanced at Maya. *Do I talk too much? You know, not really talk, but send too many thoughts?*

I like sensing you, she thought. *It's way better than actual talking. That was tiring me out.*

Watt frowned and changed the subject.

Janet trusts you with her life, he thought. *Here's the lab.* He scanned his palm and opened the door. *She's braver than I am, taking risks I wish she wouldn't.*

Does Javon know?

Of course. But no one else. And even with his support, a lot of people would not be OK with it.

What would happen? Maya absently explored the lab, her mind focused on the topic at hand.

Argh. At a minimum, her presence on this mission would be jeopardized. Mine too. Worst case scenario... He couldn't finish the thought; instead, he powered up a workstation for Maya.

So why take the risk? she asked.

It's worse to stay here. You know that better than anyone. Triton is still far enough away to be safe...for a while. But humanoid robots are even less popular than telepaths inside the asteroid belt. And now the TPA...

It won't come to anything, she thought, echoing her father and taking a seat at one of the modeling stages, keying in a few basic commands before opening some of her most recent files.

You're wrong. Watt's tone was certain.

Want to bet?

No. Heck! And you shouldn't either.

Is that why you're leaving? Do you honestly think it's going to be that bad for...people like us?

Yeah, I do. But that's not why I'm leaving. We—Janet and I—are leaving because I've known since way before Mars that her kind would never be safe here.

Those were different. They were just machines.

No. They were sentient. Deeply flawed, but sentient. Bad design, bad results.

Not all of them.

Of course not. That friend of yours, the lifeguard. And others, for sure. But the bad ones were real bad.

Janet's not like them.

No. Because I didn't design her to be a means to an end. She's an end unto herself. But politicians can't tell the difference, and if they ever found out the ways I designed her to mimic a human being and pass security protocols—heck, we could both be in a lot of trouble.

So, why'd you do it? Why make her?

Why are you doing whatever it is you're doing?

Maya rubbed the silver vial hanging around her neck, listened to the *tick-tick-tick* as she moved it up and down on its titanium chain. Why was she doing it? And why was it so difficult to put the idea into words for anyone but her therapist? Was she embarrassed?

No good reason, she thought.

But later, when visiting with Janet in her office aboard *Destiny,* the android asked the same question, and for reasons she never entirely sorted out, Maya found herself at last able—indeed, desirous—to find and speak the necessary words.

"I mean to elevate the intelligence of the animal mind," she said simply. "I wish to speak to them."

At this, Janet looked up from where she scrolled through holographic images of *Destiny's* passenger manifest, systematically updating each person's profile.

"Hooray," she said, and she clapped her hands like a child at a party. "That sounds delightful. Can I help? The ethical systems of non-humans is a hobby."

Then she paused and frowned.

"Images of Jasmine have been appearing in my mind," she said. "Not deliberate recollection, but spontaneous, with no warning. I don't ask for them."

"Happens every time I swim," said Maya. Five words. Should anyone be getting so many of her dwindling store? But she didn't linger on this question for long before she recalled a message she had been given. "Javon invited us to dinner."

"Excellent! Have you met Charlotte? I think you'll like her." With a precise flick of one finger, Janet scrolled unerringly to the three-dimensional image of a woman, tiny but fit, looking somehow to Maya's bruised pride as beautifully French as her name promised, auburn hair cut sensibly short, delicate, alabaster features sculpted to win contests, and intelligent eyes, dark hazel, needing no makeup. Janet expanded the image to life size, and Charlotte DuBois, in her tech uniform, joined them in the room. With another gesture, Janet made the image live.

"Charlotte DuBois, Chief Engineer," the recorded voice said, her lips even prettier in motion.

Maya scowled.

"Each passenger answered a bank of one hundred questions for me," said Janet. "Do you want to ask her one of them?"

"Not really."

"I'm sorry," said Janet with a worried expression. "Should I not have shown you this?"

"It's fine," Maya said, and she thought of all the personal grooming she would need between now and the dinner party. "I knew she'd be amazing. I suppose you're going to tell me she sings like a bird, speaks five languages, and has never lost a fight in her weight class."

That was a lot of words.

"She does sing." Janet smiled, and with a wave, the image began a lilting rendition of a French tune that

Time Weaver

was lovely and bright and irritating as hell.

"OK, great," said Maya. "Moving on."

Janet silenced the image, restoring it to its original size and returning it to the catalog, closing the entire program and turning her attention to Maya.

"I would like to ask you those same questions," she said, almost shyly, "if you'll let me."

"I don't know."

"Please, it would mean a lot to me. We can do it while we're getting ready for the major. It will be fun! I can do your hair, if you want. I could download a braid style and whatever makeup you want."

"No wigs. And no makeup."

"Then let me synthesize something nice to wear. Something flattering, not too formal, but attractive."

"Good luck," said Maya, and she squeezed the roll around her waist, making a crude sound.

Janet tilted her head, and her brow creased.

"It may not be my place to say this, Maya, but you've been kind to me, so I feel compelled to insist that you also be kind to yourself."

"Jeez..." said Maya, and she looked down, suddenly abashed and flustered. Neither spoke for a time.

"Was my brother invited too?" Janet finally asked.

"Yeah," said Maya. "Maybe you should be *his* dresser." And she laughed to show good will.

"He could use the help," Janet agreed, then she snapped her fingers. "I have something for you."

"Yes?"

"A story, if you'll accept. Short, but lovely."

"Sure."

"It's about your father."

Maya was silent.

"Watt," Janet went on, "had just gotten kicked out of his computer science doctoral program. I was his dissertation. Did he tell you that? I was just an infant at the time, but I understand I was considered a success. But my brother has a short fuse and not much of a filter. By the time he was scheduled to present me to the diploma awarding committee, he had managed—please, don't ask me how—to alienate everyone who had supported him, and he was told not to bother."

Janet pulled up a droopy stocking.

"The next week was the celebration dinner and press conference for *Destiny's* first successful test. You were there. Do you remember?"

Maya's eyes widened.

"I knew it. I knew I'd seen him before."

"Yes, he was there as part of the public contingent. And from what I've been told, he may have made something of a fuss."

"*May* have?"

"It was understandable, you know. He had lost his university funding, I was still unable to care for myself, rent was due... He was under a lot of stress, had a lot of anger. He needed a target to vent, and your father was it. Of course, he was detained by security and questioned. And can you guess what your father did?"

"I'm not sure I want to."

"He gave him a job, Maya. He asked him many questions, shared a great deal of his valuable time, when he could simply have dismissed Watt as a crack-pot and had him thrown out—or thrown in jail. And then he asked to see me. We talked. Well. He did most of the talking. But he was nice to me. I will never forget my first impression of his face. A week later, we were on a shuttle to Triton station."

Janet paused, waiting for Maya to match her gaze.

"Your father saved us both, you know. By the time I had reached adulthood, Watt had been promoted three times—each time on the Doctor's orders."

"That doesn't figure." Maya frowned.

"My maturation rate was twice that of yours. I was an infant when you saw Watt at the conference, but I would be your older sister now. Maybe someday I'll tell you all about my childhood and adolescence. What matters now is that I was made according to Watt's most thoughtful interpretation of the Gelertner Principle."

Time Weaver

Maya stared blankly and shook her head.

"In synthetic intelligence," explained Janet, "it is the notion that the embodied experience is the most important reality, that a person's body not only houses intelligence, but creates it, that thoughts are not simply raw data but are inflected through feelings, emotions generated in a mind that roams from high logic to free association. And this mind, and the rest of the body, is always evolving. It's not like loading a program onto a chassis. That's not life. And it's not machine learning, which is the heartless accumulation and application of massive amounts of data. It's the gateway to true sentience, and some believe, to a soul. Dreams matter! Awareness of one's mortality matters! And Watt says that when your father heard him describe the principle, he started to cry. A great man, he was. A great man. Anyway, just like that, our money worries were over."

"Replaced by others, I'll bet."

"Yes. But not through your father's fault. He eventually hired me as chaplain and left it up to me to share my identity with others as I saw fit. People who know, like the major, do so because they share with me a love for your father, a trust in his wisdom."

"Geez," said Maya. "I made fun of his mustache."

"Nothing about the Doctor is a joke to Watt. None of us feel for him what Watt does. His own father was a dedicated abuser, rarely sober and not alive for long."

She smiled.

"But I promised short and lovely. Remember while we're getting ready that your father was a man of many surprises and much compassion. That is in you, also."

+ + +

What happened after the dinner drove much of the event itself out of Maya's memory. When looking back, most of the experience was impressionistic. She recalled a general feeling of welcome to Javon's humble but stylish quarters, but also high anxiety. The food was as good as ship fare could be, but she was self-conscious and ate just enough to keep her stomach quiet. It didn't help that she couldn't talk to herself. In Watt's presence—through no fault of his own—her mind wasn't the haven for privacy she would have liked.

Of course, Charlotte was brilliant and sweet.

"Nandini," she greeted, kissing her lightly on both cheeks. She so shamelessly used Maya's pseudonym that she knew at once there were no secrets here—and no judgement. Javon hugged her just as a friend would, and dutifully gave her the first-timer's tour of the quarters. She recalled him proudly showing off his collection of antique weapons, assuring her each gun worked and each blade had a noble history. He would have gone on at length had Charlotte not gently intervened.

But what had they eaten?

She could not remember.

Had there been music playing? Certainly, but what? Strings? Voices in a language she didn't know? Impeccable and subtle, those are the words she used to describe the music she remembered, but not a single song or performer came to mind.

The meal itself was informal, for which she was very grateful, having dreaded the thought of making small talk while eating. Charlotte often flitted from the room to take a call or tend to some *Destiny*-related business, and when they overheard her in conversation, Maya was surprised by how authoritative and concise such a soft voice could be.

"What can I get you to drink?" Charlotte asked, and Maya defaulted to Daada's favorite, chaang. Synthesized, it lacked earthiness, but it helped soothe her nerves and made it easier to smile and say "Thank you," when Charlotte complimented her dress.

"Not to sound boastful," said Janet, "but I selected the print, colors, and design myself."

"Well done on all counts," Javon nodded, and he raised his glass in a toast. "Couture!"

As Maya sipped her drink, she stole a glance—and

Time Weaver

found Watt was doing the same. He had remembered at the last minute—thanks to Janet—to take his lab coat off, and he had apparently made some effort to coax his hair into a type of order. Out of uniform, he seemed a different person to her, and she looked away. But even when Javon invited him to the sitting room to discuss the upcoming expedition, his attention remained on her like a warm glow, and she sensed him struggle to keep his emotions and thoughts in check.

She remembered a fascinating conversation between Janet and their hostess, recalled a second chaang tempting her to make contributions, to offer something, maybe proof that she had at one time been worthy of Javon's love, not a tongue-tied schlub. But she couldn't recall the details of the conversation, only the frequency and candor with which their hosts smiled—at their guests, at each other, at the food, anything. Had she ever been that happy? What was their secret?

Watt looked up from across the room where he sat huddled with Javon, and for the first time that night, sent a clear thought, simple and intensely sincere.

Love, he thought and looked away. *No secret.*

"You've been delightful as always," Charlotte said to Janet when it was time to go, and she kissed her lightly on both cheeks, a gesture she offered to Maya as well, adding a hug for good measure.

"Get some sleep, kids," Javon said, and he stood framed in the doorway, Charlotte wrapped in one arm.

"Bonne nuit," Charlotte waved to them. "Enjoy your day off."

Then they closed the door and the three were left in the corridor, Maya a bit foggy in the head, Janet as sharp and alert as ever, and Watt tugging at his shirt as if wishing for the return of his lab coat.

"I have therapy routines to schedule," said Janet, and she hugged them both. "Don't wait up for me."

Maya felt sure they were being lied to, but what could she say? Off went Janet, humming to herself and moments later disappearing around a corner.

Maya looked at Watt as if daring him to speak. He did not.

Does she ever sleep? she wondered.

Aye. In her own way. She won't take the whole day off tomorrow, I can tell you that.

He squirmed, seeming to wrestle his eyes away from the brown skin left exposed by Maya's dress, and to her amazement he turned a complete circle, first looking like he was going to follow his sister, then aiming the opposite direction, still tugging at his shirt, and finally back again, looking at her and biting his lip.

Are you OK? she asked.

Of course, he replied, then: *Argh. No. Heck no.*

And he leaned in and kissed her, quickly, fiercely, as if afraid she would try to escape. Her eyes nearly popped from her head, and she not so much returned the embrace as simply accepted it. But she did not run away.

+ + +

Maya's second month on Triton station passed in a blur. Her new friends, focused almost exclusively on their upcoming voyage, left her largely to her research, and she made fine progress—when she was able to focus.

Go faster, do more.

And she did. But the idea no longer came to mind spontaneously, spurring her like an impatient rider. Now she had to consciously recall it, for an amazing thing had happened, and her goals, though not replaced—never!— had suddenly been asked to share the stage.

Thanks for derailing my project, she thought.

Thanks for derailing mine, Watt replied, and he rose from their shared bed in his quarters to get dressed.

Will I see you today?

Probably not. Tons of simulations and drills. There may be a break for lunch—may be! Then debriefing and reports and…aw, heck. It's a mess. We're not ready.

Janet says you are.

Janet is. And maybe the major. No one else.

Time Weaver

What can I do to help?

Watt slipped into his lab coat and ran his fingers through his beard, critiquing himself in the mirror.

Stay out of my head, he thought. *Honestly. I dropped a case of acetone on Willie's foot yesterday, all the time thinking about you, the way you smell...*

I smell like acetone?

You know what I mean.

Maya stretched, and she rubbed her eyes. She didn't bother to ask who Willie was. Just another person in a long list of people she would never meet. Anyway, he wasn't the point of the story.

I can't be blamed for your lack of focus.

Nor I for yours.

So, what are we going to do about it?

Watt's mustache twitched. It was as close to a smile as he ever got, wry and self-deprecating, but she had come to see it also as sign of trust. As far as she had been able to tell, it rarely happened in anyone else's company. It meant disclosure was imminent.

Not a darn thing, he thought. *Not if you want my opinion.* He looked away. *I love you, you know.*

You're a dummy, she thought, and she rose from bed, unashamed for the first time in many months of her nakedness, and she kissed him. Javon's kisses had reminded her of power, but Watt's had the flavor of wit.

Whatever that means, he thought.

Stop prying!

His sharp, blue eyes found hers, and they held each other like this, minds still and voices blessedly silent. Then he tapped his fingers to his temple.

Argh! I almost forgot. You got a message. Tony someone. He kissed her again. *Don't wait up for me.*

She didn't. But nor did she sleep well that night, for Tony's message, when she was able to decode it, laced her thoughts with menace. The gist was simple:

"Don't reply. Don't return. Consider *Destiny.*"

+ + +

A.P. Malloy

Maya's third month on Triton Station felt like something from a 3V show, as if the indigestible turn of events were happening to someone else.

First came the news from Watt.

Chancellor Mulbridge was arrested, he thought when she at last found her way to his quarters after another long day in the lab. She was shuffling in, deep in thought regarding the ethics of genetic engineering, when he looked up from his desk, face tense with concern, and delivered the news. She had to resist the urge to chastise him for lack of manners—would "Hello" have been too difficult? "How are you?"—instead focusing on the obvious problem his announcement caused.

Sorry, she thought. *Who?*

Heck, Maya! Who? He frowned. *English American Chancellor? Guy responsible for leading a billion people?* He looked at her as if expecting she would at any moment light up with recognition, but a blank expression was her only answer. *Maya Nandini Sharma,* he exclaimed, much as a scolding parent, and he ushered her into a chair. *You need to watch this.* With a wave, he activated the small 3V on his desk, scrolling through video until he found what he was looking for. A woman with a heavy British-African accent stood at a podium and spoke soberly to a jostling collection of photographers and journalists.

"At five forty-five in the afternoon of Wednesday the fifteenth, English Standard Time, Chancellor Mulbridge of the English Americas was placed under arrest for refusing to enforce the recently passed Thought Protection Act. The Chancellor was warned repeatedly by System officials that his actions jeopardized rule of law in the System, but he chose to ignore those warnings and risk the consequences. System Enforcement wants this example to make it clear to everyone from the inner planets to the Neptunian moons: no one is above the law. The TPA was passed to protect the privacy of all citizens, not just the ones who—"

Maya waved her hand at the image, silencing the woman and her disheartening message.

Time Weaver

Sorry, she thought again, and she kicked off her shoes, rubbing her feet. *But I'm in no mood for politics.*

Don't be sorry. Be aware. This is exactly what your friend Tony was warning you about. This kind of politics doesn't care if you're "in the mood" or not. Do you think the Chancellor was in the mood to get arrested?

C'mon, Watt, I get it.

I don't think you do. And it scares the heck out of me. All it would take is one slip, one wrong person to get wind of the Great Doctor Sharma's daughter—a telepath!—hiding out on the edge of the System...

I'm not "hiding out." And what would they do?

I don't want to learn.

You won't. In a month you'll be God knows where. But that was a mean thing to say, and she knew it. *I'm sorry. I know you're worried.* She took his hand. *So, what do you propose? And don't say "come with me."*

Fine. I'll say come with us.

You know I can't.

You mean you won't.

I mean I don't see what good it would do. This kind of fear, this irrational distrust? What makes you think some colony in a different star system is going to have less of it? People are people...

Because it's a Company expedition, not run by the System, and your dad is the Doctor. If they knew who you were, every person on the expedition would worship you.

Was the Doctor, Watt. Was. And being worshipped sounds like a lot of work. She propped her feet on his lap.

Your refusal to take this seriously is killing me, he said, looking down at her feet but not touching them.

She sighed.

Fine, she thought. *How's this for serious? My heart is broken, Watt, torn into bits. And I'm falling in love with you. I promised myself I wouldn't, that we were just sharing time until you left. But that hasn't been true for a while now, and it scares me worse than any damn law, or the cops, or a trip to some strange planet.*

I would never hurt you.

Can you promise me you won't die?

Maya...

That's what I thought. Rub. She wiggled her toes. Instead, he kissed her feet and stood up.

I love you, he thought. *But Janet and I have a chance to make a life away from a place that doesn't respect us any farther than it can kick us. Don't come with us because you love me. Come with us because you love yourself. Or do you think they'll let you continue your research while you're relaxing in jail?*

No one's going to jail, Watt.

Tell that to the Chancellor, he thought, and he left the room, leaving her alone with the frozen image of the System official and the memory of her voice. Maya sat like that, her feet unrubbed and her eyes weary from hours of compiling data. She was hungry but couldn't make herself get up to prepare food. Was this real?

You know it is, she thought.

Watt did not join her in bed that night, and he was gone when she woke up the next morning. But the attraction growing between them had become undeniable, and no disagreement, regardless its intensity or depth, could keep them apart long. When they re-united, they clung to each other like a life raft, tasted each other's tears, and looked keenly into one another's eyes, soaking up memories for an uncertain future.

I can't leave you, he thought.

You can't stay, she replied.

And there they left it until she got pregnant.

CHAPTER TWELVE
Ozag

WELL, WHAT NOW? asks Thunder. *That could be the last we see of your queen. And any beat now this whole place could be crawling with scion. So?*

He gets no answer from the Whitetails. Piedmont has grown morose and unresponsive. Fluvial stands near him, licking his wounds and offering thoughts meant to buoy his spirits but which have little effect. He slouches, his snout nearly to the floor.

We go see this transporter of yours, thinks Lightning to the ensign. *We need an exit plan.*

It's on the top level, the ensign points to a nearby doorway. *The stairs are here.*

Sensing a decision being made, Piedmont rouses from his funk and addresses the company.

Ain't good for much, he thinks. *Pokey ol' Piedmont! But he'll stay aright here and guard on this door, howl up a storm iffin anathing gets goofy down here, see? Keep the way from gettin' blocked or ana soopriseez show up, you know? Like them blue critters you's none too keen on—no 'fense 'tended, whatchername Joy, none a-tall—but don't do havin' all us go pilin' up atop o' this tower and not able a get back down, see? Yeah?*

He looks at Fluvial.

Better iffin you's a go with 'em. Keep 'n eye on the

two o' them—no 'fense 'tended, he thinks to Ensign Morales, *but you know, gotta do the work o' that one we knowed as Pounce, bravest Sugarfoot a ever was, and he—no 'fense 'tended—wasn't too sure 'bout the pair o' these, yeah? Whether they's the trusty type, see?*

Fluvial does. And so, with Piedmont staying behind and the bipeds leading the way, she accompanies Lightning, Cliff, Thunder, and Joy as the party begins the long climb to the tower's top floor. It is Thunder and Fluvial's first experience using Moondweller stairs, and Lightning is not surprised by their dislike for them.

"So," says the captain as they climb. "Not to pry, but what's so special about that thing you're carrying?"

Joy buzzes, hugging her sling.

Why do you care? asks Lightning.

"I just want to know what my enemy is so hellbent on getting hold of. Can we use it against her?"

I don't see how, thinks Joy. *At least, not directly.*

"Could we take a look at it?"

No, thinks Lightning, and this, when translated, stymies the captain, who falls silent the rest of the way. For this, Joy is grateful. She does not distrust the captain, but his interest feels invasive somehow, and she needs her focus. Since arriving at the dam, the artifact has been scanning for its missing Reader. The more clear her mind, the more help she can provide.

What are you finding? she asks.

Not what I had hoped, the artifact replies. *I sense nothing of my Reader—or anyone else. But this is a large facility, and I am far from the height of my power. If he was hiding, I would likely be unable to locate him.*

Why would he hide?

No reason I can think of. Which makes me fear the worst. But I will continue to scan.

As they reach the top level, the ensign opens the door, allowing the kezel to squeeze through.

The transporter's this way.

I knew it, Lightning exclaims when they arrive at the small, cylindrical room, accessed by a single sliding door. The device matches exactly the two others she has encountered. She refuses to enter and warns the others away, explaining what it can do.

How is that possible? Thunder wants to know.

Yeah, thinks Cliff. *How?*

Fluvial steps away and curls her lip as if the room might somehow reach out and pull her inside.

Actually, thinks the ensign. *Where we come from, it has only recently become possible. The humans who colonized this planet would not have had transporters this good. We don't know how they were upgraded, but they were—at least five of them.*

The maison, the bombas! thinks Joy. *We could go back!* Her clicking is rapid, her eyes alight.

Yeah, thinks Lightning. *Assuming it works. The last one of these we used let us out but wouldn't let us back in again. So where does this one go?*

They're all part of a network, thinks the ensign. *Any one of them should allow you access to any other. But there are security protocols, and they can be modified to limit travel between certain sites, under certain conditions. That's why the one you're talking about didn't work. But we've fixed that. It should work now.*

So, we could go back to the moon cave?

If you mean site four—that's how it's designated— the one in the foothills west of here, the answer is yes, as far as we can tell. Or any of the other sites—unless that Sister Janet we mentioned has been interfering.

Joy's clicking turns to an excited whistle.

We must go back!

Sorry, thinks Thunder, *but one thing at a time. We have a queen to wait on, don't you think? Or have we satisfied our promise? We got her here. Is that enough?*

Lightning growls.

That would be nice. But I don't know. Stop all this for a while and let me rest my head!

But she has no sooner thought this than the android on Fluvial's back begins to exhibit signs of life. Its eyes, already lit, become focused, glancing at each mem-

A.P. Malloy

ber of the party in turn, its neck creaking.

"Good afternoon," it says.

Everyone is, at first, too surprised to answer, and Fluvial scrambles to untie the thing, placing it none too carefully on the floor before quickly stepping away.

"I don't believe we've met," it says, its voice hollow and scratchy. "I am Delta One. Who are you?"

+ + + + + +

The scion soldiers lead Shimmer and her depleted entourage out of the tower and across the bridge that leads to the dam. The bridge is of the same style and materials as the tower, evidently built by the same creatures (*troublesome vumierre,* she thinks), but once they reach the body of the dam itself and step inside, they find themselves in a world as thoroughly scion as any hive they could imagine. They make their way through a network of carefully bored, six-sided tunnels, empty and silent, where each of the hexagonal rooms—also unoccupied— tessellates perfectly with its neighbors.

They are said, she thinks to Ozag's magister, *to be part of the greatest hive on Aranae. And yet she sees none but them. Explain!*

He does not turn or pause when he answers.

The Fabulous and Unknowable does not need a hive great in numbers but great in loyalty, intelligence, and courage. Does she doubt the Undying's might?

What she doubts is none of its concern. Shimmer clicks a harsh staccato. *Can it speak to the events at Albion? Does it know the reasons behind its drought and the Circle's destruction?*

The Appalling and Wise will have her answers.

And that is all he will say.

They are led down one level and then left, angling back and forth between empty, amber hexagons, lit by the sun through south-facing windows, high above the downstream side of the dam. When they reach what Shimmer estimates is the center of the structure, they see before them an elaborate entrance, each of its six sides intricately adorned with carving, clearly the work of scion, but skillful and detailed beyond anything Shimmer has ever seen, abstract but somehow fateful. She tries to keep her wings from a nervous flutter, and she chastises her entourage when a low buzzing spreads among them.

They all guess the same thing: Ozag lies beyond.

They will wait here, thinks the magister, and he and his team of soldiers pass through the entrance and into the amber light.

This will be their end, he is sure, thinks the highest ranking of Shimmer's soldiers. Once a humble drone, he has now been promoted twice, simply by merit of staying alive. Shimmer numbered him Seven, but in any healthy hive he wouldn't have made it to Seven Hundred.

Her eyes glitter as she scolds him.

He will meet his end in the service of his queen, she thinks, making certain the entire party senses her. *What else matters to him? Or to any of them? The Undying awaits! They will comport themselves accordingly.*

Queen is wise and brave, thinks her silvery prime, *but she wonders: if the Vengeful and Just herself brought ruin to Albion, what hope is there?*

Hope for revenge! thinks Shimmer. *Now they will still their minds and let her think! Time is short...*

+ + + + + +

"We're explorers," says the captain to the newly-awakened android, for no one else has a response. "Just visiting your fine planet. And these are our friends. We had to borrow some clothes..." He gestures to the ensign. "I hope that's OK."

"It is with me," says the android. It peers down at itself, its neck squeaking complaint. "But I am at a loss. Whatever happened to me? I seem to have suffered some trauma. Do you have my lower half?"

I'm sorry, thinks Lightning, because Fluvial shies away, refusing to respond. *From what I understand, that's the way you were found. In the mountains.*

Since the translation comes from the ensign, the android addresses her, seemingly unaware that the answer had come from someone else.

"The mountains! Heavens. I was an archivist, being re-trained as a technician. How did I end up in the mountains?" But no one can answer this question. "Well. I thank you for returning me here to my work station. But I will not be very productive without legs." It tests its arms, flexing and extending, and it wiggles its fingers.

Where are the others? Joy asks a question of her own, thinking of the Book. *There were three humans.*

"Oh dear. I was hoping you could tell me. Are they not here? This is bad news indeed." The android is silent for several moments. "I am unfamiliar with your species," it says to Joy. "What are you, if I might ask?"

I am a hybrid, she thinks, though she knows it is not a very detailed answer.

The ensign translates this, adding:

"She and the kezel can understand you, via translation, but they don't speak our language."

"I see," the android replies, still looking at Joy. "But surely there are others like you?"

No. They're all dead.

"Delta One," says the ensign. "I'm detecting transmission and reception on a radio frequency band. Who are you communicating with?"

"My fellow work-bot, the last of the Betas. He has confirmed that the humans you refer to are not here, but he can't say where they are, or how I came to be in such a condition. He has been very busy with *Destiny's* pre-flight preparations, you know."

The captain leans forward, his eyes narrow.

"You don't say. She's flight-worthy?"

"Oh my, yes. And about to embark on a most important mission, for which we had great hope."

"Had?"

"Indeed. We were always very understaffed, you know. And if the humans have come to a bad end, then I consider the odds insurmountable."

The android's gloomy message worsens Joy's own mood. The Book's continued scans have not revealed its other Reader. Had he indeed come to a bad end?

"And where is she?" asks the captain. "*Destiny*?"

"Geosynchronous orbit. Dark side of the planet."

"Well," the captain's voice takes on a hungry tone. "We're very helpful folks. Maybe we could lend a hand— or a couple of legs, as it were."

"Could you? That would be splendid."

Hold on, thinks Lightning. *I don't give a dow's honker about your stupid* Destiny *thing.*

"Of course," says the android, once the ensign has translated her message. "I understand. But kezel are not privy, perhaps, to the exigence we face."

Speak clearly, Thunder growls.

Yeah, thinks Cliff. *No...mumbledygum.*

"I mean," says the android, "that the planet is in grave danger. The moons have been disturbed in their orbits, and if we don't act soon, there will be a collision that will end in Aranae's destruction. *Destiny* is our only hope to avert the disaster."

Lightning glances at Joy.

Flying vessels! she thinks, her impatience growing. *Dark sides of planets! Disturbed moons! It all sounds like splatter to me. I'm more interested in the here and now.* She looks at Thunder. *I'm starting to think you're right; we should consider our promise kept.*

You mean go home, thinks Joy.

Yes, thinks Lightning. *And then to the maison. But away from this place, and right quick.*

Fluvial's mood is easy to read; returning to familiar turf appeals strongly to her. For its part, the Book is uncertain. Its other Reader is not to be found, and Sister Janet might be on her way. Remaining may be unwise. But it wishes to hear Delta One's plan.

For nothing matters if the rogue moon is not addressed, it thinks, which Joy shares with the others.

"It is true!" Delta One agrees, nearly tipping over.

"Without our mission, what will become of the planet?"

You tell us, Thunder growls. *What about this moon business? Is the threat real?*

"I wish it wasn't," says the android. "I could show you, but my projector has been broken." It creaks its head around to look at the ensign. "Am I correct in identifying you as a synthetic?"

"You are."

"If I share a video file, could you project it?"

"I can try."

The android opens a small panel below its left temple, and the ensign inserts the tip of one finger.

"Carmela..." the captain says in a warning tone.

"It's OK, sir, I've scanned; it's clean."

And to the kezels' great surprise, beams of light emit from the ensign's eyes, creating in the air in front of her highly detailed, miniature images of what Lightning recognizes immediately as Aranae's five moons, and at their center, an unfamiliar shape, a large, bright blue sphere, streaked in white.

What's that big one? she points.

"That's Aranae," explains the android. "It's the primary, and those are its satellites."

Aranae is flat, Thunder objects.

"Actually not," says the android. "If you were to keep walking, you'd walk all the way around."

"Here," the ensign blinks twice. "A little animation might help." And just like that, the moons begin to orbit the cloud-wracked sphere at their center. "And maybe the sun, too." She blinks again. A moment later, the largest sphere yet appears, a ball of pale, yellow fire. As the moons swing around the planet, the planet circles the sun, always the same face lit and the other dark.

"Distances are not to scale, of course," the android says, and it points. "Here's where we are."

Lightning and the other kezel stare, mesmerized by the celestial dance but struggling to comprehend the new perspective. Joy clicks an even pattern.

Remember the dark side? she thinks.

Time Weaver

Lightning does. Ari had shown it to her using the Eye, but this is not how she imagined it.

Where is the Wall? she asks. *Is that it?*

"That is the terminator line," says the android. "The point at which sunlight can no longer reach the surface. But it is because of the planet's curvature, not because of any physical structure. There is no wall."

Fluvial grumbles at this, and Thunder curls his lip; the idea seems sacrilegious even to him.

"Fast forward, please," says the android.

The ensign blinks. Suddenly, the orbits quicken, the moons spinning in a blur, the planet cycling around its sun faster than Lightning can count, only slowing down when the android waves a creaky hand.

"There," it says. "Regular speed, please."

The action slows to its original pace. The smallest of the moons, the violet Wabi-la, has drifted off course, and on its next revolution, it brushes Api-kan, the Blue Father. It seems a minor collision, but it leads to a second, much larger, between both Api and Ami, the result of which is disastrous for Brother Orange. At last, fat old Gapi-kan the Red, lumbering the wrong way as always, is steered astray by competing gravity, until he plunges in a stately arc into Aranae, resulting in a blinding cataclysm that disappears, along with the rest of the images, with a final blink of the ensign's eyes.

+ + +

"I'm afraid," the android says, gloomy but certain, "some variant of that simulation is inevitable."

"Unless *Destiny* gets flying," says the captain.

"That is correct. And soon."

"But how does that help?" asks the ensign.

"Simply," says the android. "She is meant to deliver a payload that, if detonated at exactly the correct time and place, will create enough force to alter the lunar perturbation of the rogue moon, sending it out of harm's way and avoiding the billiard-ball effect."

A.P. Malloy

"That must be some payload," thinks the ensign.

"It is. And it's already aboard *Destiny*. But it's no hope. Two of the three humans were to have run mission control from the surface—the third was too young—while Beta Three and I crewed *Destiny*. He was going to be the pilot, and I the technician. But as you can see..." The android looks to where its legs should be, as if their absence is answer enough.

"Well, shoot," says the captain. "Then it's a good thing you have Morales and me. Morales and I? Whatever. You're not looking for an English teacher are you? Ha! One problem, though. I'm not saying we're volunteering, but if we were—if!—how would we get to *Destiny*? Last I checked, some nut-job nun stole our ship."

"We have a shuttle," says the android. "Did you not notice the runway on the far side of the dam? An easy walk for those with legs. It's fueled and ready. The mission itself should take no more than a matter of hours. We've planned very carefully."

"OK," the captain says. "But what happens after we're done saving the day? Not that I'm committing, mind you, and not that we wouldn't do it for free, of course..."

"Are you suggesting a reward?"

"Nah, nothing like that. I mean, maybe a plaque. Or a statue. But mostly what I'm suggesting is that one good turn deserves another. If we help you with this, you help get our ship back—and help us find our friend."

Here, he explains to the android the situation with Sister Janet and Lieutenant K.

"Are you certain she has your ship?"

"Certain is too strong a word, but last we checked, it was flying toward your refinery."

"The refinery does require constant supervision. Perhaps that was her motivation. If she did take your ship, you can be sure it was necessary, and she will return it when she is done. She would never harm anyone, least of all a synthetic. I can't explain why you lost your friend's signal, but the odds against Sister Janet being the cause are...prohibitive. She is our champion! In any case, I'm just a work-bot. I am hardly the one to ask. But for your valor, I have no doubt you will be rewarded."

Lightning has sensed enough.

Go ahead, she thinks. *Be heroes. But you'll be doing it without us. All this…this…* She scowls generally at the space where the images had once circled. *Whatever this is. It's beyond me. Us. Am I wrong?*

Thunder growls his agreement, and Fluvial sits on her haunches, scratching her head in bewilderment.

Not wrong, thinks Cliff.

"No worries," says the captain. "This is right up our alley. We'll check out this shuttle and see if everything's legit. If it is, we'll take care of that moon."

Don't expect us to wait for you, thinks Thunder.

"Of course not," the captain replies, but the battered android waves its creaking arms.

"If your intention is to examine the shuttle," it says, "you'll need me to get past the security."

No one objects to this, least of all Fluvial, and Ensign Morales hoists the android from the floor.

Do you need this? Joy asks, and she holds out the locator badge the captain had given her.

"Keep it," he says. "Who knows? If this moon mission doesn't play out, we might need to find you again. If nothing else, it can be a token of good will."

Lightning feels she should offer something.

Listen, she thinks. *If this "disaster" turns out to be real, and you prevent it from happening, we'll be in your debt, OK? And we'll do what we can to help your friend and all that—but you'll have to take your turn. We're up to our neck in overdue promises!*

"That's all we could ask," says the captain when he's absorbed the translation. "Just remember: there's a character out there who wants what you have." He points to Joy's sling. "And she's nothing to mess with, in spite of what Shiny here thinks. Well," he says to the android. "Guess it's time to show us this shuttle of yours."

"It's not fancy, perhaps, by your standards," says Delta One, "but it's reliable."

"I'll take reliable over fancy any day." The captain waves. "Don't be strangers," he says, shouldering the ensign's pack, and they depart, she carrying Delta One, and he murmuring softly to her as the android guides them to a passage at the far side of the tower.

They pass through a door and are gone.

What do you think about that? Thunder asks once their footsteps have faded to silence. But Lightning surprises him by steering the question to Joy.

I think it's real, she replies. *The disaster, I mean.*

And what about you? Lightning thinks to Fluvial.

It's all very confusing. The bibija's snout wrinkles. *But the pictures were pretty.*

The next moment, a short, sharp warning call rises from the lower level, muffled by the door. Piedmont is summoning them—but to what?

+ + + + + +

For how long will she be made to wait? Shimmer demands when the Undying's magister and his party finally returns. He whistles calmly.

Ozag, Superlative and Peerless, rules her time as she sees fit. The supplicants will know she is ready when she tells them so.

And he can be bothered to say no more. Shimmer wishes he and his soldiers would go away and leave her to communicate freely with her pluripotents, but they remain stationed before the glowing entrance and show no signs of moving.

They will have left her by now, she thinks, referring to the kezel and others. *They were always eager for the first chance to break their vow.*

It is possible, her prime replies. *But Queen needs no help from such as them. She bears the memory of Albion. That will be her strength.*

This is a fine sounding idea in principle, but the longer Shimmer is forced to wait, the less sure she feels. Revenge had been a heroic ideal, justice a lofty, bold concept. Imagining both had given her the will to travel far from home to the very doorstep of the closest thing she has to a deity. But now here, she feels small and impetuous, a foolhardy drone pretending to royalty.

She will be derided, she thinks. *Scolded for her temerity and stripped of her rank. Queen of a ravaged hive will also be queen with the shortest reign. Ozag will see to it—if she sees her at all!*

But this thought has no more left her mind than the magister's eyes glow like sea-beams.

The Undying summons, he thinks.

It was never in doubt, Shimmer replies, and she gathers her retinue into a proper formation.

No, thinks the magister. *She will go alone.*

Shimmer begins to object but checks herself. Her party isn't getting past these bristly-legged soldiers, no matter how determined, and rejecting the terms of the summons might be deemed prideful or cowardly.

Then they shall carry her offerings, she thinks, hoping for an imperious tone. *And they will move aside or lead the way. She will not be herded like a babelrack.*

As she wishes, the magister bows, and on his command, three of his soldiers lift the woven parcels, lumpy and bulging, to their backs. This done, they join the others in a double column, passing into the amber light. Shimmer hesitates only a moment, glancing at her pluripotents. They have nothing to offer, their wilting antennae and lightless eyes telling her as clearly as thought that they are glad to be left behind.

They will stay alert, she thinks. *She will return.*

But they do not reply.

+ + +

Shimmer steps through the doorway and into the rich, amber light. The magister and his company have not waited for her but are already marching ahead, and she moves as quickly as she believes proper for a respectable queen. By the time she has caught up to the soldiers, the

A.P. Malloy

light has grown to fill the entire space, and soon after, she sees why: to her right, a huge portion of the southern wall has been cut away, opened to the sun. Such practice is common in Albion, but here, where the wind is bitter and the snow frequent, the opening has been covered with a perfectly clear substance, like an unmelting, flawless sheet of ice. Directly opposite this window, high on an amber dais, there sits an intricately woven basket, regal, glittering in gold, and empty.

Ka-poof!

Shimmer looks away, as a blinding flash of light envelopes the basket, followed by a single, mushrooming ball of angry smoke. The room is filled with a smell like a dozen queens gathered at once, and when Shimmer looks back, there, in the basket, revealed slowly by the clearing smoke, stands Ozag, Severe and Just.

For who else could it be? She is larger than any two queens combined, brighter and richer than any boast could do justice, with eyes as splendid and terrifying as the Great Saline itself—and when she ruffles her wings, Shimmer, who has never heard music, knows for the first time what it is and feels its power. Were they to have met in the middle of the plains, unadorned and alone, she would have known at once she was in the presence of the Undying, Perceptive and Judicious, and she would have done what she does now, bowing so low her antennae graze the floor, her eyes made dim.

Mercy, she thinks. *Forgiveness.*

Ozag's clicking voice comes from every direction, sonorous but delicate, a delight to the ears.

"She will use the language of scion," the clicking says to her. "Not that of vumierre. Slavers made words of our thoughts, but the ancient language is ours alone."

"Yes," Shimmer clicks in reply. "She is sorry."

"She has brought an offering?"

"Yes, may it please Ozag, Monumental and Gracious." And without looking up, Shimmer indicates the parcels placed on the floor by the magister's soldiers. They open one and hold it for the Undying to see.

Time Weaver

"Sacred pilars," Ozag clicks softly.

"Yes, oh Queen, the last of those stored in Abion. Is it not still Her wish that they be handed over to Her for safekeeping? That has been the practice, has it not? To keep them safe should vumierre ever return?"

"It has. But this is not the approved means of delivery. None are to approach Ozag's Hold."

"Forgiveness, oh Queen, but she had no choice."

"She may forgive," Ozag clicks. "She may not. Only time will tell. For what reason has she come? Why violate the Prohibition and disturb the Undying?"

Shimmer's antennae begin to quiver, and her legs grow weak. Where to start? She had been a presumptuous fool to come here, full of her own false authority. Who could ask anything of the Undying? But then she recalls Albion, the Circle devastated by fire, and thousands of larvae, left to slowly die of hunger.

"Oh Queen," she clicks, "surely She knows the plight of Her children in Albion. She needs no pretender to a throne, no trifling poser, to tell Her what has happened over the past moons."

"She does not," Ozag clicks serenely.

"Then She knows as well the tale of the black-scaled derka, the tiny one who died warning Princess of the pending doom."

"She does," Ozag clicks. But Shimmer wonders; had there been a slight hesitation before the reply? "Tell Her," the Undying prompts. "Is she sure the derka is dead? Did she note the color of its scales?"

"She...she did note. They were as black as when it first came flying to Albion. But it was no longer breathing. And so, she laid it to rest near the Royal."

"That derka," says Ozag, "was not dead."

"Oh Queen!" Shimmer replies, and her clicks betray a tremor. "Double is her contrition. She is a speck in the eye of the Undying, an unworthy waste of skin."

"Undoubtedly true. But there may yet be hope."

"Glory! What must she do, oh Queen? For the derka was interred on the Bacca."

"All in due time. But again! Why has she come?"

"To determine the path to justice or revenge, oh Queen. To humbly place herself at the Undying's service and beseech: how can she help Albion's many larvae be emancipated from their suffering? Who can be made to pay?" She chooses her words with the care of someone stepping across thin ice, and when done, she waits, trembling, to plunge into deadly, cold water.

But Ozag's tone is a soothing balm.

"She has traveled all this way for that cause?"

"She has, oh Queen."

"But how," asks Ozag, "has she come to be traveling with sharksha?"

Here, Shimmer tells of the scion raid. Ozag clicks harshly when she hears of capture and weapons theft, and Shimmer fears she will be held responsible.

"If it displeases the Undying, Her servant swears it was not her doing. And even now, she works in concert with a sharksha she herself healed—one of two such. These who travel in her entourage are allies, beholden to find succor for those suffering in Albion."

This seems to appease Ozag, for her clicking grows smooth, and her eyes lose their angry fire.

"And yet," she notes, "the larvae she refers to are not of her own making."

"No, oh Queen. They are poor Benica's."

"Why does she wish to foster another's progeny? Why not instead create her own?"

"She...she hadn't considered this, Queen. She felt it must be her duty to seek justice for the murdered and salvation for the innocent."

Ozag does not answer at once. She begins whistling a low, contemplative tune with the depth and resonance of a dozen pluripotents harmonizing in perfect unison. Shimmer yearns to look up, to match the glory of the sound with the Undying's image, but she dares not.

At last, Ozag replies.

"She will worry not about the abandoned larvae. Ozag will care for them. Waste not a moment fretting for

Time Weaver

their well-being, for the Sagacious and Charitable is their tender now, and what could be better?"

"Felicity!" Shimmer clicks. "Gratitude and praise! Nothing indeed could be better. But what of the villains who perpetrated the carnage?"

"Whom does she suspect?"

Shimmer thrusts her way past memories of accusing Ozag herself—what a fool she had been!—and focuses instead on a more likely target.

"She suspects the vumierre, oh Queen."

"Is she aware of her history?"

"To the limit of her feeble ability, yes."

"Then she knows this Hold once belonged to the slavers and was taken by the Undying Herself."

"It is known to the youngest in Albion," assures Shimmer, "and remembered by the oldest. Or it was."

"Very good," Ozag clicks, sharp and clear. "But what she does not know is that not all of the vumierre were exterminated when Ozag rose against them. Some she allowed to live because they were free of blame, not slavers, but virtuous representatives of their kind."

"This is a revelation, indeed, oh Queen. She hopes one day to meet such a vumierre."

"She has met a descendant of one already."

"The brown one!" Shimmer exclaims. "And its pale companions as well. Are those the ones?"

"Not those. They are newcomers and untrusted. And what is more, the two pale ones are imposters, machines posing as vumierre. No, think again."

Shimmer considers carefully.

"The Oddity! The mutant vumierre!"

"None other."

"Ozag, Inexplicable and Stellar," Shimmer rubs her forelimbs together and whistles. "How can it be? For it seems impossible by all she has been taught."

Ozag's tone grows harsh.

"All things are possible with the Undying!"

The glorious queen buzzes like a string quartet, and Ka-poof! another cloud of scented smoke mushrooms up from her basket. Shimmer cowers, her antennae limp. But when the smoke has cleared, Ozag's temper has settled, and she continues.

"It is a sign. The work of the Undying Herself, a symbol of what will be in the cycles to come: scion and vumierre, living in peaceful co-existence."

"She would never have guessed," Shimmer replies, her mind struggling with this news. "But then what of the newcomers? The brown one and its companions? Are they to blame for the drought and destruction of her ill-fated home?"

"Can it be doubted?"

"But they swore their innocence."

"As the guilty would."

"They blamed one called Sister Janet."

"Slanderous! That is a vumierre beyond reproach, one of the original Virtuous spared by Ozag, and one who now serves the Undying's every whim as Envoy."

"Then these newcomers shall be made to pay!" Shimmer clicks fiercely. "How shall they be brought to justice, oh Queen? What should she do?"

"Nothing." Ozag replies, and her buzzing settles like a choppy lake grown calm. "Justice has already been arranged. They will serve Her purposes, then be made to pay. Let there be no doubt of this."

"Never, oh Queen, never. She fills her servant's mind with wonder, and each of her hearts with gladness." Shimmer's chittering is unseemly for a Royal, but she is helpless to stop. "Her mission is complete!"

"Not quite," Ozag corrects. "First, she will answer: What does she know of the Weaver?"

Shimmer is caught off guard.

"She is feeble-minded, oh Queen. It is a name she has never heard before."

"Then she will answer this: Does she recall the tale of how the Undying came to be?"

"Yes, oh Queen. It is said vumierre slavers bred queens to increase the number of eggs and thus the number of their slaves. It is said they kept these queens in proximity, and that with so many so close, their minds joined, and one among them was changed, was made the First Thinking Queen."

"It is true. And where did the queens come from who gave rise to Ozag?"

"From other queens, it can only be supposed."

"Indeed. And they? From whence?"

"Others before them, and then others, oh Queen, all the way back to the crossing of the Great Saline."

"And what of the time before that?"

"That is beyond her, Bountiful and Spectacular."

"And yet, there must have been something."

"Unquestionably."

"And something before that something?"

"It would seem, oh Queen. Perhaps there is no end to how far back scion go. Was there a beginning?"

"The beginning was the Weaver."

"The very first scion, oh Queen?"

Ozag clicks like laughing pebbles dancing down a mountain face, some of which seem to plunk Shimmer on the head, as if rebuking her naivete.

"No, simple neophyte. Not the first scion. The First. The One from which all others come, all forms of life. Every babelrack, virble, scion, and dow. Even Ozag Herself can be traced back to the Weaver."

This is difficult for Shimmer to grasp.

"Would she insult the Undying with a question?"

"She would not."

"From where, then, does the Weaver come?"

Ka-poof! Smoke and a flash of dazzling light.

"Ask not!" clicks the mighty queen. "The Weaver talks to Ozag, Ozag does not talk to the Weaver—certainly not to ask such questions! Not even to *answer* questions does Ozag address the Weaver, for no questions does the Weaver ask. It is a Teller, not an asker. The Weaver gives orders, relays instructions, explains, prophesies, lectures, trains, and directs; the Weaver has Command. You have walked in the company of one who carries a Tool of Power, is it not so?"

"It is."

"She has seen it?"

"She has. It is like a...it is...it is most strange, oh Queen. She knows she has seen it, but she cannot now recall what it looked like."

"Indeed. For it grows stronger in the presence of the Oddity, and it is a Master of Disguise. Much wisdom and energy went into its making. But even its long-lived creators trace their beginning back to the Weaver, before whom the artifact is a plaything. Ozag knows all that passes within Her domain, but the Weaver knows All, for the Weaver *is* Power."

"Then the Undying honors her, sharing this revelation," Shimmer clicks carefully, "for she had been ignorant before now. And still, hers is a tiny brain, poorly schooled; she cannot see what it means for her."

"It means," Ozag clicks in sharp reply, "that the Undying is a ruler, but also ruled, and Her reign comes to an end. The Weaver calls Her to other duties, Splendid and Honorable, and another must take Her place."

It may only be Shimmer's imagination, but she feels for a moment the great queen is hinting at something, is proffering an opportunity.

"But," she wonders, "who could be worthy, oh Graceful and Robust? Whose wings could fly so high? Whose eyes see so far? Whose scent intoxicate so thoroughly? She can imagine no one."

"Only one who dares to take the test," Ozag clicks placidly. "And only one who passes."

"And what test is this, oh Queen?"

"Can she not see? Does she not understand? It has already begun!"

Shimmer's antennae tingle; she struggles to reply.

"But...but she is small and weak. She sought nothing for herself, only redress and revenge."

"And so she shall find, if she passes the test. And much more, beside. Or does she consider the Throne of Ozag beneath her? Is it an unworthy reward?"

"Never, Regal and Luminous! The opposite indeed;

Time Weaver

she is unfit for such. She has but a paltry retinue, a hive brought to ruin, and an insignificant span of cycles..."

"All true," Ozag replies. "But hers is not to question, only to decide: will she continue on to the test's conclusion, or succumb to her fears?"

"She lives to serve, oh Queen. What must she do?"

"Brave apprentice," Ozag clicks softly, and the compliment warms all three of Shimmer's hearts. "If she is indeed prepared to take on this responsibility—"

"She is!" Shimmer clicks, apologizing the next moment for her interruption. "If Ozag wills it."

"Ozag does. Now she will attend carefully. This is what must be done. First, about those sharksha weapons..."

+ + +   + + +

Lightning leads the party down the stairs, and when they arrive, Piedmont wonders at the absence of the bipeds. But he has no time for answers. Shimmer has returned, and she is tightly wound. Whatever the details of her audience with Ozag, it has left her excited as if preparing for a race.

They will rejoice for her, she declares. *Ozag has seen fit to honor her beyond measure.*

Super, thinks Lightning. *Because we're leaving.*

Ozag has foreseen this. She gives permission. The sharksha may depart; they have fulfilled their promise.

Not that we need her approval, thinks Thunder.

Yeah, thinks Cliff. *Not that we do.*

They shall still their foolish thoughts. Shimmer's wings slice the air. *Ozag senses all! Do not enrage Her now that She has granted the sharksha their wishes.*

Meaning what? Lightning asks.

A reward for their bravery and compensation for their loss. The Oddity as well. And here Shimmer looks at Joy, her buzzing subdued but her gaze avid. *Ozag knows its deepest, in-most desire.*

Yeah? Lightning growls. *How does she know that?*

With ease. All minds walk bare before the Undying. But enough! Their reward shall be this: in all things from this point forward, there will be peace between scion and sharksha; they have earned this for their kind.

I'll believe it when I see it, thinks Lightning.

It is ever the cynic. Shimmer clicks like jabbing needles. *But it will indeed see; Ozag is True and Enduring. If peace She grants, peace there shall be.*

Swell, thinks Thunder, growling. *And what about that compensation?*

In exchange for the sharksha lives lost to the ill-advised and unsanctioned scion attack and subsequent captivity, Ozag offers the lives of this queen, and all her subjects, a life-debt of servitude. If ever an Albinite can be help to any sharksha—or the Oddity with whom they travel—let it be so! None from the great City of Six Towers whether at home or abroad shall deny a sharksha in need. They shall obey the Oddity as if their own queen. So says the Timeless and Phenomenal!

Yeah, right, thinks Lightning. *If that's true, then here's a need. I—we—have two oti-kans we lost when your kind invaded our home. If they're alive, I want to know, and I want them back—unharmed.*

Ozag has foreseen it, thinks Shimmer. *She cannot say which are the sharksha that yet live, for she bothered not to dwell overlong on their displeasing form. But she knows this: in Cyclonia are captured sharksha that were given to the queen of that hive as a gift. They were to be kept alive in her Garden, but they shall be made free! With Ozag's blessing, Queen Shimmer herself will see to it.*

Thunder scowls.

Lots of nice promises, he thinks. *Why didn't you tell us this a long time ago?*

It was not her place to do so! Shimmer thinks to him as if addressing a simpleton. *She has no Command in Cyclonia! But Ozag rules. Queen Allura will bend to the will of the Undying like grass before the wind. Queen Shimmer will simply be the messenger.*

I'm going to hold you to that, thinks Lightning. *I've*

got a long list of things to do, but if you don't keep your promise, biting you will be one of them.

It wastes time with threats. Its work here is done. Ozag commands they be off.

Gladly.

And what about you? asks Joy.

She will not enter the horrid vumierre device, of that they can be certain. No, she and her heroic company will make the long voyage home, then to Cyclonia. They may never meet again, but the Oddity will be remembered. And they will be shown this honor: Queen Shimmer will see them to the device and wish them farewell.

And this she does, though no one asked for it.

+ + +

But when they arrive, Piedmont and Fluvial are nervous and reluctant, unhappy with the smell of the device and glaring at it from a distance.

Yous all so sure 'bout this here? thinks Piedmont. *Reckon it's a no-gooder by the stank 'vit, some kinda trap mebbe? How's a kezel sposta bleeve he's gonna, what? Go flyin' a hundred thousand strides in a blink, all cuz o' this here doodaddly? Don't seem natural a-tall! And whats aboot them dirty Redteeth? Sure an we aint gonna find a scad of 'em waitin' for us on the other end? Real nice welcomey party when we open the door?*

The way ahead is clear, assures Shimmer. *The Undying has foreseen it.*

In spite of this assurance, the Whitetails remain unconvinced, circling the transporter and scowling at it. But Lightning, with great patience, eventually persuades them both. It is, after all, the only way home that doesn't include a trip through hordes of kish. Taking a deep breath, Piedmont goes first; he is too large to share. When they press the buttons as Ensign Morales had demonstrated, the expected two-dimensional images appear, glimmering and lively. Piedmont selects the one depicting the moon cave island. The door closes, a whirring sound emits, and the door slides opens again.

Gee, thinks Fluvial, sniffing the empty space.

Yeah, thinks Cliff. *Gee.*

The two of them go next. Slide. Whirr. Slide.

So far, so good, I guess, thinks Lightning, sniffing carefully and stepping inside. *You ready?*

Thunder and Joy are. They have seen all they care to of Ozag's Hold, associate it with nothing but memories of Pounce and foul, inescapable scents. They squeeze in next to Lightning, and only Joy says goodbye to the scion.

Good luck finding justice, she thinks.

She needs no luck, thinks Shimmer. *She has the Blessed and Ubiquitous at her side.*

OK, thinks Joy.

In her presence, no button pushing is required. Five images appear with no prompting, and a voice speaks inside her mind.

Select your destination.

Joy concentrates on the picture of the moon cave island, and the others diminish until it alone remains.

The door slides closed.

+ + +

The moment it does, Shimmer steps forward. One of her pluripotents passes to her a small black device taken from the woven parcel borne on its back. This device, the size of her head, blocky and gray, she places against the door, where it locks in place, the attraction magnetic and unbreakable. A red light begins to blink.

So let it be, she thinks.

+ + +

The whirring sound, the sense that the floor has dropped away from beneath their feet, the blurring rush of light: all these are expected, and in moments, Lightning knows, they will come to an end.

But then there is a new sensation, as if she is be-

Time Weaver

ing squeezed in a giant fist, and she can neither breathe nor move, sure that at any time she will simply pop, her insides turned out by the pressure.

Then it passes, and she is at last able to breathe. The floor settles, the sound dies, and her vision clears.

Is it always like that? Thunder gasps.

But Lightning doesn't answer. Something has gone terribly wrong; her ringing ears and dizzy head are sure of it. She can't say how or why, but they have been sent to a space completely unlike the transporter she had expected—and they are nowhere near the moon cave.

Where are we? she asks.

But when Joy refers this to the artifact riding in her sling, its answer is disconcerting and vague.

At the risk of cliché, it replies, *a better question is not* where *are we, but* when.

The adventure continues in

Volume Five of the Moonstorm Series

available at moonstormseries.com

A.P. Malloy

www.ingramcontent.com/pod-product-compliance
Lightning Source LLC
Chambersburg PA
CBHW021954170626
46808CB00001B/158